MATTHEW YORKE was born in London in 1958 and works in Leeds as an engineer. He is author of *The March Fence*, for which he won the John Llewellyn Rhys Prize, and the critically acclaimed *Chancing It*. He also edited *Surviving: The Uncollected Works of Henry Green*.

Pictures of Lily

MATTHEW YORKE

corsair

Constable & Robinson Ltd
3 The Lanchesters
162 Fulham Palace Road
London W6 9ER
www.constablerobinson.com

First published in the UK by Corsair,
an imprint of Constable & Robinson Ltd, 2010

TO TOM

'It is one thing to mortify curiosity, another to conquer it.'
Robert Louis Stevenson, *The Strange Case of Dr Jekyll and Mr Hyde*

ONE

So here I am back at Faversham House: second time in nine months. Not good news, as Roger would say.

There's that same smell of cooking, which reminds me of school only it's worse. And there's the same sound of people playing pool down the corridor in the common room. If I listen hard enough to the click-clack of the balls hitting against one another I get wound up, a sort of hot, impatient feeling like I'm going to go mad and there's not one thing I – or anybody else, come to that – can do about it. When that happens I look into the pit, the place I can see into when I close my eyes. It's full of people mainly, but there are strange creatures in there too, ones I can't identify. But, then, who are we to think we've discovered all the species that inhabit the planet?

'Can you spell me the word "world" backwards?' Dr Murdo asked, when Roger and Diane brought me in and we were all sitting together in the consulting room. And I couldn't. It was like I was staring down a kaleidoscope and the letters were twisting and turning, exploding into colours.

1

'And what you were doing last Tuesday?'

Now it was as if I was looking over the edge of a well and couldn't tell if what I couldn't see was a few inches or a few miles away.

'I don't know.'

'Georgia,' Roger whispered, 'we were in Barcelona. In Gaudí's cathedral – don't you remember?'

I looked at him. The way he had said my name had brought me up, made me swallow. 'Can I go home now?' I asked.

And I didn't really need the answer. I already knew.

Dr Murdo cleared his throat. 'No, Georgia. I would like you to stay here,' he said. 'For a few days anyway . . . just to see how you get on.'

Pause.

'Ideally I'd like you to say you'll stay voluntarily.'

I knew what this meant, too. 'Okay.'

Roger and Diane left. Through my window I watched them talking in the car park. Diane had her head bowed; Roger was holding her by both elbows. After a bit he hugged her. None of that bothered me. What got to me was seeing Fudge sitting in the front seat of our car. He knew what the deal was. His ears were pricked, and even though I couldn't see his eyes I could tell they had that worried expression he gets when people slam doors or start shouting in our house. I wanted to stroke him, tell him how much I loved him and needed him, tell him how everything would be okay. And because I couldn't I began to get that intense feeling again. So I lay down and closed my eyes.

*

Dr Murdo came back into my room about half an hour later. 'I'd like you to take these,' he said, placing a small plastic phial on my bedside table with two blue pills in the bottom.

'What are they?'

'They're sedatives, Georgia. Once you've had a good night's rest you're going to feel a whole lot better.'

I knew he was right. So I took them.

'And I want you to read this,' he said, placing a folder next to the empty phial.

'Read what?'

'It's what you wrote last time you were here.'

Dr Murdo took a step back and folded his arms, trying to be less doctor-like, trying to give the impression that he wasn't in charge of 'a thirty-bedded in-patient unit for people of all ages, with mental-health problems, who require specialist care during an acute phase of their illness'.

'I have to say, you're a very good writer, Georgia,' he said.

'I know that.'

'How do you know that?'

'Because I got an A in my A level.'

He had one finger on the folder, as if he was pressing a button. 'That doesn't surprise me in the least, Georgia, not in the least,' he said. Now he had a hand on the door. 'Once you've read it again and you've had a good rest then we can talk about it. In the context of your present situation I think we'll find it a good starting point. Okay?'

'Okay.'

The next morning, I started to read.

TWO

Adopted

What's so strange about wanting to find out where you've come from if you're adopted? Let me tell you: it's the first thing you want to know. Who your parents are. How they met. What they thought, said and did when they discovered they were pregnant with you. How come they decided it was 'in your best interests' that they give you up? And how come it's 'give up' and not 'give away'?

I think about my mother a lot. More than I do about my father. Did she die in childbirth? In pain? Did she have me in prison? Was she a murderess? Or was she a prostitute – what Roger calls a tart and Diane a working girl? Or was she nothing more than just a 1990s version of a chav or a scally? One of those girls you see in the market, with a big belly and pink, pimply skin?

Sometimes when I'm in town, waiting for the bus or just hanging out, I find myself staring down at the pavement and thinking, Yes, I must be the child of a 1990s version of a chav because I know that gutter, that paving stone. This was a place my real mother used to bring me in my pushchair before she gave me up; this place is part of my old life. I don't like the idea that I may have been two or even three before I was given new parents. It freaks me out.

'We got you when you were five weeks old,' Diane told me, in her matter-of-fact way, when I asked her about this. Not that I believed her then any more than I believe anything she says now.

'And did you choose me?'

'In a sense.'

'What do you mean, "in a *sense*"?'

'Well, really you chose us.'

'How come?'

'There weren't as many babies up for adoption in 1991. We had to join a very long queue. Roger used to ring up every day.'

I think even Diane could see that she was digging a hole for herself. Don't adopting parents usually tell their kids they went up and down a line of cots and finally chose the special one – you, of course? Now she was saying how it was.

'So basically it was me or nothing.'

Diane was chopping something at the breakfast bar. She looked like that guy in *Psycho* when she stopped what she was doing, looked up and started stabbing the air with the knife.

'Georgia, when we saw you we couldn't have been any more sure,' she said, with one of her lights on-off smiles.

It's not as if it's been a truly burning desire to know about my parents, but it is a need that is always there, like a sleeping dog. The dog gets disturbed and stands up – it might just flop down the next minute and go on sleeping, or it might start moseying around; it might even start digging. Just like Fudge. You can never tell. All you know is that the question is there, like a dripping tap or daylight around your curtains when you're trying to get some sleep. In the end you're going to have to get out of bed and sort it out.

I *am* going to find my parents. It's possible – more than possible, actually. In fact, if I don't track them down I'll be one of the unlucky ones. I'm not naïve enough to think that everything's going to be super-cool once we make contact. I've sat in front of the news often enough to know that the world is a pretty unpredictable place and the one thing you shouldn't ever forget is that you never know what's around the next corner. But at least having some of these questions answered is going to stop the spirits.

Barrett

Barrett's an interesting guy.

His dad has got kids the world over, so Barrett's got a brother in Seattle, a sister in Rome, a brother in Miami, another in Frankfurt. He's only seen his father three times but on each occasion he's brought Barrett one of his records as a present. Barrett keeps these albums on display in a locked cabinet, which he says he used to call his museum when he was a kid (and still does now, if I know Barrett, because even though he's twenty-three he's the kind of guy who still sucks his thumb on the quiet).

'That's my dad there,' he told me once, pointing through the glass at the record sleeve, which was a flag of red, gold and green, with the band silhouetted in black in front of the red bit. They all had a lot of hair.

'Was he a Rasta?'

'Still is.'

'Where does he live now?'

'Between the sea and a river. He's a fisherman when he's not touring.'

Barrett's dad used to play with Bob Marley and the Wailers and Peter Tosh and King Tubby. I'd heard of Bob Marley, of course, but not the others – not until I met Sula and started going to the gigs. You can't really tell if it's true about him playing with the Wailers. I mean, shouldn't he be rich and famous, then? But quite often it's really not important what's true and what isn't. It's more important what you feel to be true. On the whole feelings are more reliable than knowings.

But what interests me about Barrett and his dad is that it just goes to show that you don't really need a father – all you need is to know is that you've got one. I mean, what apart from three pieces of vinyl has his dad ever given him? Nothing. But if he hadn't got those albums, if his mother had just told him, 'Sorry, I don't know who your father is, it all happened late at night in a car park', then Barrett would be like me – forever wondering.

Ben hasn't got such a colourful past.

He grew up in Wales in some mountains. His father had a stroke when Ben was twelve – 'One morning he woke up and it was like he'd frozen, Georgia' – and his mother is a colour therapist, which is something she trained to do to help Ben's father, and which is something that earns her good money now. It's true what they say about good stuff coming out of bad, that every cloud has a silver lining. If it didn't the world would be in trouble, I suppose. But sometimes I see Ben looking real sad. It seems the only time he is properly happy is when he's playing bass. Then you see a smile light his whole face and all of a sudden he's so relaxed, as if he's managed to dodge ahead of his trials and tribulations, like you can in a crowd when you think people are following you. So there's someone with a dad absent through illness. You can't win, can you?

Sula has had sex with Ben and Barrett, but only at the beginning when Ozymandias got together. Girl singers usually have sex with the band. That's rock 'n' roll for you. I sleep with her now. If ever we have to stop over we go somewhere like Hotel Ibis, Etap, or Novotel and we'll take a double.

'I really like the smell of you,' I told her one night.

'I really like the smell of you, too,' Sula whispered in my ear, and that seemed like such a perfect compliment it made me wonder if I hadn't unconsciously complimented her to get it back. Which then made me feel a bit insecure. But what's weird is that I've never been properly jealous of Sula. I've seen boys trying to pick her up and I've seen her half flirting back, but it's never bothered me. Maybe I'm not possessive or maybe it would be different if we were having sex – we're not, though.

Ben's brother, Drew, is training to be a shaman.

Clockwise

If I take Fudge for a walk in Meanwood Park, I go clockwise: down to the beck; over the bridge; through the woods; turn right to where the old lady lived in Sunny Nook until she moved and the house was vandalized; then back down to the tennis courts and home.

And that was something I did unconsciously, well before things started to come on top.

They should do a study. Get some athletes to run clockwise and anti-clockwise around a track and see how different their times are. Or get people to write down their dreams and see whether they turned left or right when they were asleep.

A couple of times I've done experiments of my own: gone anti-clockwise around the park on purpose, or into town from the Burley side, rather than via Mabgate. And always something has happened. One time in the park Fudge got into a fight; another time he just vanished for twenty minutes, and that always puts me in a spin. Once by the bus station a weirdo tried to abduct me: 'My cat has just had a litter of kittens and they're all mackerel. Would you like to see them?' Yeah, right!

I used to think it was my vibe that was deciding these things: that Fudge was behaving differently because of me. Now I realize it's not. Most definitely not. There is energy inside you, and there is energy external to you. The problem is, the boundary between the two is always shifting, like a patch of quicksand. When I take Fudge around the cemetery at the far end of the park, for instance, one day he'll piss on the headstones, the next he'll stick to me like a piece of chewing gum. Why? Because without you being aware of it something has moved.

'Knowing how to handle psychic energy requires training,' Drew is fond of telling me. 'You wouldn't try to tune an engine without knowing about mechanics, would you? Exactly the same principle.'

Dub

Dub. Dub-step.

I like the bass so deep it's sub-bass, so low you can't actually hear it – just feel it in your spine. And it holds you there, like you're a jelly quivering in a bowl.

Oh, Lord! Pull up! Rewind.

In fact, I like all the bass frequencies: the ones that crackle in your ankles; the ones that fizz in your knees; the ones that make you feel like you're sandwiched between two mattresses and every ounce of air is being pushed slowly and surely out of your lungs. The ones that make your teeth rattle like they're going to fall out on the floor in front of you. *Watch the ride!*

One morning I had missed the bus and Roger was driving me to school. We were listening to *Desert Island Discs*, and there was this guy on who was explaining how he had come to choose a song. He was saying that when he first heard the first line of the first verse – the one that goes something like '*Well, bless my soul what's wrong with me?* – he knew he was home: he had arrived.

'That's *just* how it was for me!' Roger said.

'Same song?' I asked, trying to sound interested.

'No, mine was "Rock Around The Clock" by Bill Haley.'

'Oh, right.'

But if I'm being honest, that's exactly how it was for me, too. And it was such a weird sensation. I queued up for the gig, paid my five pounds, got a stamp on the back of my hand, went in – and bang: there I was. It was as if it was just a question of time before I got there. And what was so odd was that I didn't even know I had been looking for it until I found it. Talk about the Lock and Key Theory.

Ozymandias is Sula's band. Sula's going to be a star. I love Sula.

She's older than me by four years, but when I got invited back to their place by her brother one day we just hit it off. Another of those Lock and Key moments, I took one look at her and thought, This person's going to be a friend and she's going to make some kind of a difference, a big difference.

I think the fact that I'm adopted fascinated her. To begin with anyway. She would paint her own fantasies on me. 'Perhaps your father was a sailor and he sailed away and he didn't even know he had left you behind,' or 'Perhaps your parents want you back, Georgie.' That used to freak me out, the fact that someone had actually said that to me. But that's Sula for you – she speaks her mind. 'Everything is the truth; even lies are the truth because they exist,' she's fond of saying.

It was Sula's mum, Christine, who came up with the name for the band. Christine wants to be a writer and when she went on a creative-writing course 'Ozymandias' was one of the poems they had to study. As soon as the band heard the word, they knew it was right. Yet another of those instances where you know something is meant without having to think about it too carefully. The poem was written over two hundred years ago. I don't think any of us has read it through, but Ben puts some of the lines on the flyers, random stuff, like 'Look and despair, ye mighty', or 'King of Kings', or 'The lone sands stretch far away'.

I love the gigs, every second of them. Ozymandias play weddings, christenings, birthdays – they've even done funerals! And then, of course, they play bigger venues in places like Liverpool, Birmingham and Bristol. At those gigs you have some heavy-duty sound systems, which means the night invariably turns into pretty full-on Drum 'N Bass roast. But at around three in the morning, doesn't matter where you are, you get what I like: dub.

Dub makes me feel totally eerie. It's like potholing – there's no better way of describing it – dark, endless, mysterious, like you're walking through dripping caves: drip, drip, crash, crash, echo, reverb. And you can see and hear what you want to in there, as if the songs have a dialogue going on, as if the bass lines are a series of questions and answers. A song might start with de-de-de-de-doh-dah-dah, which could be 'Did you ever think you'd see me again' – and the answer, dah-dad-dah-de-dah-dah, which could be 'I wasn't sure but I hoped so bad'.

E

When you're rushing and the party is really swinging . . . there can be no better feeling.

Who cares if it's not real? As long as you remember you've taken a pill and this is why your forehead fizzes like one of Diane's Solpadeines in water, and this is why you can feel the music talking in your bones and you can't help talking back, and this is why everyone in the room looks like they're your oldest, bestest friend – as long as you can remember all this . . . while you're in the zone . . . I can't see the problem.

Fudge

Fudge just disappears. One minute he's in front of me, the next he's gone. And I can't see him anywhere – there are just too many people. It was like the time Roger, Diane and I went to Parliament Square in London for Year 2000 celebrations. You couldn't see the pavement for people.

So I'm shouting: 'Fudge, Fudgie . . . here. Fudge, *please* come back.' And all the time I'm thinking what a bloody idiot I am because he wasn't on his lead; in fact he wasn't even wearing his collar. And I start to get that sinking, collapsing sensation when all you can feel in your stomach is an empty pain. I suppose that's why they invented the word 'gutted'.

To be fair, some of the people in the crowd do stop and help, or try to. A couple of them even point and shout at me as if they've spotted him. But when I stretch to see what they're pointing at it's not Fudge at all: it's another dog, someone else's dog, one's white, another's black – nothing remotely like my very own fudge-coloured Fudge. It seems these seconds of hope are designed to disappoint me over and over.

And then I do see him. He's the other side of a road. It's quite a busy road, the one in front of Big Ben. He looks lost and I can tell that he knows it, too: he keeps looking up at the people either side of him who are waiting to cross. Every time he lifts his head I see the cream patch he has under his chin. I'm so happy I've found him. I'm standing straight again and all's well with the world.

And then he sees me. First his tail goes up, then his ears, then he bounds forward. Some of the people who are waiting for the lights to change try to stop him. But he is too quick. He doesn't see the lorry coming. Why? Because he is looking at me.

This is a dream I have quite regularly. And always I wake up gasping. Like I've been swimming under water and have burst through the surface, which looks like a shimmering ceiling of mercury from underneath. Which isn't a bad analogy really, since being woken suddenly from a nightmare is a bit like crashing through from one world into another.

It takes me hours to get back to sleep after I've had this particular dream. I just can't get the images out of my mind, can't believe I've lost Fudge, who at that time is my only friend. The sound of traffic doesn't help either. We live two streets back from the ring road, and all night long cars and lorries sweep up and down it. There's traffic in my dreams, traffic outside my window: it's hard to keep the two places apart.

Grandma Myers

So there I was, standing one side of the grave between Roger and Diane, with Uncle Rob, Aunt Yvette and Orlando the other side, like we were in a mirror, trying to connect and stayed connected to my feelings.

Not that I'd thought I had too many feelings for Grandma Myers. Not since I was about twelve and we were in Filey (I was always being shipped off to Filey: Grandma Myers had a share in a flat there) and it had been a very hot day and we had a raging row, and Grandma Myers said, in a deep, booming voice: 'Now, you listen to me – you're a very lucky young person.' Which I took to mean if it hadn't been for Roger – and her as well, of course, because she was Roger's mum – if it hadn't been for them, well, I would be in the gutter, wouldn't I? Why? Because of all the usual reasons.

But there was something else. Grandma Myers had said, 'Now you listen to me,' in such a way that it seemed to imply she *knew* my real parents. She had that sort of adult, knowing expression. And it got me thinking and thinking. In fact, I could never really get her words out of my mind after she came out with that. Not until a few years later when I found those letters in Roger's safe and things began to make a bit more sense.

So there we were, standing by the grave, and I'm afraid to say I wasn't thinking about Grandma Myers and how much I was going to miss her and how much I hoped God was going to take her into his care and look out for her. Not at all. I was actually thinking about Sula, Ben, Barrett and the rest of the crew and how at that moment in time they'd be driving to Preston, where they were playing that night. And I was thinking how much I wished I was with them. They would be on the M62, passing the house that refused to move when they built the motorway and so the road had to go either side of it, pulled apart like a massive elastic band. Then they'd arrive at the venue and start setting up. If I had been with them I would be helping Barrett with his kit – he lets me carry the tom cases and some of the cymbals, but that's it: I'm not allowed to touch the hardware.

And all the while the priest was reading from his prayer book. 'In my Father's house, there are many dwelling places. If there were not, would I have told you that I am going to prepare a place for you?'

And suddenly I began to feel proper guilty. Was there something wrong with me? Here I was, standing three metres away from a corpse in a box, surrounded by Grandma Myers's friends and relations, all fidgeting and sniffling into their hankies, wishing I was in Cumbria with my friends. 'Grandma Myers is dead, Grandma Myers is dead,' I kept repeating to myself, staring hard at the roots that the gravediggers had exposed when they were digging down to get to where Grandpa Myers was. And for a moment I was frightened.

But not for long, though, as it was then that I had the distinct impression I would see Grandma Myers again. And perhaps not before time. I was staring fixedly at the grave, which was like a doorway into the Underworld. There didn't seem to be anything weird or frightening about the realization. The Egyptians had antechambers next to the tombs of their dead, didn't they? Where they brought gifts and offered prayers to the spirits on the other side? And the Greeks had the Oracle, didn't they? And the Amazonians . . .

'The shamans in the jungle fast on special diets of plants and herbs,' Drew told me one dawn, as we watched the sun rise from under us (we were sitting in the Devil's Chair – at least, that was what Drew called it, a sort of amphitheatre of stone in an old quarry in Leeds). 'They do these ceremonies deep in the jungle where they go into heightened states of consciousness, where they meet with spirits: the spirits of the trees and plants . . . animal spirits and spirits of the dead. The shamans are wizards, Georgia: they transcend time and space. Where they go, everything is alive. There is no such thing as death in the Western sense of the word.'

'They're tripping, you mean?' I tried to interrupt him.

'They would be insulted by that interpretation – because for them the places they visit and the people they meet during their ceremonies are just as real as reality is for us.'

Head

The time I came into the sitting room and found Roger giving Diane head!

Diane was standing with her back to the door and Roger was kneeling in front of her, pretty much out of sight. All I could see were his ankles. In the split second of walking in on them I thought he must be proposing marriage or something, like Prince Charming. Then I caught up with myself, and thought, Hang on a minute – they're married already . . . There's something else going on here. And then I saw Diane's knickers lying on the floor, right in front of my feet.

There was a girl at school, Belinda R, who told me she often heard her parents shagging and how it really upset her to the point of being traumatized and how she couldn't listen but was in the room right next door to them and couldn't help it. The weekends were the worst. Her parents would get back from the pub, pissed up, and might be at it for an hour or more. And it was so rough the windows rattled in their frames.

We had just started psychology A level and we had an answer for everything in those days. Belinda was envious of her mother, who was getting it when she wasn't. Belinda was witnessing the conception of a new brother or sister and was already jealous of it. Belinda was a repressive degenerate who hadn't come to terms with her own sexuality and therefore couldn't come to terms with anybody else's. Belinda was a mess: if she'd been more sussed, the sound of her parents enjoying themselves wouldn't trouble her – why should it?

But seeing Roger and Diane like that, so suddenly, took me completely by surprise. Diane had one foot up on the arm of the sofa. She was wearing her pleated white tennis skirt, which was short anyway, and with her in this position I could see both cheeks of her arse. Roger had one hand on the back of her right thigh, the straight one, and the skin was white where he was digging in. He had his other hand in front of him and, with his fingers outstretched to form a pyramid shape, I remember thinking how he looked like a sprinter waiting for the gun at the start of a race. Diane wasn't exactly moaning, but she was breathing hard. And even though she had her back to me I could tell she had on that stony expression of hers.

I could have backtracked without even turning around and I don't think they would have been any the wiser. But I didn't. Something in me wanted them to know I was there, that I had seen what they were up to. It wouldn't have been any good just to sneak off.

'Oh, *sorree* . . . !'

You should have seen their faces, first Diane's, then Roger's.

It was Roger who spoke first. 'Georgia!'

Then Diane: 'Georgia, out . . . Now!'

So this was them having sex, only it wasn't the type of sex that was capable of having me.

Insurance

Roger is always on about insurance. Insurance this, insurance that.

'It's a way of spreading the risk.'

'"Spreading the risk"?' I asked once, and wished I hadn't.

'Well, if a hundred people each own a valuable painting,

worth, say, ten thousand pounds, and they each pay an insurance premium of one hundred pounds a year, then when one person has his picture stolen the insurance company can give him the ten thousand pounds to buy another.'

'What happens if two people get their picture stolen in a year?'

The answer to this was cryptic, if that's the right word for it. 'Maybe in the year following no one would have their painting stolen.'

What I don't like about insurance is that it's all about the future. It's got nothing whatsoever to do with the past, and what is the future, or the present come to that, without the past?

And what pisses me off is that when Roger goes into money-making mode he makes out I'm so immature about what he calls responsibility. Not that I want his imaginary painting. But when we were having this discussion about its being stolen I could see a look in his eye that sort of said: 'Don't get excited, I might not burden you with the responsibility of giving you this painting – when the time comes maybe I'll give it to someone else who appreciates its value and how precious it is.'

I don't like it when people go into coin mode – they go weird. It makes me feel like shouting: 'I don't want your fucking painting!'

You can see what Diane is thinking, though. Just keep quiet. She knows which side her bread is buttered. And this pisses me off, too: the way she handles Roger. I know how to handle him just as well as she does, but I'm not going to nod like one of those animals you see in the back window of some cars.

I want to be myself. I'm going to be myself. And to be that I have to know who I am and where I've come from. Past. Present. Future.

Jobs

Jobs equal money and I know Roger would approve of me saying this, but I actually enjoyed my job at Holland & Barrett. I also enjoyed him taking an interest in it.

'Tell me what an open question is again,' he kept asking me, when I got back the first day.

'You don't say, "Have you got a sore throat?" You say, "What kind of symptoms have you been getting?"'

'Incredible!'

'And then you ask, "How long have you been having the symptoms?"'

'Brilliant!'

Each morning at breakfast, he would spend a good ten minutes turning my house keys over and over in his fingers, reading the bullet points on the key ring they give you as soon as you start your training, bullet points to remind you of the all the open questions you've got to remember to come up with. 'Medication; Lifestyle; Diet; Allergies?' 'Try any Holland & Barrett product before?'

'Do you know? I want a job at this place!' he would say.

So when I borrowed sixty quid from the till to get Drew and me a train ticket to Manchester and a cab home at two a.m. and got caught out by Claire the following Monday and got finished, I had to be careful what I said to Roger. I told him that unfortunately I'd had a personality clash with the manageress.

'Yes, that *is* unfortunate,' Roger said grimly. 'Very unfortunate.'

When Barrett learnt I'd got the push, he was understanding in a Barrett-like way. 'Nah, you don't want to get involved in that thieving, Georgie. Do it often enough and it'll become a habit. Why don't you do the door with Hazel? You can earn a few quid that way.'

Which was sweet of him, seeing as I'd just owned up to having my hand in the till.

And Drew gives me a few pills to sell, too. It's amazing how much you can earn in just an hour or two, because although they're cheap, these days, the punters buy more of them. In fact, when someone comes over to check if you're juggling, that's your first question: 'How many do you want?'

And joggers.

I see them every day, rain or shine, when I walk Fudge. I know most of them must be regulars and I must see the same ones over and over, but there's only one or two I recognize. And that's on account of their tracksuits, which goes to show how sexy they are with the dark patches of sweat between their shoulders, their running shoes and their drinking bottles shaped like baby's rattles. You hear them running up behind you . . . bam . . . bam . . . bam . . . and then you have to get out of the way to let them pass, because if it's raining they stamp in the mud and you get splattered. They carry on as if it's their bloody park.

Sometimes when it's been a long night and I'm still buzzing, in that twilight space where you're still up but you're not, and I'm in the park trying to clear my head, these joggers really get me down. When they run past you they create turbulence in the air, and they manage somehow to get into your space. Lately I've been finding I have to hold my breath as they come up behind me, then when they've gone past expel it very slowly, and sometimes in a special way, to prevent it getting back into me, to get rid of their energy once and for all.

Ketamine

I'm not doing ketamine again. Not after Blackburn. And I never went anywhere near the keyhole.

To begin with the high was so pure and buzzy, and even though I was stumbling and falling into stuff I knew I would be safe, that no harm would come to me. It was like I was walking on air or a mattress of clouds; that, or I was one step behind myself, if that makes sense.

And then I felt horny. Rewind. Unbelievably horny. And so did Ben . . . for me. He would not give up gawping at me with that wanton, rampant expression he has sometimes. And I didn't want to go with Ben. Not at all. Ben was a mate, not someone you snogged, not even on a bad day. But he wouldn't let up. And that was where it went wrong.

I had my eye on a boy called Zac. He's one of the best chess-players in the UK and travels all over Europe competing in tournaments: a bit of a geek. But that night, he could have done with me as he pleased. He was dancing at the back of the hall with his shirt off. He wasn't dancing with anyone, he was just into the music, zoned, into himself. There was not a hair on his chest, only a gold ring through one nipple. My eyes were a pair of magnets: I couldn't stop looking at him. The problem was that, although he was pretending he was just into himself, he was into Sula. That was why he was standing in front of Dan as he knew that the singer and the sound engineer always have to be in visual contact, especially at the smaller clubs where the acoustics can be dodgy, not to put too fine a point on it. And even though Sula had made it quite obvious before the gig that she wasn't interested in Zac, he wasn't going to give up.

So there was all this energy going about, and going nowhere at the same time. And suddenly it was like someone had flipped over a coin: I didn't like the buzz any more. Sure I felt physically good, my arms were sleepy and light at the same time, but I wasn't happy with the mental space. And then everything came down, like a house of cards. I didn't like the number the band were playing. I didn't like the club: the toilets were scuzzy and there was a pervy bloke behind the bar. I didn't like Blackburn, period: what a shit-hole! I wasn't looking forward to the journey home in the mini-bus because probably Ben would be sitting next to me, which he had been on the way out. I wasn't looking forward to the next day. I wasn't looking forward to the next week . . . Or to the rest of my life, come to that.

I went out the back. Drew was sitting on the bonnet of a car smoking a spliff.

'You want to let go of that stuff, Georgie,' he said, after I had told him that everywhere I looked there just seemed to be doors closing, that I had that edgy feeling when you know even before you've done, thought or said anything that it's not going to work out. That everything's crap, basically. 'You want to rise above that, Georgie.'

'How can I? I can't.'

'Let go of it, just rise over it like you're flying.'

'How?'

Drew moved along the bonnet. 'Sit here. Put your hands on your knees. Close your eyes. Now listen.' And he started whistling and shaking a piece of newspaper.

'Come on, Drew . . .'

'Listen, Georgia.'

At first I just thought it was ridiculous: us two sitting in a car park doing some weird meditation; then I thought, Hey, at least I'm laughing, that's an improvement, so I listened a bit closer. Drew couldn't whistle to save his life – in fact, he wasn't really whistling at all, he was just blowing through his lips; then he started humming instead of blowing. It wasn't exactly a tune, it was more a melody. Da-la-la-la-lala-la . . . And waving the newspaper, which sounded like a wind rustling the leaves in a tree.

Still I wasn't convinced. 'Drew . . .'

'Just listen to the melody, Georgie, listen to it carefully.'

I did as Drew said. The melody was very simple. A picture came to me of someone standing on top of a mountain, blowing a horn. I could hear the notes echoing through the hills, distinct and lonely-sounding. And what was weird was that I could actually see the music: it was like a tiny comet sailing very slowly up the valley.

'Now move away from the dark . . .'

'What?'

'That dark place where you are . . . step out of it. There's some light ahead of you: go and stand in it.'

I don't know if it was still the K working on me, but it really was as simple as Drew made out. There was a patch of sunlight, actually brighter than sunlight, just ahead of me and to the right, and all I had to do was go and stand near it. I didn't even have to stand in it. And all the edginess, the blackness, the dread began to ebb out of me.

Still Drew was waving the newspaper. 'Keep going, keep going,' he whispered.

'What do you mean?'

'Stand in the light, Georgia – you're not in the light yet. Don't hold back.'

So I stepped forward. As soon as I did so Drew's whistling and humming sounded much louder. It was all around my ears, down the back of my neck, in my hair. And the rustling newspaper sounded more and more like a breeze in the branches of a tree. In fact, the sound was indistinguishable. And suddenly, out of the blue, I had a vision of myself actually sitting under a tree, the silver birch I always sit under when I walk Fudge in Meanwood Park and the grass is dry. The roots form a sort of seat, and sometimes I can sit there for hours, just staring over the valley to the Ridge opposite, peeling away the ash-coloured bark.

It all started to get weird from then on.

'And I see white or silver, Georgie . . . Can you see silver?'

'What do you mean?'

'I see flashes of silver above you and around you. You're sitting on the ground and there's silver everywhere, like it's confetti.'

'Drew, I want to stop this now.'

'We've only just started . . .'

'Drew, I want to stop.'

London

The three of us – Roger, Diane and I – went to London on a day return when I was eleven to see *Cats*. When we arrived at King's Cross Roger went straight to an ATM.

In those days he and I had a game that when he was entering his PIN he would shield his fingers as they were doing the typing, and I would pretend not to be looking when I was. I don't doubt Roger would have told me his PIN had I asked, but the point of the game was that it was a guarded secret. There was something on this ATM, however, which he really was trying to conceal. It turned out to be a piece of ordinary lined A4 paper, cut out in the shape of a heart and about the size of an orange, and stuck on to the fascia with a glug of glue.

Someone – a kid, it was obvious – had coloured the outside edge blue with biro and had written in the middle the simple words 'Dad, we love you. Call us'. They hadn't even said who they were.

25

'What's that?' I asked Roger.

Roger scratched his head. You could tell he was pretending he was confused by the machine, when in fact the screen was already saying: *Please wait for your cash.*

'What's that?' I asked him again.

'Stations, and this area in particular, are well known for home-less people,' he explained eventually.

'What do you mean?'

'Well, it looks like someone's dad has left home and not come back.'

That was when I knew that originally I was from London, that my real parents were living somewhere in this giant city with its carpet of houses, its thunder of traffic, a never-ending background loop.

Methley

It was in the Methley I saw Grandma Myers the first time after she had died.

It's a good night in the Methley – you get a load of dreads, an old-school dub scene no mistake. I know it's called I-tal Night and they're keeping it real for a reason, but they're tolerant of pills there, more so than in Leeds and Manchester. So the vibe is good.

'Try one of these, Georgie,' Drew said, once the place was about half filled. Drew's particular about this: he likes to take his gear early, which means that you peak about the time the band comes on, and then if you want more, well, you just take more. 'That way you're not chasing it, you're letting it happen.'

'What is it? A dolphin?'

'A dolphin with a difference.'

'Oh, yeah? What kind of difference?'

'Let's just say it's a pink dolphin.'

'Stop talking bollocks, Drew, and tell me what you're giving me.'

'This, Georgie, was made from a plant that grows in the Amazon jungle – they call it *ayahuasca*, or Vine of the Soul.'

I made an expression like Drew was a kid and I was the school teacher, but I did notice that he was watching me quite carefully as I took it, almost to the extent that he was swallowing as I swallowed, a bit like when you're feeding a baby. The pill didn't taste any different from anything else I'd ever taken – perhaps a bit more chalky. Rewind! The aftertaste was disgusting, so bitter it made you gag just thinking about it.

I hung out between the decks and the door. The shape of the hall in the Methley means that they have to have the stacks facing each other, and here more than anywhere you get what Sula calls pockets of calm, areas where the bass frequencies from the two stacks cancel one another out. It's a weird phenomenon, a bit like swimming in the sea when all of a sudden you come across spots where for no reason the water's freezing cold or proper warm.

I was surprised how quickly the pill came up – within twenty minutes, which is unusual for me. To start with it was quite visual, a load of floaters, weird green shapes billowing and moving like those amoeba cells they make you stare at in biology lessons. It didn't matter if you had your eyes open or closed or whether you were looking into the light or away from it: the shapes were just there. I was thinking how unlike anything they were that you could draw – you could see them to study them, but it just seemed impossible for some reason to copy them or put them on paper – when suddenly the floor opened up in front of me and I was left standing on a precipice. I was scared now.

When things threaten to come on top the key is always to listen to the music: feel it, own it, be part of it. Because if you let the conscious bit of you take over, if you listen to yourself, you're going to get into trouble. 'Don't be so cerebral,' Sula is fond of telling me, but for some reason I don't find it easy to turn my thoughts off. They were playing a King Tubby mix, one of those tunes where you have a lot of guitar on its own, *chukah, chukah*, and you can hear the silence in between the strokes and the buzz of the static, and then suddenly the bass comes in, boom, boom, and you can just imagine the scoops vibrating in their cabinets.

It wasn't that hard to keep the fear at bay, not with a dub like that. In fact I was beginning to feel a little over-confident, like you do in an aeroplane which is going through turbulence and you're convinced you're going to die – then all of a sudden you're out the other side and, surprise, surprise, you're going to live after all. So I dared myself to look down at my feet again. This time I wasn't scared – just amazed. Because in front of me there was a staircase, I tell no lie, circular, like a helter-skelter or one of those shells that go round and round and you can't see further than the first bend. I heard myself go, 'Whooaa.'

I felt the fear come up again and I saw it off. But now a sort of knowledge had been given me, literally posted into my thoughts, that I must go down this passageway, there was something there I had to see, there was someone there who had something to show me. Yeah, right, I thought, I'm not taking even one step down this passage, but my feet seemed to have a different idea. Every time the bass went boom, a piece of the ground would dissolve in front of me and I'd sink a bit further. I was literally being swallowed by the floor.

Barrett was standing next to the decks. I tried shouting to him. 'Barrett! Barrett!'

But of course he couldn't hear me.

I started flailing my arms. 'Barrett! Barrett!'

Eventually he looked over. I could see his lips say one word, 'Easy . . .' which in my trip I took to mean: 'You'll take care of this, Georgie, you'll be cool.'

So I let myself sink.

At first it seemed just like any subterranean tunnel, pretty much identical to the one in the Dales we went down for my twelfth birthday but had to come up in a rush because Diane started breathing really hard and feeling dizzy. This tunnel in the Methley had the same rocky walls and smooth path underfoot and it seemed to be lit in the same way: you could see where you were going if you looked hard enough, but you had to go careful. Then I realized there was one big difference. In the walls there were windows, rectangular openings the size of large bricks. These windows had shutters of stone and were closed, but you could see chinks of light around the edges. The idea – again, it was like it was posted into my thoughts – was that you could push open the window and learn something. I didn't feel frightened, not at all at this point: I felt weirdly in control of myself yet open to the unexpected – and this was cool, too.

I stopped in front of a window. No, I wouldn't open this one; I went on a bit and stopped in front of another. I remember saying to myself, 'If I think about it long enough I'm going to chicken out, so what the hell? I'll have a look.' The stone shutter crumbled in my fingers and now I could see what there was on the other side. And I found myself looking down on a rave on a beach, two or three hundred kids dancing around a fire, Alex Garland style. What an amazing sight! There were palm trees bending in the breeze, great blankets of white surf unfolding on to the flat gold sand. And beautiful music. I don't generally like techno but these tunes were skipping and melodic: you wouldn't be able to keep still if you were at that gig. I must have spent an hour staring down at this scene, wishing I was there, but at the same time quite content with my perch, high up on a cliff behind the beach. The kids were really going for it, waving their arms in the air, doing all the 'big fish, little fish, cardboard box' hand movements they do at those raves. I thought, Good for them. Respect! You guys know how to enjoy yourselves.

I knew I needed to keep going. So down I went, passing two, maybe three windows that didn't seem 'right'. Then I thought, Okay, I'm going to have a look through the next one, it doesn't matter how it feels. Again the window crumbled in my fingers. And again there was a view of a beach – only this one wasn't nearly so enticing or interesting. It was just like the beach at Sands End, with a grey sea and grey clouds and grey sand. Not something I wanted to stand in front of staring at any longer than I had to. The only thing to look at was two lone people walking hand in hand. They weren't old and they weren't young; they were just quiet. The energy wasn't good. I felt sad for them, because you could see that they obviously weren't connected. In the distance, like it was sitting on the sea, was a ship. And the weird thing was this ship had a good energy, and the more I looked and thought about it, it seemed there were two poles, like masts, one of good energy and one of bad.

The third window was more difficult to shift: this one didn't crumble at all, it seemed to swivel on a hinge, and I had to go on tiptoe to see through the bit that opened up to get a glimpse of what was on the other side. And guess who was on the other side. Grandma Myers! Shit! I couldn't believe it. It couldn't have been for real. But it was. There she was, walking on yet another beach, as clear as day, with her hands behind her back, exactly like Grandma

Myers, staring into rock pools, every now and then stopping to gaze into the horizon. Even though I was well above her and to one side of her, she turned around the moment I spoke to her.

'Grandma Myers?'

'Georgia?'

'Grandma Myers, is that really you?'

'Of course it's me, silly.'

And 'silly' was an affectionate term of Grandma Myers's: it made me more convinced.

'I thought you were dead.'

'I am dead.'

'So what are you doing walking on that beach?'

'I'm looking for something.'

'What are you looking for?'

Grandma Myers did not answer immediately. Then she said, in a quieter voice, 'I've forgotten, I'm afraid, and until I remember I'm going to be stuck here.'

'How do you know that?'

Once again Grandma Myers sounded rather pathetic: 'I can't remember that either. Silly me!'

'Is there anything I can do to help?' I asked her, after a period of not knowing what to say.

'No, no, don't you worry about me. Kind of you to ask, though.'

I spun the stone shutter to the closed position, then almost immediately tried to open it again: I wanted to ask Grandma Myers a few more questions or I wanted to say sorry for thinking all those things when she was as cold as a stone in her coffin. But it was locked. I spent what seemed like an age hunting for secret buttons, shouting through the cracks – but nothing.

When I say an age, there's no telling how long *anything* went on for in that trip: the dimension of time, a dimension that should have been straighter than an arrow, was as twisted as a DNA molecule, totally warped. All I can say was that when I got back into the Methley and found myself standing next to Barrett, breathing his smell of coconut, the centre was much fuller than I remembered it. So perhaps even two hours could have passed.

'Has the band played yet?' I shouted into Barrett's ear.

And from the look on his face I could see how gone he thought I must be.

I stayed where I was for about another twenty minutes, just to make sure I could handle things on my own and didn't need Barrett, then headed off to find Drew. If he had been in the main room he would have been with Dan in the front-of-house desk, and if he had been in the back room he would have been by the monitor, and he wasn't in either of those places. So I went outside.

What's cool about the Methley is that on a good night there's actually more people outside than in. Just hanging, smoking spliffs, passing the time of night, because at a dub venue the sounds are almost as loud out as they are in and you can go along for free, socialize and hear some good plates. There was a good vibe that night. Two mobile food stalls were open for business: one selling jerk chicken, the other cheeseburgers in hard dough. Outside I reckon it was eighty per cent students, ten per cent dreads and ten per cent crew. Eventually I found Hazel.

'Seen Drew?'

'Last time I saw him he was outside the toilets pouring water over his head.'

And that was exactly where I found him, in the passageway where the toilets are. He was sitting down, his back against the wall, his feet straight out in front of him like he didn't care whether people trod on him or not. He had taken his shirt off;

his whole body was drenched in water. I slid down beside him.
'Drew!'

'Whooaa, Georgie!'

'You okay?'

'I seen some shit, man!'

And I had the satisfaction of saying to him, 'You call yourself
a shaman?'

Normal

Maybe that was the first time I thought things weren't quite so
normal.

To start with I was okay, I'd never ever slept as good as I did
the morning after that trip. Talk about organic. It was like being
dropped in a bed of moss: everything smelt fertile and earthy,
rich and cloying. What I didn't like about it was the fact that
the floaters didn't go away. Every time I closed my eyes I saw
those shapes, shapeless shapes, the same shapes you get when you
see oil in a puddle of water and it shines rainbow at you. Only
these ones were greeny brown – the colour of the moss I felt was
my bed. They were there the following night and they were also
there the day after. Tuesday evening they were still in evidence:
I was waiting to get the bus into town and they just started moving over the pavement. I felt my heart begin to pick up speed and
my breathing, too. It was only with the sound of traffic that I
managed to calm myself down. A traffic dub!

I found Drew in a KFC later that same night.

'They'll go, Georgie, don't worry.'

'Who said I was worried?'

'Well, if you are, don't be. This time next week you'll be wondering where they've gone.'

'You were a bit lost, weren't you?' I said, wanting to tease Drew because he always comes over wiser than thou, like he's done everything first and better.

'That's because I took two.'

'You took *two*?'

'Yeah.' He was nodding. 'I had to really hold it together.'

'That's not what it looked like to me.'

'What did it look like to you?'

'It looked like you were proper goosed.'

Drew shrugged. 'There was some heavy stuff going off in there, Georgia.'

I was laughing, trying to take the mick. 'Yeah, right!'

'Yeah . . . and some of it around you, too.'

That took the smile off my lips. 'What do you mean?'

'Just that there was plenty of action . . . if you could see it.'

At that moment a big lorry came screeching past the window we were sitting behind. I looked up in fright and for a second it seemed the lorry had a face and it was looking at me with its headlights, me and no one else. I couldn't tell whether it was me or the lorry who had got things wrong, if that makes sense, and I was scared, really scared, for a minute.

I wasn't sounding so cocky now. 'See what?' I asked.

'The energy,' was the answer.

'So what did you see?'

'Just light and dark.'

'"Light and dark"?'

Drew was sitting well back in his chair, like he was lording it over me – which he was. But at the same time I could see his eyes working fast, as if he wasn't sure he wanted to explain himself. Then it seemed he had made up his mind, and he sat forward and pushed away the cardboard carton of chips.

'When you're on the bus, on holiday, in town, wherever you are . . . you know what it's like: you see people who are dark, don't you? Unhappy, depressed people. You can tell they're unhappy just by the way they walk, the way they talk, the way they carry themselves . . . and usually by the darkness, the black rings, they have around their eyes. Isn't that right?'

I nodded.

'And you also see people who have a clean energy, people who are at ease with themselves, people who are relating in a cool, positive way to everything around them. There's nothing dark about the way they look. The opposite in fact: everything about them is bright and light. Not that it's something you can always actually see. You know what it's like: you can just *tell*, can't you?'

There seemed to be no point in contradicting this. 'Yes,' I answered.

'It's the same on a psychic level too, Georgia,' Drew went on, rotating his mobile on the tabletop, pointing it this way, then that way, then back again. 'Some people are dark; some people are light. There's really nothing more to it than that. In varying degrees, of course. When you take *aya* you just get to see it better.'

'So what have I got?' I tried to joke.

'You've got your share of darkness, Georgia.'

'But no more than anyone else?'

'Probably not.'

Even though I was careful not to appear too interested in what Drew was telling me, my curiosity was obvious.

'The shamans in South America believe that darkness can attach itself to you,' he continued, unprompted. 'Like a parasite attaches itself to your gut, stuff happens to you – traumas, pain, grief, general shit – and you take a hit.'

'What do you mean, "you take a hit"?'

35

'The same as getting physically ill . . . Maybe your immune system is poor . . . You get exposed to infection . . . and bang . . . you're ill.'

This seemed quite logical.

'The shamans also believe that you can be born with that darkness. In other words it's there from previous incarnations or previous generations from what's gone off before. Remember in *The Shining* when the chef's talking to the kid about ghosts? And he says that when bad things happen they can leave a trace . . . like the smell of burnt toast?'

'I don't believe in that stuff.'

'What stuff?'

'I don't believe in ghosts.'

Drew was smiling and shaking his head in that patronizing way he has. 'You've got them, I've got them, we've all got ghosts.'

I was shaking my head to say, sorry, I didn't agree.

'Okay, okay, try this.' Suddenly he sat forward. 'This will show you what I mean. You ready?'

I nodded.

'Think of the most embarrassing thing that has ever happened to you.'

'Drew!'

'Go on. Don't tell me what it is – just think about it.'

'Okay, then.'

Pretty much the most embarrassing thing that ever happened to me was when I was twelve. We were having lunch with Uncle Rob in his castle and it was a posh do and they had people helping and waiters serving. And this waiter came to offer me my dinner, and I couldn't really get it together, the business of getting the food off the serving plate: he was too far behind me and I was all crunched up. Anyway, the whole lot, *everyone's* dinner, ended up on the floor. And Uncle Rob just said (and there must have been over thirty people there for lunch): 'I think that means beef's off. Everybody okay with scrambled eggs?' And there was this dreadful silence.

Drew had closed his eyes and was rocking backwards and forwards in his seat. He still had a piece of chicken in one hand, which he was half waving from side to side, and because of this I couldn't really tell if he was making fun of me. 'I can feel the energy, Georgia,' he whispered eventually. 'You're feeling that feeling all over again, aren't you? Right now. There's a feeling of shame and there's a feeling that everyone's looking at you. Am I right?'

'You could be.'

'That's what I'm trying to tell you. That energy you're connecting with now . . . it's a ghost, a spirit, a darkness that has hooked into you. And it's *never* going to let go. Why should it? It's getting nourishment off you. It loves making you feel bad. You're going to go on feeling that shame and embarrassment for a very long time, Georgia. Do you follow me?'

'Sort of.'

'And some people are born with ghosts. Everywhere you go you see them. You know what it's like: people who look like they're weighed down, which is what they are, literally being dragged down, consumed by darkness.'

Drew was looking at me very carefully now. He knew I was adopted and, judging by how he glanced away from me and started to pick at the tabletop again, I think he was wondering whether he had gone too far, opened a door for me.

'But the good news is that there's an answer to it,' he said simply. 'Just like there's a positive to everything negative in this world.'

And Drew explained how when night came down in the Amazonian jungle, thick and black, the shamans gathered in special ceremonial buildings, buildings constructed from timber and mud, where they would call upon the spirits for guidance, knowledge and healing. 'The shamans are doctors, Georgia. But instead of dealing with physical ailments, they are trained and skilled in working with psychic energy. They can identify darkness and they can cut it out, just like a surgeon can remove a tumour or fix an artery. In camp last year a woman told me that after one of the ceremonies she felt as if a wet blanket had been lifted from her shoulders. She was telling me about this and her eyes were burning silver, burning silver.'

Orlando

Is such a lech. He goes to one of those posh boys' schools: Radley or Rugby or Uppingsomething.

We were in the folly in the wood behind Uncle Rob's castle ('Not a real castle,' as I overheard Diane explain to Valerie, one of her tennis partners, years ago, 'but a copy built by a Victorian mill owner. You know: a folly.'). I was sixteen. Orlando was seventeen. It was autumn and there was a smell of bonfires and the sound of snapping sticks in the air. We had been smoking a spliff and I remember thinking how much better Barrett's yard weed was than Orlando's skunk. We were both feeling pretty high, though.

'Come on, Georgia, give me a kiss,' Orlando said, after he had sidled up to me like a crab coming out of his hole.

I couldn't tell him straight up I didn't fancy him – I should have done – so he kept coming.

'Just let me kiss you.'

So we snogged. His mouth was dry and his teeth were cold and hard and when they banged against mine I felt a shudder go down to the bottom of my spine.

'Oh, Georgie,' he moaned, and he started trying to put his hand up my shirt. His fingers were cold and hard and stubby.

'Please, Orlando, don't!'

'But I fancy you, Georgie. I *want* you.'

And he was trying to lever his knee between my legs. That was it. I put a hand on each of his shoulders and pushed him away. 'For fuck's sake, Orlando! Get off!'

First he looked hurt, then angry. 'What's your problem?'

'*I* haven't got a problem.'

'So why won't you let me touch you?'

And he came at me again, this time holding my wrist and dragging my hand on to what I could see was his hard-on. 'I know you want it. I saw you looking at me last night.'

'You saw me looking at you?'

'I can see you want it, but you're scared, because . . . we're related.'

'You *what?*'

'Well, we're cousins, aren't we? But that's the whole point: we're not. We are on paper. Of course we are. But there's no blood between us. We can do what we want.'

And there was a similar thing about blood when I was much younger, say six or seven, and we were in the car – I think we were driving to Scotland and the journey was going on for ever. And I heard Diane say to Roger something along the lines of 'If there was an accident with Rob, you know, and the family, where would the castle go?'

And I was so young I thought she meant, was the castle going to fly away or something crazy like that.

'The castle would pass to me and then, well . . .'

'You mean, not to Georgia?' Diane whispered.

'I'm not sure, darling.'

'You mean it would bypass Georgia?'

'As I say, I'm not sure . . . and it's not really something I can check up on very easily.'

After that we drove the rest of the way to Scotland in silence, and even though I was six or seven I had a sense of what Roger and Diane had been talking about. Coin is like that: it talks to you on many levels.

Preston

The second time I spoke to Grandma Myers was in Preston.

The venue is rubbish. It's down in the basement of an arcade in the city centre, where the ceilings are so low you can reach up and touch them, and where they have this ventilation ducting that vibrates to pretty much every bass frequency there is. When you're standing by the decks you could be in the belly of an aircraft as it shakes and shudders into the air at take-off.

But it was an Ozymandias night and everyone had done their best to make the place look as good as it could, especially Dan with the lights. You couldn't actually see Barrett or any piece of his kit. He was behind a peacock's tail of green, blue and silver, as if he was sitting the other side of a waterfall, the place where you can keep as dry as a bone when in front of you there's a sheet of foaming water.

Third song in they played that Lloyd and Claudette cover and things began to happen:

> *I don't care what the people say*
> *I know that this is the way*

Sula was skanking up and down the stage, a tambourine in one hand, her shoulders down at her waist, rolling with the bass, then stopping, with that righteous pose she has, to sing over and over again:

I, I, I am the Queen of the World
I, I, I am the Queen of the World

Even though you could see that she was pushing it (sometimes you can't tell whether Sula's being serious or not) the dreads were really digging it. There was a bunch of them by the amp racks, some in boiler-suits, their heads sinking into their shoulders as they skipped to the beat. They looked like a group of elders at some weird prayer meeting.

I had taken some 'shrooms that Ben had given me and I was thinking how poor they were compared with Drew's *ayahuasca* – all I had was a fizzing on my forehead and a bit of a high, floaty feeling – when suddenly I started to see shapes again. This time they were like falling autumn leaves: no matter where I looked shapes were fluttering to the ground. And once again it was as if thoughts were being posted into my brain: now I was convinced that these shapes weren't an hallucination, that they were there all the time, existing in a world of their own, and it was just the drug which had pulled the curtains so that I could see them.

I remember thinking that 'shrooms had never done this to me before and how perhaps it was the *aya*, which was still somewhere in me, bringing it on, and I got to worry a bit. But it wasn't a serious worry: it was just a passing energy, if that makes sense, chameleon by nature. One minute the energy could be a happy one, then a sad one, then a pissed-off one.

Which was what it became. Pissed off at a tall white kid who had come up to the stacks and was dancing right in my space. He was trying to build a spliff like the dreads do when they're skanking, breaking the weed in the palm of one hand, and you got the impression that he thought the whole club was checking him, seeing how cool he was, waiting to see what he did next. And then – would you believe it? – even though he was standing one metre away from the stack and you wouldn't have made yourself heard even if you were being eaten alive by a wild animal, he answered his mobile phone! That was it: I was going to tell him what a retard he was, and why didn't he just go home and save everyone the embarrassment, when my phone started ringing too! Or, rather, I could feel it vibrating in my pocket.

And even though I was closer to the cabinets than that guy and there was no way I was going to hear one syllable of anything anybody said, it seemed the only thing to do was to answer it.

'Hello?'

The voice the other end was crystal clear. 'Georgia, it's Grandma Myers.'

'Grandma Myers! Can you hear me?'

'Of course I can hear you, silly.'

'What are you doing?'

'What do you think I'm doing? I'm talking to you.'

'That's incredible. You sound so close.'

Grandma Myers was using her business-like tone. 'I just wanted to let you know I'm all right,' she said. 'Last time we spoke you were kind enough to ask how I was, so I thought you'd be interested to know I'm through to the next level now.'

'The next level?'

'That's what I said.'

'What does that mean?'

'It means I found what I was looking for and I'm on to the next thing.'

'I'm really pleased for you,' I said.

I couldn't see Grandma Myers, of course, but her voice was so clear and so much hers that a picture came to me of her. Her hair was immaculate. She must have been to the salon that morning. She had on her oatmealy twin-set and the pearls she wore on special occasions.

'That's all I wanted to say,' she then said, and I could tell she was winding up.

I had a panicky feeling, the type you get when the phone's breaking up while you're trying to get directions, or something equally important, and you haven't got them clear in your mind. 'Grandma Myers?'

'Yes, darling?'

'While you're on, has anyone been asking about me where you are?'

There was a slight edge of suspicion in Grandma Myers's voice, as if she knew you were about to try borrowing some money off her. 'Asking about you?'

'You know – people who are interested in me?'

'My dear, everyone is interested in everyone here. That's what's so marvellous.'

'No, no, I mean special people.'

'Darling, this isn't a cryptic crossword.'

That was Grandma Myers's way: she had a knack of making you come out with it.

'No, no, what I mean is the people I'm connected to, the people I'm really related to. My real mum and dad's families. Those people.'

I could tell by the way Grandma Myers hesitated before she replied to my question that she wasn't going to be straight with me.

'I can't really say, Georgia.'

'Why not?'

'Because I'm not allowed to.'

Now I could see her frowning and sort of wringing her hands, or pretending to wring her hands.

'All I can say is that everyone is looking out for you; everyone wants you to be happy.' And she half winked.

'But have you met anyone related to me?' I persisted.

And again Grandma Myers wasn't quick to reply. 'My dear, we are all related in one way or another.'

'So you have met them?'

'Georgia, you're putting words into my mouth.'

'Just tell me, please! I need to know.'

'All I can say is that once you're here everything makes sense.'

And that was it. End of conversation. The phone just went dead. It was as if the selector had turned off his dub-plates mid-stream. I stayed put for a good twenty minutes, trying to get myself back to where Grandma Myers was. I felt there was a chance: sometimes when you're in the middle of a dream and you wake up you can get back into the dream if you try hard enough. But it wasn't to be.

Queen

Sula is queen, while Barrett and Ben, the crew and all the scenesters are the worker bees. And that includes me. Except I'm a worker bee who gets to spend a bit more time with her queen than most. And that makes all the difference.

We had done a gig in Manchester and we had got back to the Ibis at about five in the morning. It was starting to get light and Sula spent a good ten minutes standing on a chair in front of the window, making sure that each bit was blanked out by the blinds. Then she got into bed. It was pitch dark.

I hadn't done any drugs that night but still I was moving with the sounds of the dubs, just like when you step off a boat on to dry land.

Sula was spooning me. I could feel her breath down the nape of my neck. She smelt of the club: the cigarettes, the alcohol and a mixture of perfumes, none of which, I knew, belonged to her. But she also smelt of Sula: of her sweat, a delicious, deep, and only-her scent. Smells are weird. You can glance at someone and you get to see enough of them in that one look, but when it comes to their smells you have to take your time. Just like Fudge does in the park.

Sula kissed me beneath my ear. 'I'm mashed,' she said.

I snuggled backwards and into her. 'I love you, Sula,' I whispered.

'And I love you, too, my little Georgie.'

'I wish I was a boy.'

'Why do you wish that?'

'Because if I was a boy then I'd marry you.'

Sula pushed me away a fraction as if she was getting a better look at me, which she couldn't as there was no light. Then she laughed. 'Who said anything about me getting married?'

And suddenly I had the impression that I *was* a boy and that I was madly in love with Sula, like I was careering out of control, and wanted to marry her, and she had just told me that she didn't feel the same way. The feeling was so real, an icy sensation, that it almost took my breath away.

'What's up?' Sula asked.

My eyes were sore with tears and I was hot and cold all at once: hot because I was so grateful that Sula loved me, and cold because I feared she might give that love to someone else. And then where would I be?

'I don't know,' I replied, in a cracked whisper, and we both heard the despair like a black hole in my voice.

'You're tired,' Sula said, and she took me in her arms again and began to stroke my shoulder. Her flesh was tacky with sweat; as she moved her wrist it dragged at my skin. I felt myself falling into her and I closed my eyes.

'I need to find my real parents,' I murmured.

'I know you do.'

'I need to find them so bad.'

'You can find them when you're eighteen, can't you? You haven't got long to wait.'

'But what happens if I can't find them? What happens if I look and they're not there?'

'Then you'll have to come to terms with that, Georgie. If that's how it turns out then that's exactly how it should be.'

'Was it as it should be that I was given away?'

Sula took a moment before answering. 'Yes, Georgia, it was. At that moment in time it was exactly the right thing.'

'How can you know that?'

'Because it happened.'

Rochdale

I first met my mother a month later. In Rochdale.

It was the second time I took some of Drew's *ayahuasca*. At once I wished I hadn't. Forget about the club, the people, anything around me – I had to get out into the street and sit down. And the need to puke! I had my head between my knees, staring at the tarmac, retching from the bottom of my guts.

The feeling of terror was unlike anything I had known, only it had hardly started. I was literally like a rocket on countdown – I could feel the engines growling, then shuddering into life, then booming and screaming – and I was going to be sent high up into the air. And from there, there was only one way. Down.

I tried to concentrate on the music. I was just the other side of the fire exit and the wall I was leaning against was fizzing with the bass, but the music only made the chaos worse. It seemed to accelerate the effect of the *ayahuasca*, bring it on. I looked up. Where was Drew when you needed him? Nowhere.

I knew the free-fall was only a matter of seconds away and before it came I rolled on to my back. In this position I could pull myself up better, I thought, as all around me there were semi-invisible threads, a sort of glistening spider's web, that I could hold, grip and climb. But it was a losing battle: I was sinking, I was headed for the bottom of a pit no matter how much I climbed and tried to save myself. And the fear was all around me, thick, dark. One moment there were bats in my face, the next I could see into the next millennium – and it was just pitch black, as black as a well.

Once I had reached the bottom it seemed pointless trying to climb any more. I was in a massive cave, a chasm, with dripping water splintering around me. I was calmer now. Okay, I thought, here I am, lost to the human race, I've only got myself to blame, as Roger would say, so just pipe down. And I was proud of myself, proud that I had got through the worst – and then, as if I was being punished for thinking I had got through it, it came on again, much stronger than before.

'Please, please,' I could hear myself moan. 'Help me, save me.'
And then silence once more. And now someone real to look at. A young girl, maybe four or five years old, wearing a gingham dress, a red bow in her fair hair. I stared at her for what seemed like a year in time. I could tell she was spoilt. She had everything a little girl could want – dolls, a pram to put them in, and a heap of other toys and picture books – but there was something not right with her.

'What's up, little one?' I asked.

The little girl just looked at me. I couldn't tell whether she was sullen or scared, but her mouth was buttoned up and she wasn't going to answer.

I was determined to make her speak. 'Haven't you got enough toys?'

Again no answer.

'Things can't be that bad, surely?'

And even though the little girl was too young to know whether things were bad or not, she began to cry.

'Darling, I'm sorry, I didn't mean to upset you.' I tried to soothe her. 'Please don't cry.'

'It's not your fault,' another voice said.

'Who's that?' I asked.

'It's me.'

And beyond the little girl, seated in the type of hollow you get in a bee's honeycomb, there was a young woman. The light was so thin I could hardly see her.

'Who are you?' I demanded.

'I am the little girl's mother.'

'Then why aren't you cuddling her?'

The young woman did not answer immediately. 'Because I can't,' she said eventually, and there was a note of such sadness in her voice it was as if the whole world was going to break under its weight.

'What do you mean, you can't?'

'I wish I could but I can't.'

'This is all you do,' I said, and I was going to step forward and take the little girl's hand – but I couldn't. Just like in one of those dreams where you find yourself powerless, I couldn't even lift a finger. I looked imploringly at the young mother, who remained expressionless. Then she turned away and bowed her head in the grey, still light; she resembled a statue now.

'Hello?'

No answer.

'Hello?'

Again no answer.

'Little girl?'

The little girl had not turned to stone. She was looking at me as if her eyes would burst with tears.

'Little girl. What is your name?'

The little girl swallowed before answering. 'My name is Georgia.'

Safe

'And if anyone asks if we've got a safe, what do you say?'

'We haven't got one,' Diane and I would answer, in singsong voices (this was when I was much younger and things were better between us all).

'And what if the robbers say, "We know you've got a safe. Open it up"?'

'We'll say we don't know the combination.'

This satisfied Roger. 'Very good,' he would answer.

The safe in our first house was behind a picture in the hall. The safe in our house now is in the dining-room floor. 'Sunk in concrete,' as Roger once explained, dead chuffed. 'They'd have to chain it to the back of a car to pull it out . . . probably a four-by-four at that.'

Once I had turned thirteen and the babysitters stopped, getting into the safe became an obsession. As soon as Roger and Diane were out of the house that was where I'd be, pulling back the square of carpet in the corner of the dining room, playing with the dial. I didn't know what I'd discover in there: gold, silver, diamonds, wads of cash. But I was never going to find out – not on my own. Not until I enlisted the help of Harry, who lived on the other side of the park and whose father was a detective super-intendent – at least, that was what Harry told me his job was.

'You've got to listen to the clicks,' he said, and he would be lying with his head over the dial, twiddling it backwards and forwards. I felt a bit guilty letting this boy into my home and giving him the job of safe-breaker, but I half fancied Harry. And standing behind him I could take my time staring at his body spread-eagled on the floor, with his long blond hair matted into the carpet. There was such a distant look in his eyes, as if every bit of energy he had was going into trying to hear the mechanism, such an intense and such a faraway expression, that the more I looked at it the less I could understand it.

After a few visits Harry had a different idea. 'What's your father's birthday?' he asked.

'Second of August.'

'Second of August what?'

'I've no idea.'

'Okay. No problem, let's try oh two oh eight.'

'And your mother's birthday?' when that didn't work.

'She's not my mother.'

'You know what I mean.'

'Fourteenth of November. She's a Scorpio,' and I pretended to pinch Harry's arm.

'No good either. And your birthday?'

'My birthday?'

'Yes, yours.'

'Eleventh of February.'

'Eleven oh two. And the dog's?'

'Fudge's, you mean?'

'Yes.'

And the door pulled open. 'Fuck me!' Harry said. 'We've done it.'

I wasn't going to let Harry see what was in the safe and we ended up snogging on the sofa, which was the best way I could think of to distract him. And although we were only kids and he was rough when he was touching me, the thought of that door, which was like a secret opening into another realm, made everything a whole load more exciting.

'Georgia, you're hot,' he told me, and then blushed the colour of a setting sun.

I didn't get a chance to open the safe again until Roger and Diane went to a Chamber of Commerce dinner about a month later. I made it into something of a ceremony, dimming the lights, drawing the curtains so there was not even a chink of outside visible, double-locking the front door and leaving the key in the lock, so that if Diane had one of her attacks and they had to leave the dinner early at least I'd have the warning of them banging on the door before they got in.

There were some valuables inside: a brooch and a gold bracelet, which I think had once belonged to Grandma Myers; some dollar bills held in a tight roll by a blue elastic band; some pieces of thick paper, each of them with the words Share Certificate written at the top; and then there was the brown envelope with 'Georgia' written in biro over the front. This was it: the envelope that I had known would be in there without knowing it, if that makes sense.

The flap wasn't glued so there was no problem in taking out all the papers. There weren't many, I remember thinking, and I was disappointed. But what was there was pretty earth-shattering. The first started something like this: 'Dear Mr and Mrs Myers, I am pleased to tell you there is the possibility of a baby girl in whom you may be interested. If so, please will you telephone me either first thing in the morning or on Monday? Yours sincerely'.

The next letter was the one I read over and over again.

Dear Mr and Mrs Myers,

Further to our telephone conversation, I am glad to know that you would like to come for baby Lily. Here are a few details about her. She was born on 11 February when she weighed 6 lbs 11 ozs. She has made good progress and her medical certificate is satisfactory. She will have to have a blood test before the court stage is reached.

Her mother Elizabeth is from a good family. Her father works in the City of London, and her mother before she married was a florist. Elizabeth went to a good school where she obtained eight O levels but failed her A levels. After she left school she worked in the tourist industry. She is twenty years old.

Baby's father in twenty-six years old. He is a joiner. He is dark with brown eyes.

Elizabeth is an attractive girl with fair hair who is most anxious to do the best for baby Lily. She has thought carefully about adoption and feels that it is the right thing to place Lily for adoption so that she may have a secure home with two loving parents.

I am pleased to tell you that we have arranged for you to come for Baby on Wednesday, 20 March, at 1.45 p.m. Come prepared to take her straight home with you, so bring a small empty case for her things and an extra shawl or blanket. Please would you confirm these arrangements?

Yours sincerely . . .

So this was it! The answer to all the questions! I was really called Lily and my mother was called Elizabeth; she was from a good family; she had eight O levels; she wanted to do the best for me. I was thirty-six days old when I was given away; all my belongings fitted in a small empty suitcase. My father was dark and he was a joiner. A big lump had been forming in my throat as I read and reread all the details, and as soon as I finished the letter I burst into tears. I didn't know what specifically the tears were about, but they were tears all right: hot and wet, maybe tears of relief.

There were other letters, most of them typewritten, which had all the practical details about me. There was a long one from a case secretary to a Mr Stuart whose job title was county children's officer. It started in a pretty formal way: 'Thank you for your letter informing us that you have been appointed as Guardian *ad litem* in respect of an application to adopt the above . . .' Blah blah.

Then the interesting bit:

> The father of the child is twenty-six years old, single,
> and is employed in the overseas construction indus-
> try. They met abroad and went out for a matter of
> months only. He was informed of the pregnancy and
> broke off the association . . . From the report of your
> own department, from the reports of our visitor, and
> from our observations, everything is completely satis-
> factory and it would appear that the making of an
> Adoption Order would be in the best interests of the
> child.

For some reason I did not want to read any more at that first
sitting. I needed time to digest. I dropped the door to the safe and
spun the combination dial as if it were a roulette wheel. There
was nothing startling about what I'd read; in fact, compared
to the fantasies I'd built up over the years, all the details were a
bit tame. Although I have to be honest and say I was relieved.
I liked the bit where my mother's family was described as 'good'.
I know it's not very PC to say it but if my mother really had been
a chav that would have been quite a challenge to my pride and
self-esteem.

Over the next few weeks there were plenty of opportunities to
get back into the safe, but I dragged it out, relishing the snippets
like a good meal: City of London; florist; good school; O levels
but no A levels (good on you, girl!); tourist industry. And brood-
ing over the others. So it was my father who hadn't wanted me. It
was he who had broken off the association, abandoned my poor
mother. Bastard! But still I was relishing the prospect of what I
felt sure remained to be discovered.

And then, as always, pride came before a fall. Or in this case pride came before confusion, which is really worse than a fall.

No one had been in the safe since I'd last been in, I could tell: everything was exactly as I'd left it – the roll of dollars standing on its end but at a bit of an angle, the diamond brooch staring out from the corner of the steel box. This time I spread the papers in a great fan shape on the floor. I had all the time in the world, as Roger and Diane were having dinner in Halifax at Uncle Rob's and I had refused to go, saying I had homework, but in reality I didn't want the hassle of dealing with Orlando, his big arse and stubby fingers.

There was one more letter from the case secretary and several from a case worker, a Mrs Walker, with sentences like: 'We confirm to the best of our knowledge that the mother is single and there is no order or agreement as to maintenance in respect of this child. With our good wishes.'

There was another dated six months after I was born. 'Dear Mr and Mrs Myers, Many thanks for your most generous donation to our council. Your support is greatly appreciated. We now enclose our Covenant and Banker's Order, as you requested.' Which made me sit up. So, as usual, money had changed hands! Surprise, surprise. Coin!

Then there was the medical certificate with loads of questions. For instance, under General Condition: Skin; Eyes; Ears; Nose and Throat; Speech; Alimentary System; Nervous System (including fits). Against these was written: Normal or Not Available.

Then the three letters, which were literally like a door into yet another room. It was as if you had explored the house, acquainted yourself with its layout, then suddenly another corridor was leading off into a part of the building you had no idea was there. The first was a photocopied letter of Roger's on one sheet of A4.

It read:

Dear Mrs Walker,

Here is a letter about Georgia for Mrs Peddar. We were sorry to hear about her unfortunate circumstances and hope news of Georgia will help in a small way. So that you may pass the letter on I have written it on a plain sheet and know you will respect our anonymity in spite of the very unfortunate situation. I enclose a photo and leave it to you – knowing Mrs Peddar – as to whether you think it should be passed on to her.

Yours sincerely . . .

Then Mrs Walker's reply:

Dear Mr and Mrs Myers,

Just a line to let you know I have had a letter from Mrs Peddar and she wishes to tell you how grateful she is for the photograph and news of Georgia. It is a great comfort to her to know that Georgia has grown into such a beautiful little girl. Thank you very much for your kindness in writing.

Stapled to this was a Xerox of the letter from Mrs Peddar herself. The address at the top of the A4 sheet was PO Box 148.

Dear Mrs Walker,

Thank you so very much for the photograph, which I will always treasure. Georgia is a beautiful little girl and I can see how well cared for and loved she must be. Would you please thank her parents for the news they have sent to me, also for the photograph? Thank you once again for all you have done to help me. I feel now that part of Ralph is close to me.

Yours sincerely . . .

So my father was called Ralph. That wasn't exactly what I was expecting! But the fact was something had gone off with him. And it sounded pretty bad.

Tennis

I'd got off at the wrong bus stop because I'd been so busy talking on my mobile, and I was doing a short-cut through the Tong Road Tennis Club car park, when I came across a couple snogging in a Porsche Boxster.

I knew it was Uncle Rob's Porsche Boxster before I knew it, if that makes sense.

And I knew the woman was Diane, even though it was semi-dark, also before I knew it; but really, I suppose, because of the shape of the back of her head and the way she was turning and leaning over in her seat.

If I had seen them a few seconds beforehand I might have stopped out of view to see what they were getting up to, but I was already just about passing the bonnet of the car with its poxy badge.

Fate's a funny thing. It had me walking in front of that very car in that very car park and at that very moment in time. And it had Diane and me look at each other, too.

I wasn't exactly going to stop and exchange pleasantries, as Roger calls it, but I wanted Diane to know that I had seen her: I had to let her know that. And she did. In the flash of the next second our eyes locked, and there and then we both knew the game was up. I, Georgia Myers, had caught Diane Myers snogging Uncle Rob, Roger's brother, her husband's brother, in a Porsche in the Tong Road Tennis Club car park.

But that night, as she made herself busy about the kitchen, with Roger and me sitting at the breakfast bar, having our evening chat (one of the last, as it turned out), she had the gall to pretend she hadn't seen me. She just looked at me as if she was looking through me, or like a curtain had come down between us. And I thought, You cow! You bitch! As Grandma Myers would say: 'What a liberty-taker!'

I didn't tell Roger I'd seen Diane snogging Uncle Rob. I couldn't. How could I? And I wasn't going to confront Diane when we were alone either. That wouldn't be cool. But I let her know that I knew she knew.

'Have you been playing tennis today?' I asked her, with Roger reading the paper right next to me.

'No,' she answered, with her head slightly to one side. 'Why do you ask?'

'I thought Thursday was your tennis day.'

'Not this Thursday.'

'Been in town, then?'

Now Diane fixed me with her eyes and they were level and still. 'No, I've been with Valerie. Why do you ask?'

'Just interested,' I said, in my most ordinary voice.

That's when I reckon I became an adult, that night. Not that I think Diane is an adult any more than a teenager is. But to drag me into her sordid affair like that and make me lie to Roger, even if Roger hadn't actually asked me a question that would have meant me having to lie, it seemed like I had been dragged into the lion's den with the door slamming behind me. Fucking great!

I felt so sorry for Roger, poor innocent Roger, that I found myself hoping he had a lover too. Only I knew he wouldn't dream of making out in a car park. His affair would be in Paris or Stockholm or somewhere interesting like that, when he was on business seeing clients. It sounds sick but I would be rooting for him. If we were driving along and pulled up alongside an attractive woman at the lights, I would be trying to get Roger to have a look by telepathy, by saying loud and clear and silent: 'Roger, there's this gorgeous woman sitting a matter of feet away to your right. She'll treat you better than Diane. Have a look.'

Underpass

Drew and I were in Birmingham, making our way from New Street to Aston, trying to cross a dual carriageway to where the bus station was. It was a massive junction. There was an underpass and a bridge over the road for pedestrians.

'I'm going under,' Drew said.

'It's quicker to go over,' I said.

'Well, I'm going under.'

'Why? It's twice as far.'

There was a firmness in Drew's voice. 'Because I am. That's why.'

So I went over. Because I reckoned I would be on the other side much sooner than Drew, I stopped halfway. It was weird staring down at the traffic zooming underneath me and imagining Drew the other side of that with loads of earth on his head. The thought of Drew being underground made me think of Grandma Myers's funeral, and I took time out to talk to her for a minute.

'Grandma, you okay?'

Grandma Myers answered immediately. 'I'm fine, darling. Things are going better for me than I thought here.'

'How do we get to Aston?'

'You get the bus, silly.'

'Which bus?'

'The number eight.'

It felt good to think that I could check in with Grandma Myers whenever I wanted to, and I took the steps down to street level two at a time. But Drew was nowhere to be seen. So I went into the entrance to the underpass, which smelt of piss and rain. It was dark and there was no light ahead, nothing to walk towards. Suddenly I began to feel cold and alone, and to keep my thoughts at bay, without really thinking too much about the lyrics, I began to hum that Toots dub, which Sula sings with a voice like she really is lost to the world:

> *And I swung right out of the belly of a whale*
> *And I never get weary yet*
> *They put me in jail and I did not do no wrong*
> *And I never get weary yet*

Weird! Here I was, Jonah, trying to get out of the belly of a whale, the tiled walls all shiny with slime, the stomach a vast chamber with everyone's footfall hollow and empty-sounding. I got to what must have been the middle of the road, with other tunnels leading off in loads of directions to other points in the junction, like the spokes on a bicycle wheel, but still no Drew. So I followed the arrow back towards New Street Station. And found him more or less where I had left him.

'Dude! What you doing?'

Drew wouldn't answer. There was a look in his eye like he was listening very carefully for something, a snapping twig, the faintest whisper.

'Drew, what's going on?'

'There's something not good here, Georgie.'

I looked back into the underpass. There was a mother with a pram just coming out of the darkness. 'I know,' I said. 'There *is* something weird here. I felt it in there just now.' I pointed back towards New Street. 'Let's go.'

There was a grim look on Drew's face as he shook his head. 'I can't,' he said.

'Why not?'

He gestured ahead. 'I've got to go through there.'

'What do you mean, you've got to go through there?'

'You can't run away from this stuff, Georgia.'

For a second I was frightened. 'Drew, stop talking bollocks!'

'Georgia, you go on. I'll catch up with you later.'

'Like hell.'

'Then just stand behind me and follow me footstep for footstep.'

And Drew started to hiss and blow through his teeth, a sort of sucking in reverse, as if he was blowing the seeds from a dandelion or he was trying to get the best score he could by blowing into one of those tubes they use at the doctor's to measure the strength of your puff.

'Zzooh, zzooh . . .'

Every last ounce of energy was going into pushing something out of him, and you could tell he wouldn't be able to keep it up for ever: already there was sweat glistening on his forehead and his cheeks were the colour of dough. Between breaths he shook his head, just like you do when you're back in fresh air having dived into the sea and you're getting the water out of your hair and ears.

'Jesus, Drew! What are you doing?'

When Drew turned to answer, he looked at me and through me in the way he does when he's tripping. I hate seeing the whites of Drew's eyes: it freaks me out.

'There's spirits in there, Georgia, bad spirits,' he said. 'We've got to take our time . . . do things right.'

I could hear myself swallowing over the sound of the tunnel's silence.

'We've got to go around them . . . only go where they can't get us.' And once again Drew went through the motions of hissing and blowing, only this time he was scrunching the ground with his feet as well, as if he was screwing out a cigarette butt.

It took us about an hour to reach the bus station. We would get back to the middle of the underpass where the tunnels radiated in different directions only for Drew to shake his head and we would have to go back to where we had started.

He told me later (and, what was weird, I knew exactly what he meant) it was as if there were curtains hanging all around us and ahead of us. Sort of shower curtains. And if you walked past them too fast or carelessly, they stuck to you and stung you with their venom. Just like when the fronds of jellyfish that wrap around your arms and legs and sting you, you don't get to know you've been stung until afterwards, when it's too late. It was a question of choosing the right tunnel and then swimming stealthily past the spirits, letting them know that you were there, that they couldn't attack you, that you were too strong to mess with. Finally we got ahead. And do you know which way we went? Over the road! On the same bridge that I had crossed originally!

And listen to this. The bus to Aston was the number eight.

So Grandma Myers was on the money!

Violence

I hate violence. One night in Leeds we were just getting under way and word came through from the door: 'There's a load of hoodrats and they're jacking the punters.'

And we all rushed outside and there was this big bouncer – Chessy, they call him – who had one of the hoodies against the wall and he was giving him a good hiding. You could hear the sound of the punches smashing into this guy's face and it made me think, Shit, just imagine if this bloke was hitting me.

I was fascinated – there and then, and afterwards – about everyone else's reaction to this event, this beating. Barrett was standing there, nodding, dead cool, like a spectator at a snooker match; Sula was looking on with that serious, righteous expression on her face, the one where you can't really tell what she's thinking or going to do next; Hazel did seem shocked, but nowhere near as shocked as I must have appeared. Ben was smiling. And there were a few other people who were shouting and jeering, encouraging the bouncer to let rip. The whole thing made me sick. I went into the back room and sat in the corner furthest from the bar. The place was completely empty.

Why did I feel so scared? It wasn't me who was getting a beating; it wasn't going to be my turn next. So why was I shaking? Why did my knees feel like they were trembling to a bass that wasn't there? Maybe it was a sub-bass, it occurred to me then: a bass frequency so low that you couldn't actually feel or hear it, but one that was there anyway, doing its business. A sub-dub.

I could hear Barrett talking to Chessy at the door, calming him down, reasoning with him. It's funny how the bloke who does the beating can sometimes end up sounding like the one who has taken it. And I began to wonder, just like I'd done so many times before, where this fear came from. Not from Roger, that was obvious – his favourite television sport is boxing. On *Fight Night* we've got to eat early and you get to hear him shouting: 'Stop it, Ref.' Or: 'Go on, finish it now!' This fear was from somewhere buried very deep, I knew then for sure. It was something I could only have inherited from my birth parents. Where else? So were Elizabeth and Ralph cowering cowards like me? Was that why I had been given away? Had they done the cowardly thing? Had they been too scared even to look at me?

But did they now regret it, having realized too late that fear is, as Drew told me after that second *ayahuasca* trip, fear of fear, and nothing more?

Water

The water in this place sucks. Maybe there're drugs in the hospital mains and that's why it tastes so bad. I get my supply from the shop in the foyer.

There's a whole lot of stuff going off here, a whole lot of bad energy. There's plenty going off in the main bit of the hospital, where people are dying and suffering, them and their folks; and there's enough going down in Faversham House, that goes without saying. The eighteen people here have got mental-health problems. I haven't got mental-health problems. According to Dr Murdo, I'm suffering from nervous exhaustion, exacerbated by some of the street drugs I've been using. I'm free to leave whenever I wish.

That wasn't what they told me when first I got referred.

'She's psychotic, responding to hallucinations,' I overheard Dr Murdo tell Roger and Diane, after I'd been asked to wait in the corridor, 'and she needs specialist attention.'

Specialist attention! I get to take two tablets four times a day; and I get to talk to a trainee psychiatrist lady called Kathleen. I wish she'd read her notes before our sessions as she tends to ask the same questions over and over again. 'Have you ever been abused?' and 'Do you ever dream you're flying or travelling very fast?'

When I got admitted here – what a fiasco. Dr Murdo was asking all these questions. What day was it? What month was it? Who was the Prime Minister? Could I please spell 'eagle' backwards? Would I please take these pills?

'No, I don't want to.'

'You must,' Diane said.

'I think you really better had,' Roger agreed.

'I'm not going to,' I kept on repeating, until that butch nurse I can't stand mumbled, in a matter-of-fact sort of way, 'I think that means it's Plan B, then.'

The room was dark when I woke up a few hours later, alone, hot and thirsty. To be honest, it was a relief not to be at home, having to see and talk to Diane, and feeling sorry the whole time for Roger, who had got to look so worried lately. I lay in the bed for what seemed like a year, staring at the door, wondering whether it was locked or not, but my legs and arms and body felt so heavy I couldn't even move to check. Finally I pulled myself up and sat with my head between my knees, the room sparkling, like I was at a gig and the whole place was dissolving into a crescendo of sound and light.

I made it to the door. It was not locked. I pulled it towards me and looked out into the passage. There was a black woman outside, standing guard like she was a sentry, with a gold and red badge on her shoulder that read: 'Joyce, Health Adviser'.

'How are you feeling, Georgia?' she asked.

'Like shit.'

'Can I get you anything?'

'Some decent water, please.'

Xylophone

There isn't too much you can say about a xylophone. The only time I've heard one is on some of Roger's jazz records. By a musician called Roland Kirk.

'This is the type of stuff Grandpa Myers used to like,' Roger explained to me loudly, over the tinkling, fluttering sound. 'Grandpa Myers liked his jazz.' He nodded with a faraway look. 'Poor old Grandpa Myers.'

I'd never met Grandpa Myers, and I'm not sure Orlando had either; and if he hadn't I'm not sure why either he or I had to call him Grandpa Myers. But he was evidently a man to be feared or respected. Whenever anybody speaks about him, they do so with that distant gaze.

This was about three weeks ago.

I wanted to talk to Roger about my mother. I wasn't exactly going to tell him I'd *met* her, and that I was worried about her because there was something not right about her energy, but I wanted to broach the subject anyway. And maybe end up by saying that when I was eighteen I was going to undertake a search, that there was this website called adoptionsearch.com that helped reunite families (it wasn't just adopted people and adoptees they helped: families got split up for all sorts of reasons). That there was a photo of a woman called Heather Cross, and that this was the person I was going to ask to help me: I liked the look of her – there was just something *right* about her. And then probably Roger was going to ask how much it was all going to cost. Which was the first thing he says about any plan. And why didn't I use Social Services? And I was going to say I couldn't be doing with Social Services, to which he'd say: 'Of course you can't, Georgia. I shall pay for the search.'

But the conversation never took place. Because Roger looked so fragile. I reckon he had found out about Diane cheating on him – in fact, I know so. If I had asked him all the questions I didn't ask him and then asked him what he felt about it all, I know he would have said, 'I want you to be happy, Georgia.' And because I knew that he'd say this before I had even asked him there was no point in talking about it in the first place. I knew it would be hurtful to talk about my birth parents, and this wasn't the moment to pile on the hurt when he was already being deceived by one of the women in his life. That Diane: she's a bitch, you know.

Y

?

Zener

There are twenty-five cards in the Zener pack, which Drew keeps
in a drawer next to his cooker. Five squares, five five-pointed stars,
five plus signs, five circles and five cards with three wavy lines
going from top to bottom.

The person conducting the experiment sits at one end of
the room, the subject at the other. After shuffling the cards the
experimenter withdraws one card from the pack and holds it
blank-side up to the subject, who has to use his ESP – according
to Wikipedia, his knowledge of the outside world through something that cannot be explained by the five senses – to determine
which card is being shown him.

If you get five out of twenty-five, you're average at twenty per
cent. If you get eight per cent you're considered to have a negative
ESP; if you get thirty-two per cent or more you're considered at
have a 'budding' ESP.

The first time I did it I got sixteen cards right out of twenty-
five: sixty-four per cent in other words.

Drew was staggered. 'That's amazing, Georgia.'

I shrugged, just like I did on holiday in Scotland years ago
when I dangled a bunch of worms into a river and caught the
salmon Roger had been trying to catch all week.

But the second time I did it I scored just eighteen per cent.

We did it for hours. It seemed the harder I tried the worse was
my score. And the more I tried not to think about what was on
the reverse side of the card and tried to concentrate on something
else really absorbing, the better I did.

'That's exactly how it is,' Drew said. 'You can't force
clairvoyance.'

'What is the hell is clairvoyance?'

'*Clair* means clear. *Voyance* means seeing. Seeing clearly. Nothing more.'

'You think people really *can* see stuff?'

Drew laughed his most patronizing laugh. 'What do you think?'

THREE

I finished reading my A–Z.

Some things were apparent. I had a sense of humour now. I should never take myself too seriously (probably the same thing). And that if ever I was confronted with a similar situation in wanting to know something as big and dangerous as this . . . don't bother.

'I think you're right, you do have more of a sense of humour, Georgia,' Dr Murdo said, as we sat in his George Street office, him in his chair, me in an armchair by the window. 'You were very serious last year. Everyone remarked on it. Why such a difference?'

I shrugged. 'I was younger, I suppose.'

'Not by much, though.'

'It feels like a long time ago.'

He nodded. 'Which, I suppose, in a sense, reading this,' he said, his hand on the folder, 'it is.'

Dr Murdo let the silence grow. Most people get uncomfortable when they don't know what to say, and they end up just saying any old thing to hide their nervousness. I could hear John Silver and Mack shouting in the common room and I could hear the sound of the laundry trolley being wheeled down the corridor. And I could hear the silence between Dr Murdo and me. But for some reason this time it wasn't making me nervous.

'Do you want to tell me what happened after you left Faversham House on the second of August last year?' he asked.

'Not much . . .'

'Can we talk about it?'

'We could.'

'Do you think it would be helpful?'

'I don't know.'

'Do you think that writing the A–Z was helpful?'

'It was a bit random.'

He laughed. 'That's its purpose!' he said. 'And let me tell you, you're not the first person to write about xylophones!'

Pause.

'But do you think it was helpful? That was my question.'

'Up to a point.'

'Can you say to what point?'

'It fixes stuff.'

'But what do you mean it fixes stuff? For you or for other people?'

I must have looked nervous.

'Not other people in that sense, Georgia,' Dr Murdo reassured me. 'You know we have an understanding: whatever passes between us does so in strictest confidence.'

Silence.

'It "fixes stuff"?'

'Once you've written something you can't unwrite it,' I answered.

'A bit like a photograph?'

'If you like.'

'And if you say something, recount it, tell it, then it's not as . . . valid? Is that what you mean?'

'I didn't say that.'

'I beg your pardon, I know you didn't. But I'm struggling to understand exactly what you do mean when you say that "Once you've written something you can't unwrite it."'

His words were beginning to crowd in on me, like giant butterflies with broad, feathery wings.

'It's just that writing it makes it more real, I suppose,' I said.

Dr Murdo nodded in his Dr Murdo-like way. 'I see.'

There was another silence. This time it was like that padded sound you get when there's snow all around you: heavy and thick.

'Perhaps it might be better for you to go on writing about what happened, Georgia,' he went on eventually, 'rather than for us to sit and talk about it. Perhaps things would become clearer for you if you put them down on paper again.'

I said nothing.

'Does the thought of that worry you?'

'Not really,' I lied.

'So: do you want to go on writing, or shall we talk?'

I didn't answer immediately. There were definite black spots in the room, the type you see after you've been lying flat on the beach and think you haven't been looking at the sun when in fact you have. I had to keep them back. 'I could write some of it, I suppose,' I answered. 'But not . . . all of it.'

'O-*kay*,' he murmured, and I could tell that he didn't really want to go on questioning me on an indefinite basis, but that because he was a doctor he had to. 'Is there a reason that you can't write about all of it?'

I didn't want to bring Phoebe Evans's fat envelope into the

discussion, the envelope I had just managed to slide behind the print of Van Gogh's *Sunflowers* above my bed – everything in Faversham House is screwed to the floor or the walls. Not now. 'Because I don't know everything,' I said absently.

Dr Murdo sat up. 'You don't *know* everything?' he repeated.

'That's what I said. Look: I'm happy to write about some of it, but not all of it . . . not the end. Okay?'

'Will you be able to *talk* about what happened at the end?'

'I won't know until I get there . . .'

'So you don't know what happened at the end?'

I didn't answer.

'Sorry, Georgia, I just want to establish this point, it's important. Is it because you don't want to talk about what happened that is preventing you? Or is it because you don't actually know what happened that is stopping you talking or writing about it?'

'Both.'

And we started laughing.

'Okay, let's cross that bridge when we come to it, eh?' Dr Murdo sort of huffed, a bit like Roger does when he's reading the paper and finds something funny to laugh about. 'But in the meantime I think you *should* write about what happened – just go as far as you want. My only advice is not to think about it too much – just write it. Okay?'

FOUR

I was wrong about Heather Cross. I can see now that I was probably wrong about a whole lot of stuff. Maybe my expectations were too high. But when I saw her photo on the net, with the caption underneath that read, 'Heather Cross, Intermediary with 15 years' experience', for some reason I convinced myself that my problems were half over.

I emailed her at adoptionsearch.com and got a reply the same day.

> Hi, Georgia, thanks for yours. As I can see you
> already know, there's not much we can do in a
> practical sense until your eighteenth birthday –
> we could meet, though, to discuss the possibility
> of working together. Let me know. Kindest
> regards, Heather

I didn't reply for some weeks, not until I was admitted to Faversham House the first time around and Joyce let me access my Facebook and hotmail accounts from the staff room when no one was looking.

- Please come to see me if possible [I wrote]. I'm
  in hospital in Manchester.
- I'm sorry to hear you're in hospital [she replied].
  I am collecting a friend from the airport
  Thursday p.m. We could meet then.
- Yes, please. I'm in Faversham House – annexed
  to the Infirmary.
- I'll be with you 3.30 p.m. Kindest regards,
  Heather

I remember thinking how much Roger would have disapproved – not with me contacting a specialist in tracking down birth parents, but with someone who signed off their emails 'Kindest regards'.

'I abhor "kindest regards",' is what he would have said. 'Can anybody tell me what's wrong with "yours sincerely"?'

Heather Cross was nothing like her photo. She looked like that homeopathic doctor Diane used to take me to, before she died, whose house smelt of cats' piss and boiled cabbage. I was a bit unnerved that I had got her so wrong. And clearly she hadn't done her research either: not a brilliant start for an investigator. She had no idea she had come to visit someone in a place where the staff believes that 'quality holistic care is dependent upon a multi-disciplinary approach'.

'Do the . . . doctors know who I am?' was her first proper question.

'I told them you were a friend of the family.'

'But what happens if some of your family walk in now?' she

whispered, looking over her shoulder, like she was checking her shadow was still there.

'They won't. They visited this morning.'

I wasn't sure whether Heather Cross was going to walk straight out of the door that second, but eventually she took off her coat, folded it into a shape the size of a piece of luggage, and sat at the end of my bed. 'I thought you'd broken your leg or something,' she said, still glancing around her. 'I didn't realize you were in *here*. You understand: I do need to ask. Why are you in here?'

'They're calling it nervous exhaustion.'

'Nervous exhaustion?'

'I promise you, it's no more than that. Things just came a bit on top.'

We made small-talk to start with – or, rather, she did: how the park-and-ride bus had been delayed by an argument between the driver and an old lady who had three dogs, not the two which is the maximum you're allowed to travel with. How the air quality in Manchester was so much better as a result of improvements in public transport. All the time she was still looking around the room, though.

'My, what a lot of paper!' she remarked, pointing at my A–Z.

'They make you write a lot of stuff in here.'

'Is that so?'

Finally she launched into her spiel. It was well rehearsed or well versed or both, and pretty much standard for 'a preliminary meeting when the fee structure could be established'. She had started her working life at the Preston General Infirmary, where she had trained as an orthopaedic nurse but had found herself gravitating towards the children's ward. That was why, once she qualified, she had taken a job at Barnardo's. And subsequently at an adoption agency. She was absolutely passionate about her work. But about two years ago she had had to take early retirement, something to do with her husband. Working freelance was, if anything, more rewarding, she told me: there was more scope and unlimited time to get properly involved in individual cases. She had known Margaret, who had founded adoptionsearch.com in 2001, for over twenty years – since Barnardo's days, in other words.

'In that time we have reunited more than six hundred families – not all of them involving adopted children, you understand. We get enquiries from all sorts of people who for whatever reason have lost touch with one another.'

The more she spoke the more she came to look like Diane's homeopathic doctor, or the more Diane's homeopathic doctor came to look like her. Just for a second I thought perhaps I was being deceived and this really was Diane's homeopathic doctor, back from the dead, sent by Diane (and Roger) to check me out. And because the two women could have been twins in the physical sense, naturally enough they shared the same taste in clothes. Heather Cross was wearing a rainbow-coloured shawl just like her double's; she was also wearing the same type of chunky crystals around her neck. I knew instinctively that things would work out better if I came straight to the point.

'On your website I read that when I'm eighteen I can send off for my original birth certificate,' I said. 'Is that right?'

'Yes, that's perfectly correct.'

'And it said that my parents' names and addresses will be on the certificate. Is that right, too?'

'No, I don't think the website does say that. Your mother's name will be on the certificate, yes, but not necessarily her address. And not necessarily any of Father's details. More often than not, Father's details are absent.'

I didn't like the way she had referred to my father as 'Father', not 'your father' or the 'adopted person's father'. It's a bit like calling a baby just 'Baby', not 'the baby'. Maybe it's a nurse thing, but it's very over-familiar.

'But if my mother's address was on the certificate . . . I could find her, just like that?'

Heather Cross suddenly looked very worried, and it started her hunting around the room all over again. 'It would be most unwise to make an approach of that kind,' she said.

Of course I knew this, but at the same time I thought it as well to get it spelt out. 'Why?' I asked, in a quiet voice.

'*Why?* Because you might both have seizures,' she answered, with a pretence laugh. There was a long silence as she studied me, like a school mistress, over her spectacles. 'No, seriously, Georgia,' she went on, drawing herself up, 'once you have details you would be strongly advised to seek the services of an intermediary. If not me then someone like me: a counsellor with very specific experience in this field.'

And she went into a long speech about how it was like standing outside a house in the middle of nowhere. Inside there was a gathering of relatives you had never met before: uncles, aunts, brothers, sisters, grandparents, cousins, all sorts. There could be loads of them or very few: there was absolutely no way of telling.

'Some of them you may like; others you may take an instant dislike to. Conversely some of them may not like you, may resent the fact you exist, even. You need someone to announce you,' Heather Cross finished, 'someone to introduce you. My job is to prepare all parties: you, your birth parents . . .' she paused '. . . and not forgetting the parents who adopted you, to prepare them too. I mean, are your adoptive parents aware that you intend to make enquiries?'

'Not yet.'

'Have you considered how they might feel?'

'Not really.'

'How do you think they would react?'

'I think Roger would be supportive and Diane wouldn't want the hassle.'

'Roger and Diane are their names, right?'

I wasn't going to answer a question like that. 'So do a lot of people get the address and just turn up?' I pressed her instead.

'Very, very rarely,' Heather Cross cautiously replied. 'I can't say it hasn't happened, because it has. But in ninety-nine cases out of a hundred people are very sensitive to the feelings of others, not to mention their own feelings. And, in any case, if you think about it, the likelihood of a person being at the same address fifteen, twenty years on – even if the address given *was* the actual address – is remote to say the least. I mean, there's a possibility that you discover the street name but find it no longer exists: it's been demolished to make way for a new development. I've seen it before – admittedly with older clients – but it's still a possibility . . . a very real possibility.'

There was something about the thought of this that made me nervous. I could see myself flying over London, like a bird, looking for somewhere to land and there was nowhere, and I was getting more and more tired. In the end I was going to fall out of the sky.

Her point made, she then said: 'And you may also have to come to terms with the fact that you'll find no one.'

'No one?'

'Well, it's possible that the searches will not return any meaningful leads, that the trail goes cold.'

'That's not the way it is for me.'

'How can you tell, Georgia? You can't.'

'I just know.'

Now there was a sort of bullying tone to Heather Cross's words. 'And you may even discover you were, like me, a foundling,' she finished.

'A foundling?'

'I was found in the doorway of a hospital in Birmingham. Yes, I was. There was a bit of heather stuck in my shawl. And I wouldn't stop crying for a week. That's why they called me Heather Cross.'

I could tell Heather Cross was waiting for a reaction to this: me finding it funny; me being amazed; me thinking it through and taking on board that I might be a foundling, too, and us being in the same club, so to speak. And I could tell she was disappointed that my expression gave nothing away at all. I might have been keeping a straight face, but my brain was racing, really racing. Even though I knew one hundred per cent that I was not a foundling, the idea absolutely terrified me.

Again, I had the impression that she was trying to assert herself somehow. 'That might be something we'd need to spend some time on,' she added.

And I didn't like it. 'But I know I'm not,' I told her.

'Not what?'

'A foundling.'

'Georgia, how can you know?'

'Because I've met and seen my mother,' I replied, simple as that.

The meeting pretty much degenerated after that. I couldn't ask her to leave – or thought I couldn't – so the only way out was the bathroom. I excused myself, ran the taps and sat on the toilet. I had to get this woman out of my hair, the smell of her out of my nostrils, and the thought of this foundling business out of my mind. It wasn't easy. It was as if I had to blow it all out through my mouth, like I was smoking a cigarette in reverse, as I had seen Drew do in the underpass in Birmingham, then breathe in very carefully through my nose: if I didn't do it right I might suck in the bad stuff I had just expelled.

The next thing I knew I was staring up into Joyce's face. Heather Cross was at the back of the room, framed by the open door.

'Are you okay, love?' Joyce whispered.

'I just feel a bit sick.'

And when I looked back into my room Heather Cross was gone.

*

And even though I didn't particularly like Heather Cross or think that she could help me, I knew somehow that she was part of the puzzle. I really didn't want her to be involved, but the more I looked at her portrait on adoptionsearch.com's website, the more convinced I was that she was going to come up with some of the answers. What was weird was that they changed the thumbnail of her on the homepage, out of the blue, just like that. One morning I looked and she was sitting on a grey sofa with a table behind cluttered with framed photos; the next she was perched on the same sofa, but the table was gone and this time she had a chinchilla cat in her arms.

*

As soon as I got the certificate – seventeen days after my eighteenth birthday – I took it around to Sula's house. And it was really Sula who decided me.

'Whoooaaa! It's even got the address. You need to show this to that counsellor woman,' she said. 'You should scan it and send it to her.'

'I'm not sure. I didn't really like her.'

'That's not what you told me, Georgia. You told me she had a good energy and that you had made a sort of connection with her – those were your exact words.'

'I may have been wrong.'

'Listen: you need help with this, Georgie. Do yourself a favour and send it off.'

We were staring at the certificate, a sort of spreadsheet of pre-computer days, coloured red against pink. The registrar, a T.W.J. Auty, had filled in the details with a fountain pen. His handwriting was spidery and childish. Where some of the boxes were empty ('Father: Name and surname; Place of birth; Occupation. Mother: Maiden surname; Surname at marriage if different from maiden surname') there was just one diagonal line, faint at the bottom, thick at the top where, if you looked at it long enough, you could actually see the nib lifting from the paper. The top edge of the sheet was serrated, where it must have been torn from a pad. Sula had her thumb next to the box with the heading 'Mother'. She was shaking her head; there was a faint smile on her lips – not a funny smile, a wonder smile.

'Elizabeth Florence Dunne,' she whispered, rolling the names on and off her tongue, slowly at first, and then quicker, and then she sang them. 'Elizabeth Florence Dunne, why you do what you done?'

I snatched my birth certificate from Sula's hand. Even though she was my best friend I didn't like her owning the names, feeling them, sounding them out before I had had a chance to be familiar with them. There was an awkward moment and neither of us knew where to look. Of course I wanted to go on talking about it, so I pretty much handed her back the certificate straight away. 'Look at the address,' I said, pointing.

If I'm being honest this was the thing I was most relieved about. Because when I read Pond House, Fitzroy Avenue, NW1 in the box where it asked for 'Usual address (if different from place of child's birth)', I took it to mean that Pond House was a house on its own, with a gate and a gravel path leading up to steps and a big front door with pillars either side and long, deep windows that shone in the morning light. A house much grander even than the one we used to visit in Edinburgh, which had belonged to Grandpa Myers's older brother before he died.

'I always knew you were posh,' Sula whispered, 'and now you're even posher.'

I was laughing now and Sula was laughing, too. But I felt as if at any minute I might start crying, a sort of knife-edge feeling.

'Oh, Sula, should I be doing this?'

Sula cocked her head as she looked at me, from one eye to the other, dead earnest. 'Sure you should,' she replied. But then that smile returned and I could tell she was going to make fun of me for being so serious, which is something she quite often does. Sula does the whole range of voices. This was her being a fly girl: 'You want to step right up to her and go, "Yo, baby mother, whah happen?"'

And I didn't find it amusing.

'You want to go, "Where you bin, Mama? Why you leave me alone like you did? Whah happen to your nerve?"'

I smiled weakly.

'That's what you want to ask, isn't it?'

'I don't know,' I replied, blinking around the room, which was sparkling through my wet eyes. 'I don't know.'

Immediately Sula took me in her arms. 'Forgive me, Georgie, I'm only joking. You know I am. And this is a serious business, proper serious. But I just need to hear you say *why* you want to get to know stuff about your parents.'

I had my cheek on Sula's collarbone and my eyes were screwed shut. I could feel myself melting into her, becoming part of her. If I got one ounce of this feeling of completeness from my real mother when finally I found her and hugged her, then the whole thing would have been worthwhile, I was thinking.

'I just need to know,' I answered. 'I've tried not wanting to know but – I can't help it – it won't go away.'

I could hear Sula swallowing, too. 'I can understand that. If I was in your shoes I would be as curious as hell, curious as hell.'

We studied the certificate once more.

'"Certified copy of an entry Pursuant to the Births and Deaths Registration Act 1953",' she was whispering, running the ball of her index finger over the serrated edge at the top of the page. 'I wonder if your mother was sitting in front of this when it was filled in,' she murmured, and her eyes were distant, like she was looking over into another valley half a mile away. 'I wonder whether she was sitting here, just here.'

The exact same question had occurred to me. 'Do you think she touched it?' I whispered in Sula's ear.

'I don't know. She may have done. I don't know. She probably did. What a weird thought.'

*

Drew was sure. And then he wasn't.

Then he was. 'Yes, Georgie: I reckon she touched it.'

'How do you know?'

'I think I'm right.'

I wouldn't believe him now if he came out with stuff like this, and I wouldn't have believed him when I was thirteen, say, but at that moment in time I did believe him. Maybe because I believed it myself. Since, if you thought about it long and hard enough, it really didn't take such a leap of imagination to picture Elizabeth Florence Dunne sitting at one side of a table in 1991 with Mr T.W.J. Auty at the other, fountain pen in hand.

'But, then, I don't know,' Drew said, and he made a point of laughing, almost in my face.

'Jesus, Drew! It's not funny.'

'I know it isn't – of course it isn't – but one thing you can't afford to lose now is your sense of humour, Georgia.'

Drew was smoothing out the certificate on the arm of his chair, very slowly and intently, as if he were stroking the arm of a fur coat. Then he raised it to the light and seemed to be looking through it. Still he was rolling his thumb over the paper, which made a very faint sound, like waves breaking on a distant shore. 'She's not living at this address now, you know,' he went on, much quieter.

This seemed like such a shocking thing for him to say it made me splutter.

'In fact, she never lived there . . .'

It was the conviction in Drew's voice that took the smile off my face. 'She never lived there?' I repeated.

'Pond House belonged to a friend. Your mother may have stayed there, but she never lived there.'

'Drew, you're talking rubbish.'

'You think so?'

'How can you know?'

He didn't answer; he just stared at me.

I was on the verge of calling it a day and just about to stand when Drew said, 'Can I try the cymbals?' with his hand over the certificate like he was the conductor of an orchestra, tweaking at the air.

'Feel free.' I shrugged.

Drew opened the drawer where he keeps his tarot cards, crystals and other stuff, and took out his velvet pouch. Inside was a pair of miniature cymbals tied together on a piece of leather bootlace. He held them over the birth certificate as if they were a pair of scales. Then, with one clean movement, he struck one against the other. A silvery note, oscillating like you get when you twang a tuning fork, rang out and filled every corner of the room. Drew had a look in his eyes like he was running after the sound – that, or he had just tasted something and he was trying to suss it out. And it was weird: I could actually see the sound, patches of it glowing in different parts of the room, just like you see the air move and glow in that half an hour before it gets dark – what Roger calls the gloaming.

'Can you hear it?' he whispered to me.

'Hear what?'

'That it isn't clear, Georgia.'

'Not clear?'

'Georgia, it's like a washing-machine.'

'A *washing*-machine?'

'Can't you hear it? It's everywhere.'

And he rang the cymbals again. The sound was much higher this time: it was almost deafening the way it burrowed into your ear and yet it was a closed sound, with no depth to it, just flatness, like a door.

'There's something there, Georgia. Can't you hear it?'

'What do you mean, "something"?'

'Something locked up. A secret.'

It sounds naïve of me now to have thought then there could be no secret. The secret was the birth certificate: everything would be revealed from that A4 bit of paper. Okay, in some of the boxes – the ones where it said 'Father', with its questions, 'Name

FIVE

So I emailed Heather Cross and attached a pdf of my certificate, just like Sula told me to. I got a reply the following night.

> Given the circumstances reference our last meet-
> ing I think it only prudent that we have another
> talk before proceeding any further. Could
> you come to see me in Huddersfield? Kindest
> regards, Heather

So I got the train over the following Wednesday.

Heather Cross lived at the Sunsets, high up on the east side of town, overlooking a park. There's a beck in the park with little stone bridges every hundred yards or so, some of them just slabs of stone, Flintstones-style, others proper hump-backed bridges with castellated sides. It's pretty, scenic, chocolate-boxy. That afternoon, with the sun on the water, I thought how much the beck looked like a silver ribbon, a bit of tinselly taffeta – dragged there by a giant, perhaps, who had marched over this place in another dimension of time.

Number fourteen was a bungalow nearly at the top of a cul-de-sac. There was a for-sale sign at the head of the short driveway, which was something I hadn't expected. But it made me say to myself: 'What did I expect?' There was no need to ring the door-bell: Heather Cross was waiting for me.

'Georgia, come right in,' she said, with both arms up as if she was going to give me a hug. 'Did you find us okay?'

'I got a map off the Internet.'

'It's difficult to imagine what we'd do without the Internet now? It's a good job things can't be uninvented, isn't it?'

We went straight into the back room, which might have been the bedroom once but had been extended outwards and had a wide view, like a wide-screen TV, of their garden and the park beyond. A man was clipping the hedge, not with electric clippers like Roger's: these were old-fashioned ones with yellow wooden handles.

'That's Allan, my husband,' Heather told me. 'Don't you worry about him: he won't disturb us. Once he gets started on his gardening he's lost in a world of his own. Sit here, Georgia.'

I sat on an armchair facing the sofa that I had seen on adop-tionsearch.com's website. The room was full of light and smelt clean and had a good feeling – quite unlike Diane's homeopathic doctor's house, which was dark and cold and where it always seemed to be raining outside. But there was one thing the two places did have in common, though. Just like Diane's 'late and great' homeopathic doctor, Heather Cross had loads of crystals. There were two quartz balls, really fortune-teller's crystal balls, on the mantelpiece; an amethyst geode, a sort of peaked doorway, the kind of thing you might see in a Walt Disney cartoon, on the windowsill; and some smaller pieces arranged around the telephone. I remember saying to myself: 'God, everyone's at it!'

'So, Georgia. How are you?'

'I'm good.'

'Because the last time we met things were a bit strained, not to put too fine a point on it.'

'I know.'

'You told me the doctors had diagnosed nervous exhaustion. I don't mean to pry and I won't ask again, but why exactly *were* you in hospital?'

Being blunt and quick to answer often helps. 'Because I had been using too much of that skunk weed.'

'And what is "skunk weed" when it's at home?'

'It's cannabis that they grow under lights. Some people can get a . . . How do you call it? A psychic reaction to it.'

'A psychotic reaction, you mean?'

'But I'm okay now. I haven't used any for seven months.'

I saw Heather Cross looking very carefully into my eyes as she asked, 'And are you getting the support you need to stay off it? Because by all accounts stopping and staying stopped are two different things.'

'I'm still an outpatient at Faversham House. But I'm okay now, completely okay.'

'I have to say, you do look quite a different person. You know, you're a very attractive young girl, Georgia.'

I pretended to be shy, but once again I could see that I would need to take control of the situation. 'So, do you think you will be able to help me?'

Heather Cross sat back, her face beaming. 'My! You're very direct!'

'My father, my adoptive father, always tells me not to "beat about the bush",' I replied, with a laugh, and could see as soon as she laughed back that I had won her over.

'His name's Roger, if my memory serves me correctly.'

'That's right, Roger.'

Heather Cross then launched into her speech. She thanked me for attaching a scan of the birth certificate, which she now withdrew from a folder and studied over the top of her glasses. It was pretty standard, as a matter of fact, she said, and even though I had been over the details a hundred times I let her read them out. I was born in London, in Hammersmith Hospital, on 11 February 1991; my mother was called Elizabeth Florence Dunne; she was residing at Pond House, Fitzroy Avenue, at the time of my birth. She had called me Lily Rose Dunne. Father's details were missing. Nothing unusual about that: Father's name is only shown when he is the husband or when he accompanies Mother to register the birth. But at least there was *something* to go on.

'Because, again if my memory serves me correctly, the thought of having no details was something you found difficult to entertain.'

I thought this was a strange use of the word 'entertain'. I also thought that Heather Cross, by conceding that I had been right in knowing I was not a foundling or a baby-in-a-basket, must be indirectly apologizing to me, admitting that she had been wrong to press that point when we had last met. But I also knew it would be best just to play the game.

'Well, yes,' I replied. 'I suppose for so long I'd been thinking about meeting my parents and any other relations I might have that the idea of having no one was a bit . . . you know . . .'

'Yes, I do know.' Heather Cross nodded, with a big smile, as if she was pleased I had acknowledged the great favour or service she had conferred on me by telling me something I already knew.

We both sat there in silence for a minute or two. And then the door swung open of its own accord. Which was a bit weird. It turned out to be Heather Cross's cat, the long-haired chinchilla as seen on adoptionsearch.com's website. I let it smell my trousers, shoes and hand; then it jumped on to my lap and began purring.

Perhaps the fact that I had made a connection with her cat was an added bonus, as it seemed that the further Heather Cross went the more of a client I was becoming.

'So, given the information we have, I think there's every chance you will get to make contact.'

I nodded thoughtfully.

'How does that make you feel?'

'Good!'

'Just good?'

I was tickling the cat behind its ears, the place Fudge likes to be tickled, and the cat was turning its head and staring at me with its eyes that were like the shutter on Roger's ancient camera. Then, out of the blue, it stretched its claws, and when it retracted them their tips went through my jeans and into my thigh. I didn't want to cry out as I thought that Heather Cross and I were on the brink of something, but I had to straighten my spine against the sharp, razor pain.

'That doesn't mean there won't be things you might rather not know about,' she warned me. 'I've worked with two clients this month. Shall I tell you about them?'

'Yes.'

'The first is a young mother in her twenties from Immingham. We found her father, who is now living in Eastbourne, had remarried with a new family, but she discovered her mother had died in a road accident – in quite tragic and protracted circum-stances, actually. My client was very distraught at the prospect of never meeting her mother. Nevertheless she knows now she will be able to come to terms with this. She has closure. But the joy of meeting her father! And the joy of the father! As soon as the letter I wrote reached him, he phoned. That very evening. He said, "I'm shaking. I'm hot and cold. I've been waiting for this call for years . . . years." When the reunion came it was a marvellous, *marvellous* experience for both of them.'

Heather Cross paused before telling me about her second client.

'The other, I'm afraid, doesn't have such a happy ending. This time it was a woman in her seventies, ill with cancer, terminally ill. She had given her daughter up for adoption, and wanted to make contact before she . . . passed on. I have to say I had a hunch this one might not turn out so well.'

Another pause.

'It transpired that her daughter had died at the age of two, drowned in a pond in the adopting parents' garden.'

'Oh, God,' I couldn't help saying.

'The poor woman, you see, had thought she was doing the best for her daughter by giving her up for adoption. When I told her what I had discovered, she just said to me: '*I* could have done better myself. Why did I give her up?"

Heather Cross had this way of not pulling her punches. 'Think of all the years,' she said, as if she was talking to herself, 'when the poor woman thought her daughter was growing up, flourishing, perhaps having children of her own . . . when all along she was no more. She was alive no more.'

*

My train wasn't for another hour and a half so I went into an Internet café just outside the town centre.

When you type 'Elizabeth Dunne' into Google you get 11,524 hits. When you type in 'Elizabeth Florence Dunne' you get none. Somewhere between the two is my mother, somewhere in the 11,524. When you select images for Elizabeth Dunne you get 1082 hits. I'd been looking at these thumbnails, one after the other, at home, ever since the certificate arrived. That afternoon in Huddersfield I went at random through some of the ones I hadn't accessed before. There was a cheerleader from Ohio; a french polisher from Maidstone; a Dr Elizabeth Dunne outside her practice in Singapore; a photo of a painting of an Elizabeth Dunne who died in 1879.

I was feeling weary, like I had gone for a long swim and was now sitting on a rock with the water at my feet, trying to get warm. I had got what I wanted, though. Heather Cross would make some preliminary enquiries on my behalf, absolutely free of charge (to start with anyway, to make up for the abrupt manner in which she had left Faversham House last year). She had told me that mothers who give up their children for adoption more often than not have another child quite soon after. And more often than not that child is born *in* wedlock. The obvious place to start looking was in the General Register. You didn't need to go to Myddleton Street in London, these days. All searches could be done on-line. If this brought no leads, there was no cause for immediate panic. A death search for the grandparents, great-grandparents, uncles and aunts, etc., would provide up-to-date information of the relative registering the death. Then there were the electoral registers, old phone books. And the address on the birth certificate.

'But I've already checked the address,' Heather Cross told me.

'So have I,' I said.

Heather Cross gave me that worried, school-mistressy look. 'You have?'

'Only with Directory Enquiries,' I explained.

'Well, that's where I checked . . . there and another directory we use. But, Georgia, please, please . . . when we've identified someone, let me make the approach on your behalf. Will you promise me that?'

I nodded, but can't have looked that convincing as I was desperate to find out what Heather Cross had discovered about Pond House, with its ivy-clad front and black railings. Here was another example of puffing yourself up when at the end of the day you were going to get deflated – almost as if you were doing it to yourself on purpose.

'What is Pond House?' I asked her straight up.

'Pond House is owned by the local authority,' Heather Cross told me carefully. 'It is a block of twelve dwellings. Your mother, when she registered you, did not give the flat number – just the name of the building.'

So I wasn't so posh, after all. And it had taken me a whole walk back into town to come to terms with that fact. Funny how good stuff is easier to deal with than bad.

But now that I had started on my journey proper and could imagine – or not, as the case might be – some of the places at which I might stop, I was feeling a bit buzzy, a bit light in the head. As if I had had a toke on some really powerful weed and had stood up too quickly and was trying to adjust to the stars.

I was staring at a photo of Elizabeth Dunne, interior designer. She had shoulder-length blonde hair, saucer-like eyes, and collar-bones that you could see beneath her jersey. I mean, had this Elizabeth Dunne given me away, then had another baby quickly afterwards to replace me? If Heather Cross found her through her youngest child, did this mean I had three or four brothers and sisters, all looking like her? But did I want *this* Elizabeth to be my mother? She had swimming-pool eyes (as Roger calls it when he's trying to be 'ironic' about someone's looks), but she was staring out of the screen with such a vacant expression, just like a posh chav. What about one of the others among the 11,524?

I went through a load more images, hitting any results page, then scrolling down and choosing a thumbnail at random. Perhaps this would lead me to my mother, a sort of weird Zener cyber-telepathy, I was thinking. The idea made me laugh out loud. But if the truth were told I was getting pretty fed up with these Elizabeth Dunnes. I did a big puff at the screen, like I do to those joggers to get them out of my space. If nothing else, I thought, at least this trip to the Internet café had shown me that I wouldn't be trawling through the web again. I had gone past that stage.

How wrong I was, it turned out.

I remember then feeling suddenly cold, as if the sun I was waiting for just wasn't going to show – ever again. I wasn't losing my nerve, but I hadn't liked the story Heather Cross had told me about the two-year-old toddler drowning in that pond. I don't think anyone would have liked it much. The old lady had kept a flame burning for fifty years plus . . . *fifty years plus*.

Drew had anticipated this, too. 'You either walk away from this, Georgia,' he had said, as he handed me back the certificate that afternoon, 'or you turn over the stone.'

'What are you talking about?'

'There's no half-measures where this stuff is concerned: you either go after the truth or you don't. You just have to decide what you're going to do and stay with it . . . because if you start swapping your mind all you'll be doing is wasting your time.'

'What do you think I should do?' I had asked him.

'I can't tell you that, Georgia. You know what it's like.'

'What would you do?'

'Me, I'd release the energy. And then I'd straighten it.'

Exactly what the old lady with her drowned daughter hadn't done, and her life was over – over, in a sense, before it had begun. In my mind's eye I had a picture of the boulders Roger and I used to turn over in Scotland when we were looking for worms. You never knew what you were going to find underneath as you pulled back the stone: fleshy white roots, woodlice, blue-grey worms saddled pink? But once it had been turned it had been turned: the tufts of grass that had held it to the ground now showed an edge of black earth.

I paid, left the café and walked towards town. The traffic was heavy, a background of thunder. I hadn't done any E or *aya* since before Christmas, but now suddenly I got a feeling in my stomach like I needed to go back into that space. And because I was feeling that need it put me in mind of Grandma Myers.

'Grandma Myers, can you hear me?' I asked, over the traffic.

Nothing.

'Grandma Myers. Tell me, am I doing the right thing?'

Still nothing. But at that moment a car pulled up on the kerb just ahead of me. And the letters on the registration plate? YK04 LRD.

SIX

Things were happening so fast now, I thought I'd better 'put my house in order', with Roger at least.

'My darling Georgia,' he said, as soon as I'd got to the end of my stuttery speech, 'this doesn't come as a surprise to me in the least. If you want me to be completely frank with you, I don't welcome it . . . but that's purely for selfish reasons.'

'What do you mean?'

'My darling girl, I don't want to lose you!'

I could tell that any more of this and I would start beefing. 'But you're not going to lose me,' I said, swallowing back the tears.

'I know I'm not – but the human condition seems to be so predisposed to loss, or the fear of loss, at any rate, one's imagination gets the better of one.'

I couldn't really follow this.

'What I *really* mean is that you have my wholehearted support.'

'Really?'

'Yes, really! Every day I've loved you, Georgia. I don't expect anything of you – except good table manners and a sunny disposition – and I don't expect anything of our love. It is to be enjoyed today, not tomorrow, today. Grandad Myers might have been quite an eccentric old fuddy-duddy, but he had a very sober outlook on life. And you know what he always said?'

'Hope for the best, expect the worst and take what comes.'

'You'd be hard-pressed to find better advice than that.'

I was holding Fudge around his body as he sat on the sofa next to me. I could smell his doggy smell, and every now and again I did what I always do when I'm feeling unsure about stuff or just plain upset. I give him a hot potato behind the crown of his head: this brings out his smell stronger.

'How are you going to go about it?' Roger then asked, and it felt good that he was taking an interest in the mechanics of what I was up to and wasn't going to leave it at that, like a door hanging open with nothing going on beyond.

I wasn't exactly about to tell him how I'd already sent off and got my birth certificate, and the news was I had been christened Lily Rose Dunne, that I had spent the first few days of my life in a place called Pond House (which I had thought was posh, but turned out to be a block of council flats), that my real mum and dad had met abroad, that basically I already knew a whole load of stuff about myself. So I explained about adoptionsearch.com.

'How much is it all going to cost?'

'I think the first searches are free of charge.'

'Can't you use Social Services?'

'I can't handle all those busybodies.'

'Of course you can't. Why don't I pay for adoptionsearch.com . . . if and when they ask for payment?'

And there was another reason why I wasn't going to mention the birth certificate and say what was on it and what wasn't and perhaps have to get it out and show it. And now as we sat in silence for a minute or two that reason began to hang over us big-style. I knew that my father was called Ralph Peddar, that he had brown hair, that he had been employed in the construction industry, that he had known my mother for a matter of months only, that it was he who had broken off the association. And Roger knew this too. But Roger didn't know that I knew. And what would happen if I got the certificate out and we were both staring at the empty box where it said, 'Father', and Roger said nothing? Would I be able to stop myself saying something? And even if I was able to stop myself saying something, would I be able to go about my business knowing that I hadn't been told everything there was to know?

The minutes hung over us. I was desperate to put my cards on the table, tell him I'd seen his Xeroxed letter and the reply he'd got, and get him to explain the meaning behind it. But how could I bear to see his expression change and recognize the distrust and disappointment in his eyes once I had owned up to the fact I'd been in his safe when he was out at dinner, dressed up like a penguin? Now of all times. So I bleached it out of my mind. I was going to find my birth parents without reference to the letter: I didn't need the information I shouldn't have had. And Heather Cross, good old Heather Cross, she didn't need it either: if the truth were out there, she would rootle it out, like Fudge does with a stick you've thrown into a bramble patch.

We stood up and hugged. Roger had his hand at the top of my neck. 'I love you so very much, Georgia,' he said. 'Every day has been a bonus. It really has. Please don't forget that.'

And when we stood apart I could see that he had filled up. I was surprisingly calm. And it occurred to me then, like it has loads of times since, that our roles were reversed: that I was the adult with the secrets and he was the little boy with nothing but innocence. It was another of those moments when you grow up real quick, like you've stepped over a crack in the ground and you're the other side and you're thinking about jumping back but you find you can't, because just in those few seconds the crack's got wider.

*

I don't know if 'magnanimous' is the right word for it, but Diane certainly wasn't demonstrating a 'generosity of spirit'.

The next morning I overheard her and Roger talking in the kitchen. I hadn't meant to creep up on them but I was only wearing socks and they wouldn't have thought I was up as it was too early for me to be having breakfast. And, anyway, they were so locked up in their own conversation.

'Jesus, Roger!' I heard Diane hiss. 'Our lives are over!'

'What on earth do you mean?'

'I mean, God knows who's going to be beating a path to our door.'

'Maybe no one.'

'Come on!'

'Maybe she'll find no one.'

'That's a possibility, I grant you. But people breed, you know, and she'll have grandparents, uncles, aunts – there could be an army of people out there.'

'That's something we'll have to come to terms with, if and when we need to.'

Silence.

Then: 'We'll be easy pickings.'

'Meaning?'

'Well, they might want our stuff . . .'

Even though I couldn't see them arguing I could tell Roger

was losing patience. 'Well, then, we'll have to put *our stuff* away, won't we?'

Diane was taking a plate from the cupboard, making as much noise as she could. Fudge was sitting next to me at the top of the stairs. His ears were pricked and his eyes looked heavy with worry.

'How she's going to do it anyway?' Diane then asked.

'She's found a site on the Internet.'

'The *fucking* Internet!'

'Diane!'

'Well, I mean . . . Jesus Christ!! Do we need this? Does she? Do you really think she's well enough?'

And I could tell by the tone of Diane's voice that she had her arms crossed and head back and she was giving it the you-may-think-you're-the-clever-businessman-but-you've-just-so-missed-the-point. 'She told me the other day they were stopping the medication.'

By keeping his cool, Roger always manages to have the upper hand. 'I'm sure Dr Murdo knows best,' I heard him reply.

Then Diane's voice went real quiet: 'And what about . . . you know?'

'Well, I know . . .' Roger had to concede.

And even though Diane's words were becoming inaudible, I could sense without being told that they were talking about the letters in the safe: there would really be no need for them to whisper otherwise.

'So are you going to tell her about *that*?' she finished, strong again.

'There's not much to tell.'

Sarcasm: 'Oh, no, of course there isn't!'

'Nothing we know conclusively to be true.'

'It's a can of worms, Roger – and you know it.'

I went back to my room and stood in front of the window. I had made a huge mistake in telling Roger (and Diane), I was thinking, I had been a complete fool. It would have been much better to do the business without them watching my every move, questioning my motives, asking me what stage I'd got to. It's a bit like winning the lottery. The last thing you want is for everyone to be waiting to see how much you dole out to whom, with people looking at you, saying, 'Is that all?" and 'What about so-and-so?' Big stuff like this needs to be done in private.

But now that I had other people watching me I could actually see through their eyes, imagine myself in their shoes. As I looked down the garden path to the gate with the beech trees either side, I began to see Diane's army of people: they were in such a hurry to get in they were virtually falling over each other, half treading on the flowerbeds, snapping Roger's plants with their big black boots. I found myself almost ducking sideways behind the curtains. Heather Cross had told me that discovering your birth family was like standing outside a big house in the middle of nowhere and they're all inside, and it's you who's coming in from the cold. But actually it was the reverse. You were in the house and they were beating down your front door. Heather Cross had also said that the first meeting would be on neutral ground – and with her, Heather, if that was what I wanted, and that my birth parents needn't ever know my name or where I lived. But that seemed a pretty 'half-baked' idea. What about if someone followed me back on the train, someone who had been posted outside the rendezvous where we had arranged to meet? What about me giving out my mobile number and them somehow getting my address from that?

It seemed that there really was a crack in the ground. As soon as I had stepped over it I would never get back . . . to this place, this safe place with my own dog.

SEVEN

An email came from Heather Cross exactly a week later:

> Hi, Georgia, please could you phone me?
> Kindest regards, Heather

And I couldn't. Not immediately. Not until the evening of the day after, when I finally got it together.

'I'd like you to come and see me again,' Heather Cross said. 'I have some news.'

'What kind of news?'

'I'll tell you when we meet,' she said, and there was a firmness in her voice that spelt something definite basically.

'Can't you tell me anything?'

'No, Georgia. We must meet.'

So I got the train over the following day. The carriage was half empty and I was sitting on the right-hand side, overlooking the moor. It was wet and dull and the sky was one great ceiling of puffy cloud. Perhaps when we got to Huddersfield it would be clear and blue, I remember thinking – perhaps they're in a different space over there and don't feel this roof of whiteness above them, pressing down and yet empty at the same time. Please, God, I wouldn't be feeling the way I was feeling now when I got to my destination.

But I felt worse. What was Heather Cross going to tell me? Probably that my father was called Ralph Peddar. And that he was dead. That would be bad enough. But I already knew that, didn't I? Perhaps she was going to tell me that he was alive, I was also thinking, and for a moment there were two of me, one listening to the dead news and one listening to the alive news. Or what if Heather Cross had tracked my mother down and had her waiting for me, just like in *The Railway Children*, behind a cloud of steam? Or what if my father was there, sitting forwards in an armchair, his hand in front of his face, trying to conceal the wounds that had killed him, like in *The Monkey's Paw*? Again I had the clear impression, as clear as looking into a fish tank, that this really was a Pandora's Box: it was impossible to know what might escape once it was opened and it would be impossible to squeeze back those things once they were out. I could turn around now and forget the whole thing, I told myself – but at the same time I just knew I couldn't. For a moment I thought I might literally pass out I was breathing so hard – so I took some time out and concentrated on my dub of the week, a pretty fitting one as it turned out.

Say, the road is foggy, foggy
Man, the road is so icy, icy

I made it to the Sunsets in good time. Again there was no need to knock. This time Heather Cross did kiss me – which I took to be a bad omen. And this time Allan was in the house, in the kitchen, making a cup of tea. As he came out of the door he made a point of not looking at me. So he must have known my business as well. I sat on the same sofa.

Heather Cross did not 'beat about the bush'. 'Georgia,' she began, 'I don't think I've done my job quite as well as I would have wanted to, as we should have discussed this possibility when you were here last. But the fact of the matter is I've written to NORCAP and got a reply: there is a "no-contact request".'

This meant absolutely nothing to me, although I could tell it wasn't good. 'What is NORCAP and what is a no-contact request?'

'NORCAP is a charity set up to help everyone in the adoption triangle: they give information, support and advice . . . and they also have a contact register, where birth parents and adopted people can register their wishes regarding contact. I'm afraid your mother has made it known that she does not welcome contact.'

'Does not welcome contact?'

Heather Cross could not have been any more blunt if she'd tried. 'She doesn't want to meet you, Georgia.'

My jaw must have hit the floor.

'I know hindsight is a wonderful thing, but we definitely should have discussed this possibility at our last meeting,' Heather Cross said, shaking her head. 'I don't know why we didn't. I just assumed we were going to have a straightforward time of it.'

'Let me get this right: my mother has written to this NORCAP place saying that if I make enquiries about her I'm to be told she doesn't want to meet me?'

'She wrote last year.'

'Last year?'

'She would have known, of course, that you were turning eighteen and that information would shortly become available to you . . . so she wrote to register her feelings. When *was* your birthday, in fact?' Heather Cross muttered, not asking me who might know but looking into the manila file she had open on her knees. 'Eleventh of February. Her no-contact request was dated August the fourth.'

'So what do I do next?'

Heather Cross did not answer; she just looked at me with a buttoned-up mouth. The clock on the mantelpiece was ticking very loudly.

So I repeated the question. 'What do I do next?'

'Georgia, I can only give you my advice.'

'Which is?'

'I know it's easy for me to say this, but I don't think under the circumstances you have many options.'

'You mean forget about her?'

'I'm afraid so, Georgia. If someone doesn't want to know you can't really change that fact . . . can you?'

I must have looked very grim.

'We can do some counselling to help you with this,' she added.

I didn't want Heather Cross looking at me any more, so I put one hand in front of my eyes, as if I was shielding myself from the sun. My mind was racing, my thoughts turning and churning, like massive wheels throwing up great clods of mud, never stopping. I focused on the clock, which was like a metronome.

'Do you want a cup of tea, love?' Heather Cross asked me.

'Please,' I answered, just to get her out the room.

When she came back a few minutes later with a mug that had *Sugar Daddy* written on it, I was much calmer. We spoke very quietly, just audibly: it seemed fitting not to say all this stuff too loudly. Again, Heather Cross had this way of saying things straight up, which in fact was a good thing under the circumstances.

I had been rejected at birth, she said, and now I had been rejected again, but I wasn't to look at it like that. You couldn't be rejected by someone who didn't know you. There were reasons why I had been given up for adoption, just as there were reasons why my birth mother did not want contact now. 'We just don't know what they are, and to be realistic we may never know.'

The situation might change, though, she went on. When people make a no-contact request they are asked to revalidate it every five years, just so that it can't be considered out of date, and just so that there is a chance to address any specific issue that may have arisen in that interval. They are also asked to leave a letter with basic information, sometimes spelling out why they don't want to be contacted. My mother hadn't done this when she made the request last year, but she might do so in five years' time. In fact, she might want contact in five years' time. It was impossible to know.

'The fact is she has all the power. I'm worse off now than I was before,' I said.

'It might seem that way today.'

'It does.'

'But it won't for ever. I do *know*,' Heather Cross said, trying to catch my eye. 'I spent years making searches of my own. I found out some things: a newspaper cutting, I even met the matron on the ward who was the first person to hold me and name me . . . but nothing more. I had to let go of it in the end, Georgia. It was stopping me getting on with my life.'

'I could still find my mother,' I interrupted, anger welling up in my voice. 'I'm not a foundling.'

'I know you're not. We've confirmed that much. And I've no doubt you could find her, my love. Your mother will know that, too.'

'So what's to stop me?'

'There's nothing to stop you. But you will have to ask yourself whether you want to make contact with someone who doesn't wish to meet you.'

Then, after a short pause, she finished in a quiet voice, 'And now that your mother has made her position clear we should assume that new relationships exist: perhaps there are people to whom your adoption has not been revealed.'

The cat was trying to get on to my lap, burrowing under my arm with its scaly, sandpapery nose. I kept pushing it away but its body just yielded into my hand. 'You mean that she's got a new family?'

'More often than not that is the case.'

And I went, '*Fuck that*,' under my breath.

*

I kept on thinking about Heather Cross's analogy of my family and all the cousins, grandparents, uncles and aunts, etc., etc., being inside a house in the middle of nowhere and me needing someone to knock on the door and introduce me. When all along this was the last thing that was required as the doors and windows were firmly locked and there was a notice outside on a pole that read: 'We don't want to meet you – go back to where you've come from.' It made me feel as indignant as hell.

Sula was getting to sound a bit like Heather Cross. 'I don't think there's much you can say, really.'

'Except – selfish bastards.'

'You don't know the circumstances – what's involved.'

'I'm involved, aren't I?'

'Georgia, you don't know the whole story. Your mother might be handicapped – she might have given you away because she physically couldn't have fetched you up.'

This possibility had never occurred to me, but that it hadn't no longer surprised me – each step of the way seemed literally littered with new possibilities, like weird plants you'd never seen before growing alongside a path.

Sula had her back to me. She was fixing a piece of patterned blue material in her hair, every now and then half bending to look into a mirror. She was distracted, not really talking to me properly. First she tried the material with the bow at the front; then at the back; then with her hair piled up and funnelled through the centre, pineapple-style. Finally she turned and beckoned me into her arms, and for a few seconds we rocked each other. My face was in the hair behind her ear. She smelt warm and doughy. Yet still I felt she wasn't properly there. Gently I pushed her back and stared into her face. Her skin is the colour of caramel and speckled, like an apricot or the most beautiful egg you've ever seen. Her eyes are dark brown, as dark as the molasses sugar Roger likes in his coffee. And her teeth are whiter than white, like ice on snow. That afternoon she looked gorgeous.

'Do I look okay?' she whispered.

And I knew then that she was getting ready to meet someone. If I hadn't been so preoccupied I would have realized this earlier. 'You look beautiful,' I answered, and I could feel my smile was paper thin.

Sula held my eyes like she knew that I wanted to kiss her, be folded into her, be one with her. She wasn't teasing me: she was saying it was okay to feel that; but her eyes also said that that wasn't where we were going. The sensation I'd had in the Hotel Ibis twelve months ago came over me again, like a great sheet of icy water, only colder than before. I didn't want Sula to meet someone, for her to give those lips away, for someone to float in her eyes. I wanted it to be me.

'Who are you meeting?'

Sula smiled. 'Just someone.'

This made it better and worse at the same time. 'Who?'

'A friend of Hazel's.'

'A blind date?'

'Sort of.'

I'd never, ever felt as alone as I did that afternoon.

EIGHT

So I went on a bender. The following Saturday at the Wigton. A bump of Charlie, an E and a corner of one of Drew's *ayas*. In that order.

The coke made me feel real edgy, wanting more of something, I didn't know what. And even though the place was filling up and you could lose yourself in the crowd, I kept on coming up against myself, against a feeling of impending danger or, worse, catastrophe. It was like being in one of those glass mazes at a fairground where you can't stop yourself slamming into sheets of transparency, which in reality are see-through mirrors.

Drew wasn't exactly gurning, but his jaw was chattering with what appeared to be cold. It wasn't cold, though. In fact, it was roasting in the Wigton. He had both hands behind his back, his fingers playing keyboard-style on the radiator he was leaning against, doing what he always does at the start of a trip, 'arranging' the energy.

'Can't you stop fidgeting, Drew? You're like a kid.'

But he just looked through me and past me, like Captain Kirk does in front of that plasma-telly-sized window they have in the *Starship Enterprise*, gawping into the galaxy and the Milky Way beyond, through a space that you can't see and the Vast Eternity of Time. His expression might have been blank, but other Drews were coming through. Drews I had seen before: an angry Drew, a haggard Drew, a wistful Drew; then bits of Drew much more pronounced, looking perhaps like some of his relations or ancestors might have looked when they were around. And then – just like that – it was as if he had stepped twenty years into the future. His cheeks had hollowed, his eyes were yellow, and his neck had wasted away to show you the sinews and veins right there under a parchment skin.

'Shit, Drew! You okay?'

'I'm okay,' he answered, eventually.

'Only you look a bit strange.'

'So do you.'

'Really?'

Drew came right out with it: 'To be honest, Georgia, I feel a bit weird around you at the moment,' he said. 'I can feel where you're at; I can actually *see* it. And it's weird.'

Oh, *great*! I thought.

The *aya* was coming up in gentle waves, a soft pressure behind the eyes. I found myself staring at my hands so intensely it was as if it was the first time I had ever really studied them, and I could see something too. A golden glow, a bit like the yellow band that Roger said represented shallow water in the pictures of *Treasure Island* he used to draw for me when I was a toddler, a band that followed the land into every nook and corner. In some places it turned gold, orange and red, in others black and purple. I tried stroking my fingers to see if I could feel what I could see, but the touch of my skin was something I found I couldn't handle. And so I splayed my fingers apart as far as possible, like you do when you've finished making pastry or crumble.

The gear was coming up strong for Drew, too, you could tell. His pupils were the size of saucers and every now and then his eyes rolled, flashing pearly white at me. He looked like the Haitians in that Bond movie who are about to commune with the dead in a voodoo ceremony.

'What can you see, Drew?'

'I can see a glow all around you,' he said, staring at something above my head. 'But I can also see something dark, Georgia – really dark.'

'Yeah?'

'Yes, it's more than a sense now – I can actually *see* it.'

'Tell me what you can see.'

But he wouldn't answer, and his eyes widened, revealing more whites, as if he was in fear of his life. Again he morphed in front of me, becoming an ancient, wizened sage, with skin heavy like molten wax, hooded eyes and crooked teeth stained with something tobacco-brown. I had to look away.

And then a klaxon and a silence, followed by the sound of Sula's voice, unaccompanied to start with.

The man next door,
In the neighbourhood, in the neighbourhood,
He gets me down.

Boom, boom, boom, went the bass, like the three big strides you take as you wade into the sea before diving in, your whole body submerged.

115

He gets in so late at night,
Always a fuss and fight, always a fuss and fight,
All thro' the night.

The music was just such a relief! I launched into the middle of the hall, like I was kicking away from the side of a swimming-pool, and began to feel the music in the soles of my feet, at first gently, encouraging the bass to resonate in my stomach, and then more in the frame. I had come to the Wigton to forget my troubles, to get out of it, and that was exactly what I'd do. Although I hadn't tripped for some time I hadn't lost the technique in directing the energy: to empty myself of thought, to look out on to a blanket of new snow, heavy, violet, not a footprint in sight. As the *aya* pushed, all I had to do was to turn and get it behind me, just like you do when you're surfing. Because once you're in harmony with the weight of the ocean, then you're never going to drown.

I knew all of the songs, all of the lyrics, the timing of Barrett's drag on the splash and the ride. I knew when, as a unit, without even looking at one another, the band would somehow unanimously pull up in a heap of muddled notes after the opening bars of a song. Then Sula would go, 'Oh, Lord!' and they would start the song all over again from scratch. They played 'Higher Plane', 'Step Up', 'Conscious Being' and 'Riverton City'. I was beginning to get lost. There was no parcel of fear attached to this. Quite the opposite. The melodies were enticing me, signalling for me to follow, as if I was delving deeper and deeper into a forest with brown leaves closing behind me, do a sudden left, take that right. Not to worry about finding my way out. I would be delivered back to the start point just when the time was right. I was in the zone, in other words. But I had a terrible thirst. I had to get a drink 'at all costs'.

When I got to the bar and stopped moving, all the energy came to my head. It was as if great currents were washing out of my eyes, flooding the bar in front of me, draining into each grain of wood, each nick and imperfection. For a moment I felt marooned, how you might feel when the piece of ground you're standing on breaks away and becomes an iceberg, and there you are, free to float but in prison at the same time. I had to push the fear away, paddle back to safety. Still I found I was having trouble with 'myself'. So I was blowing on my fingers, drying the sweat to leave them cold. I needed that water badly and I began waving to get the attention of the bar staff. That was when I caught sight of myself in the mirror behind the bar.

I smiled at myself and the smile smiled back. I nodded and my reflection nodded back. I hadn't remembered I was wearing my necklace with its leather shape of Africa painted red, gold and green with the cowrie shell. When I looked down and couldn't actually see it I assumed it was just me that wasn't focusing properly. I hadn't realized my eyes looked that pale, silvery and bright . . . They must have done, though. But I *did* know that the two guys either side of me at the bar were white – and that the two guys either side of my reflection were black. I stared at myself real hard; and my reflection stared back with the same open mouth. Time seemed to stop. The bass was pounding behind me, but it was leading me nowhere now.

A century could have passed for the time it took me to work it out; but once the solution had presented itself to me it was simple enough when you thought about it. There are two rooms at the Wigton, each served by the same bar, a sort of corridor that runs between the two. This girl who was opposite me wasn't my reflection: it was me – but me in the other room.

I gestured to myself across the bar, like: 'Hey!'

And the other me gestured back, like: 'Whoa.'

Then me: 'So what you doing here?'

'Come on round and I'll tell you.'

'Okay: wait there.'

To get to the other room took at least five minutes. I had to make my way back past the main doors (past the office where they play dominoes, such a weird sight: eight hundred people off their faces in the club and six old black men slamming counters on a table, for all the world as if nothing out of the ordinary is going off). And then on, around a corridor and through some double doors. When you're really tripping it doesn't occur to you that you might have taken a drug and that what you're seeing isn't there: you take things at face value; what you see is what you get. So I can't have been that out of it, as I remember half expecting not to find the person who was my double in Room Two of the Wigton, where, according to the flyer I had propped against my mirror at home, two DJs were at war: DJ Blessingz and MC Dreadnort. But I was there all right.

The other me was confident, had no nerves in meeting me. She was smiling in the way people smile at you when you're introduced to them at a party, and you know that the person who has done the introducing has told them all about you first in a few rushed, whispery seconds.

I and I, on the other hand, were totally lost for words, moved to silence. I just stood, open-mouthed, staring at my twin as if I was staring at my reflection. I had exactly the same mole that I've got just above my collarbone and the same scar, a sort of crater scar, on my right temple from when I scratched off a chicken-pox scab aged eight (and Diane said: 'What a shame.').

This was the Drum 'N' Bass room, and it was much too loud to hear anything anybody said. It was more a question of lip-reading.

'Yo!' the other me seemed to say.

'Hey,' I answered.

Then something incomprehensible.

'What?' I shouted.

And what sounded like: 'I said: "You can dance, sister."'

'I know that.'

This person I was speaking to was to all extents and purposes there, completely three-dimensional, as there and as real as the person standing next to her, but she was also a phantom. I knew this, and I also *knew* it. I was determined to believe she was real, though, so I kept on talking.

'I've got a necklace like that.'

'Oh, yeah?'

'My mate Barrett got me mine.'

My twin said nothing.

'So what you doing here?' I shouted.

Again no reply.

'Where have you come from?' I then asked, thinking I was going to catch her out.

'Leicester.'

'You're joking!'

'Not.'

For some reason I said, 'I've been to Leicester. Leicester's a dump.'

'You're wrong. Leicester's cool.'

The other me was shouting right into my ear. To let her do this I had turned my head and was staring at the floor. I could smell my twin's voice as well as hear it, full and warm and deep. And I could see her words, shards of what appeared to be splintered lumps of rock or ice or stone, rotating kaleidoscope-style as they ground into one another. Another century could have passed before I realized that I hadn't realized it was suddenly impossible for me to look up. It was as if I had cricked my neck, that, or it was held in a brace, like the one Uncle Rob wore for six months after he fell off his motorbike in France. All I could do was stare at the floor. Nothing more. But now, through a tiny speck on the dance-floor, a piece of trodden-in gum or sodden Rizla, through this miniature eye, another whole world was revealed to me. An hallucination through an hallucination. I went: 'Whoa!'

There I was in the Wigton, but I wasn't standing surrounded by a hundred skanking bodies, I was standing alone in front of a vast pane of glass, tinted brown like the windscreens you see on some of those cars owned by celebrities or wannabe celebrities. Only I was standing in front of it edge-on. Which meant there were two spaces to look at, one on one side, one on the other: one belonging to me, the other to my sister. On each there appeared to be a casino or an amusement arcade: loads of lights, spinning wheels and the belching sound you get as coins hit a steel tray. There was a very busy vibe in both, a whole lot of energy going off, and I remember thinking how like a certain type of dream all this was, where you just get to watch without being able to participate. And because you can't participate, you're not able to control anything. It wasn't a problem to focus on my side of the glass, but I couldn't see at all what was going on in my sister's. Just like my neck being cricked, so were my eyes. On my side the wheels were spinning in the one-armed bandits, then stopping long enough for me to see what was on them: horseshoes, halters, rosettes, big jewel-like eyes, flying manes, weird, random stuff that appeared not to be related to anything but was all to do with horses.

'Any ideas?' my sister whispered in my ear.

This seemed like such a patronizing thing to say that it broke me out of my trance. 'Ideas about what exactly?' I shouted back.

At first my twin looked disappointed, almost hurt; then she smiled that knowing smile a second time. I thought I'd jolt her out of her cleverer-than-thou attitude, so I tried to get hold of her arm. I knew that my fingers would close around fresh air, that my trying something on would change the energy. And so it did. There's a myth we learnt at school about someone coming out of the Underworld and he's not allowed to turn around to see if the person he loves is still following him. Same deal! My twin started to vanish in front of my eyes, first the bottom half of her, then all of her, vacuumed through the black hole of the people dancing around us.

Immediately an awful, hollow, homesick feeling begin to fill my stomach. 'Wait! Wait!' I shouted, pushing past the people around me. 'Please wait!'

I found myself being dragged into the centre of the dance-floor, chasing after me and her at the same time, following the top from Ghana that Sula had given me with its splodges of red against a honeycomb of amber, my red hair, perhaps a little darker than mine when I got to think about it later. The other me might have given me the impression to begin with that she was going to vanish, but in actual fact it turned out she was enticing me, like a siren, with a flash of the eyes here and a wave of the hand there.

I caught up with her by the fire exit, where Chessy was standing guard, checking that anyone who tried to get into the club via this door had a stamp of the lion's head on the back of their hand. It was quieter by the door: even though we were quite near a wall there must have been one of Sula's pockets of calm there.

'I didn't mean what I said about Leicester,' I shouted, again realizing how random all this was. 'But what did you mean about me having any ideas?'

'Georgia, don't be in a hurry.'

121

'You know my name?'

'Of course I know your name. Grandma Myers told me. She says you're always in here.'

And my twin gave me an enormous hug. All night I had been careful not to touch myself, and to give the other people in the club what Roger calls a wide berth, but now this embrace was the most delicious thing in the world. My twin's fingers and hands passed through me, and everywhere they touched there was a warm glow. We started to dance together, at first as if one of us was a reflection in a mirror; then we were on the same side of the mirror until finally we were inside each other and we were one. I didn't feel any sense of abandonment this time, perhaps because I knew that my sister was somewhere *inside* me. Yet still I wanted her where I could see her, just to look at her one last time. I thought that maybe by getting someone else involved I could bring her back, make her real once more.

'Chessy, this is my sister,' I shouted, pointing at the space in front of me in which the other Georgia had been standing.

'What are you like?' was all Chessy grunted.

*

I got in at five thirty, just as it was getting light. Fudge was at the door, his thick tail thumping against the umbrella stand. There was no question of going to bed, lying still in a dark room, when everywhere there were noises and colours. So I took Fudge to Hepstall Park, turning left down the ginnel by the side of the Hodges' house.

We went on the top path through the woods, the valley on our right, which you could half see through the branches that were beginning to get heavy with leaf. The whole place was full of energy and being right there in the middle of the dawn chorus, with the cawing, chirping and singing all around you, so close it was almost in your hair, was like having a bell jar sat over you. In fact, the sound had that same bearing-down intensity of the Wigton, and I remember half joking to myself that I shouldn't have thrown away the pair of DayGlo earplugs you get given at the door as you go in.

The jokes didn't last long, though. It was the trees I had to deal with first. Trees corkscrewing up into the sky, *Jack in the Beanstalk*-style, taking you to a place where you might fall out of the thin air, others buried deep in rotting earth, an army of kicking legs held in a bank of mud, all furiously trying to free themselves to stay in this world. Then *Wizard of Oz* trees, each twisted knot in a trunk a crooked eye or a tooth-crowded mouth.

If it hadn't been for Fudge, who was walking on ten yards ahead as if he was a guide dog, drawing me through streets of thundering traffic, I probably wouldn't have been able to keep it together. Because, everything, *everything*, was talking to me, clamouring, begging to get my attention: the rhododendrons with their blooms of mauve, cream and egg-yolk flowers, each colour a different key; the buds of hawthorn that were beginning to unfurl, squeak out from their cases; the beck at the bottom of the valley, whispering, muttering; the dead-damp mulch of leaves underfoot, groaning and hissing.

I sat on a wooden bench, dreading what was to come. I really was stranded on that ice floe. ('Purgatory, a living hell,' was how Roger put it when we were watching a documentary about that bloke in Antarctica who screwed up and drifted around the oceans on a lump of ice for nine months.) I began to panic, really panic, that terrible on-your-own panic, when you know that you're beyond the help of anyone or anything – you've just got to deal with it by yourself, or perish. I made a conscious effort to calm myself as well as make a physical effort too, actually smoothing the air in front of me, clearing the decks of negative energy. Drew had told me that the shamans sang *icaros* when they drank *aya*, songs to summon and placate the spirits of the spirit world, but most importantly to keep everyone anchored.

'Sometimes in the jungle, Georgie, in the middle of a ceremony, the shamans stop singing . . . Then you have to hold on because your head can go anywhere – like being on a raft with no paddle . . . You just drift aimlessly.'

So I sang the chorus of 'Man Next Door', the song that Sula had pulled up maybe three times at the Wigton. I sang it over and over.

> *I've got to get away from here*
> *This is not a place for me to stay*
> *I've got to take my family*
> *And find a quiet place*

And it worked straight off, totally worked. The walking bass line, the *chukah chukah* of the echoing guitar, the rattle of the snare just seemed to snatch me by the hand. Suddenly things were not so bad! Of course they weren't! Sure I could encourage the visuals if I dared to, see the branches swarm like the quills of a hedgehog when you poke him with a stick, the tumbling and seething parallel lines, a thousand ploughed fields of every colour. But there was nothing heavy about these hallucinations now. They were lending their weight, working to bring up a knot of warmth that was growing in my stomach, a feeling of being so completely and utterly part of the park. Never mind the spirits of the other world, the thick-trunked trees with their dark energy, I was telling myself; and never mind the spirits of the real world either, the joggers in their Gore-Tex suits with their expressions of cold disapproval when Fudge does a shit and I don't pick it up in an inside-out plastic bag that I haven't brought especially for the purpose. Why didn't they all fuck off?

I basked in this feeling of oneness, connectedness and belonging, a warm bed of moss. It wasn't the first time I had communed with Nature, realized that I didn't need a mother, a father, realized that it was only human beings who messed each other up, yet the novelty of the revelation was no less strong. People were missing the point when they put their energy into another person – this was all they needed: to be part of the universe, part of the black earth, the rust on a robin's chest, the wind in the trees. I was having one of those cheesy moments, in other words.

That didn't last long either. When Fudge barked his bark, so sudden it was as if a cannon-ball had smacked through a shop-front window, it pretty much jolted me out of my skin. He had moved maybe ten yards down the path from where I was sitting, ears up, hackles bristling, tail straight. There was nothing ahead, just a tunnel of trees and branches. But he had seen something, or sensed something, no question about it. A second later a tremor of pure fear rushed up my spine – because I was beginning to sense something too, a curtain of chill all about my ears, a fridge-freezer chill. Then there was a rumble, low to begin with but quickly growing louder.

'What is it, Fudge? Fudge, what is it?'

Fudge had turned his head, like he does when he's really listening for something; then he crept back to where he had been before, half in and half out between my legs. He was doing his lowest growl.

As he did so four horses burst into view from around a bend in the path, maybe a hundred metres away. They were galloping, really galloping, their hoofs slamming into the earth *b-dum,* *b-dum,* sending clods of mud high into the air. There didn't seem to be any time to react. What could we do anyway? Run, hide? But run where, duck behind what? The pack got closer and closer. The two horses behind were trying to overtake the ones in front, raising their heads high into the morning, tossing their manes, pushing forwards. The noise was all around us, deafening. It seemed the only thing I could do was close my eyes and hope for the best: hope that Fudge and I would not be trampled underfoot. But as they passed I couldn't help looking. It was the horse nearest me – as black as the stallion in the Lloyds advert – that seemed to be telling me to focus on him and him alone: on his flat, rippling chest; on his eye as big as a plum with its wild, empty look; on his knotted mane that shook and trembled like a nest of dreadlocks. He was checking me out, no doubt about it, NO DOUBT ABOUT IT, looking deep into me. And as he passed where Fudge and I were rooted like statues, he gave a wicked kick with his back leg, a sort of jag-jag. There would have been enough power in that kick to boot you into Kingdom Come, if you had been in the way of it.

Then – just as suddenly as they had appeared – they were gone. And now complete silence: not even the sound of birds. Had this been an hallucination? It couldn't have been. Why would Fudge still be staring up the path from where they had come? Why were his ears pricked? Why was he trembling? I was shaking too. In fact, my back was like jelly: all I could feel was a dull watery sensation at the bottom of my spine.

And then I began to puke, right from the very pit of my stomach. Wrong. I began to puke from out of the top of my guts. I was standing, holding on to a tree (a friendly one, as it turned out) with both hands in front of my head, rocking backwards and forwards, gagging. But nothing was coming out. Something *would* come out, I knew, but it needed to come out in one piece, not in bits. It felt like there was a serpent inside me, its head just behind my swallow, its tail anchored in my intestines. And then finally it did come out. Not a serpent, but a series of dark pebbles – coal-black in texture, but shiny as if they were the seeds of some exotic fruit from an other-world garden. And Fudge, fool that he was, he ate them!

NINE

A few days later Roger and I had one of our heart-to-hearts.

'I don't mean to pry but I just want to be sure you're getting on okay,' he said, as we were driving back from town after getting Diane a birthday present. I knew exactly what he meant and there didn't seem to be any point in 'beating about the bush'.

'Not brilliantly, actually,' I told him.

Roger nodded. 'I know.'

The car was so smooth it was difficult to tell whether we were moving along the ring road or whether we were stationary and the streets of houses, the supermarkets and flyovers, were flashing past us.

'I love it when you smile, Georgia, and when I see you looking . . . unhappy and pained . . . as you have been lately, well, of course, it pains me too . . . very much.'

Roger has this way of making me cry. Even when he's jokey, which he is most of the time, he's serious; but when he's serious he's really serious. He means everything he says.

There was a long silence, and then, for some reason, I said, 'I'm sorry.'

'What have you to be sorry for, for goodness' sake?'

'For wanting to find out.'

We had stopped at some lights. 'What *have* you found out, Georgia?'

I was looking at my hands. If I concentrated hard enough I could see the aura I had seen at the Wigton, a glow a bit like the one the kid has in the Ready Brek advert.

Roger was staring at me hard.

'I haven't found out anything,' I admitted.

'The agency you told me about on the Internet: haven't they discovered anything?'

And so I told Roger about the no-contact request.

'I'm very sorry, Georgia,' he said, after a few moments and with a big frown. 'That must have come as a bitter setback.'

'It did, actually.'

Roger put a hand on my knee and squeezed me twice. The tears were streaming down my cheeks now and my nose was full of snot.

'I'm afraid it looks like you'll have to go on putting up with us,' he said, and I caught sight of an expression I could tell he was trying to keep from me but which was there all the same. 'I wish I hadn't said that,' he quickly added, and there was a crack in his voice, like a twig breaking.

I didn't know what to say. It was obvious that I had hurt Roger by making enquiries and now, even though I had had the door slammed in my face, I couldn't just sweep that hurt away. It was like a stain, there for everyone to see. A pigeon was flying alongside us, exactly at our speed, beating his wings then gliding, beating his wings then gliding. I could see Roger's reflection in the glass, right over the pumping wings.

'You might not think you are, but you're very brave, Georgia,'

Roger went on, much calmer. 'You have to be very strong to cope
with something like this.'

'I don't feel very strong,' I said.

'You are, though.'

We drove on in silence for a bit. It was weird to hear Roger
talk about emotions. Up till then our heart-to-hearts had been
factual: Roger may have spoken about feelings but never about
people being weak or strong. I wasn't comfortable with it. I let
him go on, though.

'I'm not sure at all how I'd manage if I was in your position,'
he said. 'Here am I, a simple businessman, going about my life
convinced that everything's two-dimensional, explainable – or
explicable, if that's the right word. You encounter a problem? All
you have to do is break it down, take it step at a time, engineer a
way out of it. And here you are, presented with a lock for which
there is no key.'

The pigeon had gone: I looked ahead and back, but he was
nowhere to be seen. There was a dreadful hollowness in my
stomach, a weird uncertainty that I wasn't keeping up with stuff,
that if someone asked me what I'd done yesterday or what I'd
been thinking about only a few seconds before, I wouldn't be
able to answer them – like when you're getting to sleep and your
thoughts are random and intense, yet the next second you can't
remember anything about them. All I could hear were Roger's
words, repeating over and over, demanding I pay attention. The
fact that he had almost alluded to his safe gave me the last bit of
courage I needed.

'Don't you know *anything* about me?'

'What do you mean?'

'Is there nothing else you know about me?'

'Well, no . . . nothing of any significance.'

'My mother?'

'We've told you everything already, Georgia – that she was very beautiful, that she loved travelling, that she was young . . .'

'And my father?'

I could see that Roger had hesitated, and I could see that he had seen me see him hesitate as well.

'Well, nothing *really*.'

'"Nothing *really*"?'

He was suddenly very serious. 'Well, there was something,' he said, 'and I think under the circumstances it would be wrong not to tell you about it.'

I must have been looking very serious as well, as Roger was quick to tell me that when all was said and done it didn't amount to a great deal.

'When you were about three we had a letter from the adoption agency. The facts as I understood them were that your paternal grandmother' – and it sounded so weird Roger referring to some-one else as my father – 'didn't actually know that you had been born . . . that you existed, even. I forget the nuts and bolts of how she tracked down the right people within the agency, but she wrote saying that she had lost touch with her son, that she was ill herself and that her one desire . . . well, perhaps "one desire" isn't quite the way she put it, but in effect she wrote asking for news and for a photograph of you.'

I was careful to give the impression that I was hearing all this for the first time, but I couldn't help blurting out, 'How did they lose touch? Had they fallen out?'

'We know no more than that, Georgia. I solemnly promise you. We didn't want to ask. In a way we didn't want to know any-thing more. We were told that your father had vanished overseas. In Malaysia, I think.'

'Vanished?'

'Darling, I'm sorry, we just don't know. We wrote a lovely letter describing you, enclosed some photos, and sent them off via the agency. We got a letter back from your . . . grandmother, thanking us, and then nothing more.'

I had two thoughts about this. One was that my photo was out there somewhere, who knew where? The other was of someone vanishing off the face of the earth, and I got a picture in my mind's eyes of the globe and the bit that you can't see because it dips out of view into darkness.

*

It was Barrett's idea to send the letter. But only after he had given me a hard time.

'You want to stay away from that Drew: he's bad news.'

'That's a bit harsh, isn't it?'

'Autumn time last year you were in hospital, Georgia. You want to end up back there again?'

He was right – of course he was – and at that moment I would have given quite a lot to be able to look up with the knowledge that that night at the Wigton and afterwards in the park had been a dream, that I had not visited those places, encountered those spirits. It wasn't so much that I was worried I had damaged myself (sometimes you hear people say that it's possible to lose a bit of yourself when you're tripping); it was more a question of could I stop myself doing it again? Probably not. And what might happen next time?

'I know. I know,' I whispered.

'Why do you think you need to get out of it like you do?'

'I just have the feeling and I can't resist it,' I answered.

Barrett was shaking his head in his Barrett-like way. He was exposing a weakness, a vulnerability, and I didn't like it. All it did was make me feel I should be sticking up for myself.

'It's not all rubbish, you know,' I said. 'The medicine men use *ayahuasca* in the jungle, for healing purposes. You get to realize truths, get given knowledge. And it can be really beautiful: when it comes up you can actually see the music, Barrett, in shapes of colour, like in front of your eyes. Believe me, there's a lot more going on in the world than just in the here and now,' I finished, provocatively repeating one of Drew's catchphrases.

'You worry me, Georgia,' was all he said. 'The here and now is just where you need to be right now. Smoke a little weed, feel okay, but stay off the pills.'

We were in the front room of one of the flats Barrett was doing up with his brother off the Easterly Road. In the centre of the room was a mound of brick and plaster, all that remained of the chimney-breast. I liked the feel of the raw, powdery brick under the balls of my fingers and the look of the pale cement, which was like the wedge of filling Grandma Myers used to put in her sponge cakes.

'You should send a letter to that address you've got,' Barrett then said, once he was out of lecture mode.

'What letter? What address?'

'You should write to your mother in London. To that address you showed me.'

'What good is that going to do? She doesn't live there any more. We know that.'

'It would make you feel better.'

'How?'

'Did you never send Santa a letter when you were a kid?'

'Sure I did.'

'So send a letter,' Barrett repeated, much softer now.

'She won't *get* it, though.'

'That's what I'm telling you: it doesn't matter whether she gets it or not. Send a letter and it will be out there, out of your space.'

I made a throwaway gesture.

'Because you need to free yourself up, Georgia.'

'Not another lecture – please, Barrett!'

'You're angry, Georgia. You've lost your poise.'

'Wouldn't you have lost your poise if the person who brought you into this world said they didn't want to even meet you?' And I spat the word 'poise' disrespectfully, to hurt Barrett, as I knew this was part of his *t'ai chi* vocabulary.

It was water off a duck's back. 'Maybe I would,' he admitted. 'But I'd be thinking how I could absorb the energy. And then once I'd got myself balanced that's when I'd push back. You can't meet force with force, Georgia. But sending a letter: that's good.'

At first I laughed at the idea, but then it did start to make some sense. Now that I knew about the no-contact request there wasn't a great deal of point in making further enquiries, proper enquiries, to establish some real details. What was I going to do? Stalk my real mother? Spy on her? Deceive her, then reveal myself to her? Not really. But by sending her a letter, a sort of message in a bottle that might or might not wash up on a shore intact and dry and might or might not be opened by the person to whom it was addressed, and might or might not have an effect of some sort, this was a gesture at least. What the doctors call a placebo.

I had told Barrett everything the week before as we were getting ready for the Wigton, including stuff about NORCAP, with its register of requests and non-requests, a stinking bank of people's wishes and non-wishes.

'If I'm going to send her a letter why don't I send her a letter there?' I said.

'You could,' he shrugged, 'but I think you'd be better off sending it to the address in London you showed me. Send it to that NORCAP place and you might spend the next five years waiting for a reply.'

Barrett smiled. I like Barrett's smiles: all teeth, ugly and beautiful at the same time.

'You're right, you know,' I said. 'You're bloody right!'

And immediately I began to compose letters in my head – letters along the lines of the ones Heather Cross had described when we had first met last year.

A direct one: 'Dear Elizabeth, I am writing on behalf of someone you last met in 1991, who is anxious to re-establish contact.' A more oblique one: 'Dear Elizabeth, I am hoping you might be able to help. I am making enquiries on behalf of a mutual friend who is very poorly.' I could even write: 'Your daughter here, any chance you could get in touch to explain where you've been these last eighteen years?'

And it felt good that I could write that. That I could get some of the power back.

We sat for a while in silence, dunking our dripping teabags in and out of our cups, like we were those fishermen you see on holiday who sit on the quayside with a line over their index fingers. The red numerals in the music system were flashing the time at me. I wanted to move on, be on my own, but Barrett was staring at me hard and nodding, as if he could read my thoughts.

'Do you never wonder about your father?' I asked him eventually, to break the silence.

'Never.'

'Never?'

Barrett put both hands up, as if someone had drawn a gun on him. 'Look, I just go about my business. Because at the end of the day that's the deal I got,' he answered. 'If my father came looking for me, wanting to explain, blah-blah-blah, then I'd listen. Sure I would. But why would I want to chase after him? Just so that I can hear him say sorry?'

TEN

And then Fudge started acting weird. Or I thought he did. Which at that moment in time amounted to the same thing. I noticed it first the Monday following that night at the Wigton. He was slow to come when I called him, and when we finally got to the park he walked so directly behind me I kept on having to look around to see if he was still there. It was like he was stalking me, playing a game of Grandmother's Footsteps, stopping when I stopped, always keeping a distance. He wasn't interested in the usual places where there were smells; and didn't even notice the squirrels as they flew through the branches overhead, twitching their tails to tease him.

I knew something was properly up when one afternoon about a week later I called him and he wouldn't come. This was so odd it occurred to me that maybe someone else had taken him for a walk. But that wasn't possible: Roger would still be at work, and Diane never undertook 'dog-walking duties'.

I found him under the bed in Roger's dressing room. 'Fudge, what's the matter?'

And Fudge just stared at me with a careful expression, like he was wounded or that he didn't trust me any longer.

'What's the matter, Fudge? Tell me,' I begged him. 'Have I upset you?'

Still nothing. I was lying flat on the floor, like a car mechanic, with the fingers of my outstretched hand trying to stroke him under his chin. This would normally put him on his side and, if he was out in the open, he would roll on to his back and let you massage and pull his coat, so thick and loose it could have been a jacket.

He didn't want to bite me – I did know that – he just wanted me to respect his space, but when he growled that low growl and bared his teeth, I couldn't help recoiling right back to the door. I must have looked like someone standing on the shore of an island as the boat that has brought them there pushes out through the surf and rows away, leaving that person marooned.

'Oh, shit!' I said to myself, and I could hear the breath at the back of my throat, a dry, rasping what-the-fuck-have-I-done sort of sound. I didn't know what to do with myself. In the end I went and sat in the kitchen.

By the time Diane got in, about an hour later, I was in a real state. As soon as I heard her key turn in the lock I went to meet her in the hall. 'Do you think Fudge is okay?' I asked her.

'Why shouldn't he be?'

'He doesn't want to go out. He's not his usual self.'

Diane shrugged. 'Everyone has their off days,' she said, leafing through the mail.

'Diane, Fudge is not well,' I insisted.

'Well, then, we'd better take him to the vet, hadn't we?'

And the way she had said that, like a machine-gun, made me hate her. I was on my way back upstairs by now – I was going to check on Fudge again – when I found myself turning. I was looking down on Diane, like a priest stands a few steps above his congregation.

'So how's the tennis?' I asked her.

Diane shot a look at me. 'It's fine, thanks. Why do you ask?'

'Just interested. Who's your partner these days?'

For a moment I saw Diane flinch, but it wasn't a guilt flinch, more a surprise flinch. Then I saw that hard look come to her eyes. 'For God's sake, Georgia! If you've got something to say why don't you come out with it and say it?'

I shrugged, exactly like Diane had shrugged a minute before, turned on my heels and went and locked myself into my bedroom.

Half an hour later, though, I was on my way to Drew's. It seemed the only place to go. I remember thinking on the bus that Barrett was right, of course he was, and the sooner I got back on the straight and narrow the better – but the fact that Barrett had said all this only made it harder for me, in some sense. The bus was crowded, with standing room only. No one would budge: I had to go the whole way down to the bottom of the aisle. Each time the doors closed I got a feeling of claustrophobia, like I had to get off 'at all costs'. It was only the crunch of the engine, as it seemed to dubstep through the gears that kept me together. Those traffic dubs!

It was a relief to see Drew's smiling face. 'I was wondering when you'd come over,' was all he said, as he closed the door on the street and led the way, barefoot, up three flights of stairs.

Drew's studio flat is on the top floor, pretty much an attic, of a terraced house just outside the city centre. An old lady, the tenant before Drew, had died in the flat and had actually lain there for about ten days before she was discovered, so Drew had had to do a lot of psychic house-cleaning. But now the place has a good vibe.

A sort of breakfast bar divides the room in two. Drew was kitchen side, making us a cup of tea; I was seated low in an armchair (for some reason Drew has sawn all the legs off his chairs), staring up at the sky through a slanted Velux window in the ceiling. The sky was white with the faintest wash of blue.

'Perhaps he's ill,' Drew said, once I had finished telling him about Fudge. And I knew before he came out with it that he, just like Diane, was going to suggest the vet. 'Why not take him to the vet?'

'Because he's not that sort of ill.'

'How do you mean?'

'Drew, I've freaked him out. After the Wigton I took him to the park. I was tripping. He wasn't right then and he's not been right since.'

'Okay, okay. Tell me what happened.'

So I explained how I'd got in and it was too light to go to bed so I'd taken Fudge out into the dawn chorus. And how, just as soon as we got into Hepstall Park, everything had come on real strong. I described how the rhododendrons, the trees, the beck, the incessant chatter of the birds each seemed to have an individual energy and voice of their own; and how all these voices were speaking to me, moaning at me, yelling at me, cajoling me. And how it had all come together in a great crescendo of chaos.

'Shit, Drew! I was really rushing. And then I threw up like I've never thrown up before.'

'That's good.' Drew nodded. 'When you throw up on *aya* that's good. They call it a purge. What did it look like, the puke?'

The fact that Drew had asked me this made me nervous. 'It was like black pebbles, Drew, hard and shiny.'

'O-*kay*.'

'And Fudge ate it.'

'Fudge *ate* it?'

'Yes, he ate it.'

I was in tears. Having convinced myself in front of another person that it really *was* me who had harmed Fudge, I had to get back to him. But there was a bus journey between us. And what was to say that once I got home he wouldn't look at me with those same suspicious, wounded eyes? I heard myself sob from the bottom of my stomach. 'What have I done?'

Drew sat on the chair next to me. He took my hand. I had watched him turn into an older version of himself as the *aya* had come up that night in the Wigton, but now he was looking ten years younger than he should have done, as if he was Peter Pan and had caught up with a previous shadow. 'You haven't done anything, believe me,' he said, stroking my nails with the balls of his thumbs.

'But what's happened to Fudge?'

'He'll be fine, I promise you.'

Drew's explanation was completely logical. Perhaps Fudge *had* picked up on something in the park, he said. Animals were like that: highly sensitive, in tune with what was going on at all levels, not least the psychic one. They were weird that way. His own grandmother's cat, for instance. As soon as visitors got to the bottom of the street it would just vanish into the cellar. How did it know that people were about to call? There was no way of explaining. In Fudge's case he probably *had* been observing me, and seen me behave in a way he hadn't seen before and couldn't understand. And, yes, he might even have picked up on bits of my trip. You couldn't say one way or the other. I had put him on his guard: that was all. It would have been strange if I hadn't. There was nothing more to it than that. Before long Fudge would be completely cool.

'It's just a bit ironic that he ate your puke, that's all.'

I managed to laugh through my tears. 'What are you saying? That Fudge has eaten my purge?'

'Exactly that. Fudge has eaten shit!'

Even though my tears were tears of relief, I still wasn't entirely convinced. 'Oh, God, Drew, it was so heavy. He was barking at these horses,' I tried to explain, and for a moment I was right back there in the park and all around my shoulders and hair was the thud of hoofs slamming into the black earth, 'but there can't have been any horses . . .'

'What are you talking about?'

'A pack of horses just *galloped* past us, four of them. Just like that. Out of nowhere. And Fudge was barking at them. He saw them as well. But there couldn't have been any horses loose in Hepstall Park. So was I hallucinating it? Was Fudge seeing stuff I was seeing? Or had some horses really escaped? Did it really happen? I can't tell any longer. Oh, Drew, help me!'

And I was crying again, really crying this time.

'Okay, we'd better sort this out.'

And Drew did that wave, the wave he does to the spirits to keep back, like drawing a line in the sand. After a couple of minutes of this and him muttering what sounded like Spanish under his breath, '*Nunca, nunca, mallos spiritos . . .*' he came up behind where I was sitting and eased my shoulders so that they were pinned against the back of my seat. Then, with one hand formed into a funnel, he began to blow into the crown of my head. It was like a hot potato, when you start off by feeling a dull warmth and then you feel that warmth travel down to your fingertips and to the tips of your toes. Each time he leant back to take a new breath, I heard him blow through his teeth – 'zoooh . . . zoooh . . .' Drew's way of saying: 'Get thee behind me, Satan.'

Almost immediately the tension began to ebb out of me, just like it had that time when we were in the car park in Blackburn, when I moved out of the darkness and went to stand in the light. It was incredible. I wasn't mad about Drew's smell, his scratchy-looking chin, yet at that moment in time I just wanted to hug this person who had cut down to size my worries with one swing of a magician's sword.

I was beaming when I turned around to look him in the eyes, but at once I could sense that he was on guard. 'What's the matter, Drew?'

'I was wondering when I'd see you.'

'What do you mean?'

Drew sat by my side. He didn't take my hand this time. Instead he pulled at the collar of his fleece to reveal, just above his left collarbone, a love bite the size and shape of a leech, not black and inky but raspberry red and purple, edged with that waxy-yellow colour you get with bruising.

I went: 'And?'

'You did that, Georgia.'

'Don't talk bollocks!'

'You don't remember?'

'Do I heck.'

'Georgia, you were coming on to me.'

'Fuck off! I never saw you again after we were standing at the bar and the band started.'

Neither of us said anything for a minute or two. I tried to laugh, but because Drew was staring at me so hard, it was a thin laugh. There was something deadly earnest in his expression, and I knew then that he was right and I was wrong.

'You came straight over and started snogging me, Georgia. It was as simple as that,' he insisted.

'I didn't!' I insisted back. 'It was dark in there . . . you were tripping . . . you were really out of it. It could have been anyone.'

'It was you, no mistake. You smelt of you. You felt like you. I could tell. And you were wearing that necklace,' he finished, pointing to my leather map of Africa with its cowrie shell – the one I hadn't been wearing at the Wigton but which my twin sister had.

The detail about the necklace pulled me up. 'Really?'

'Yes, really!'

I was silenced but my mind was racing, racing. What the fuck did it all mean? That I had turned into my sister? But I had no memory of anything she did? Or that I had just been me, Georgia, gone into a blackout and snogging people at random in the club? The panicky feeling in my stomach was returning. I knew immediately I was never going to get to know the truth about this: where *aya* was concerned, it was impossible to be sure what was real and what wasn't. But I wasn't going to tell Drew about my sister: I didn't want to make it more real than it already was, if that makes sense. I didn't want him putting his slant on it, owning it: owning a part of me without me knowing what part it was.

'Only then it got really weird.' Drew frowned.

I dreaded what he was going to say next.

'You were kissing me hard, almost like you were a snake, with a darting tongue and strange eyes, hovering there just in front of me. For a moment I thought you were a *brujo* and I was going to get a hit. But it turned out you weren't a bad spirit: in fact, you were a good one and good stuff was flowing into me. All these pictures were flowing into me,' Drew whispered, with faraway eyes. 'From you into me . . . a thousand movies all playing at the same time.'

'What kind of pictures? What kind of movies?'

'Just random stuff. But what was weird, Georgia, was that it was all to do with horses.'

'Horses?'

'Yes, horses.'

*

I left Drew's flat pretty quick after that. And walked the whole way home. A good two and a half miles. I knew I had had a kind of warning, exactly as Barrett had said. I would never experiment with *ayahuasca* again.

And, as if it was a reward for making this resolution, when I got home Fudge was waiting for me. He was doing that snorting and smiling thing he does when you've been away on holiday and surprised him at the kennels. I was pulling at his coat, burying my nose in his scent, when Diane called up from the basement. 'That you, Georgia?'

'Yes.'

'I took Fudge to the vet,' she said. 'You were quite right. He's got a bad tooth.'

'Oh.'

'They gave him an injection and some painkillers. Poor Fudge!'

And somehow hearing Diane's voice without seeing her gave me a different impression of her. And for a moment I thought I'd been wrong about her too, and that maybe she was not so bad after all.

ELEVEN

I had my bi-monthly appointment with Dr Murdo the following day. When he sees his outpatients you don't go to Faversham House – you see him in a consulting room he has at the bottom of George Street. Which is a good job, better than walking through the doors of a psychiatric unit and hearing people like Mack carrying on – Bedlam, as Roger calls it.

We went through the usual rigmarole of me not saying much and Dr Murdo saying absolutely nothing and me thinking, I can handle the silence through the silence – then he came right out with it.

'Have you been using drugs?' he asked me.

'What do you mean?'

'Georgia, you know what I mean.'

'I've been taking the ones you prescribe me.'

'And nothing else?'

'Nothing else,' I lied.

Dr Murdo sat back a fraction and nodded. He seemed to be satisfied. 'I'm very pleased to hear it,' he said, 'because I thought I could see something.'

I gave Dr Murdo a puzzled look, when really I was nervous. 'See something?'

'I thought I could see something in your eyes,' he explained. 'It worried me, and that's why I needed to be clear on that point.'

Thinking back on it now I could have saved myself a lot of time and heartache if I'd said, 'Yes, I have been taking drugs, pretty heavy-duty ones in actual fact, drugs that the shamans and witch doctors use in the Amazonian jungle when they want to commune with dead people and their spirits, because did you know that there's more than one plane of existence? In fact there are loads of different realities going on simultaneously, each inhabited by their own populations of people and spirits all going about their busy business.' But I didn't.

'How are you coping with the no-contact request?' Dr Murdo then asked (he was doing a lot of talking today – maybe *he* was nervous).

'Okay.'

'Just okay?'

I shrugged. 'What can I say? My mother doesn't want to know me.'

'Not at the moment she doesn't.'

'Which is all that matters to me right now.'

'What about your father?'

'What about him?'

'Has the no-contact request had the effect of transferring your attention from your mother to your father, do you think? That's what I meant.'

'No.'

'You don't think about your father so much, do you?'

I spoke without thinking. 'No, not so much . . . because he's dead,' I answered, and when I heard my words come back at me I couldn't be sure I had actually spoken them for a second.

Dr Murdo sat up. 'How do you know?'

'I just do.'

'But how?'

So I told Dr Murdo I'd spoken to Roger about the letters I had found in his safe two years back, the ones I had written about in my A–Z. It hadn't been easy to talk about them because Roger hadn't known I'd seen them, of course: he hadn't known about the copper's son coming into our house, lying on our dining-room floor, like one of those athletes you see embossed on a bronze coin, as he broke into our safe. But I was glad we had had that opportunity, I explained to Dr Murdo, because, as it turned out, Roger hadn't known much more than I did, really. Nothing more, in actual fact. So now the whole subject was 'done and dusted', I said, with a throwaway wave of the hand.

'What *did* Roger tell you?' Dr Murdo quietly asked.

'Just that my father had vanished overseas. That he had been in some sort of trouble,' I went on, unable to stop myself putting my own slant on it. 'And that was the reason my grandmother had written for news of me. Apparently she didn't even know I existed until he vanished.'

'And you think that means he's dead?'

'Wouldn't you?'

Dr Murdo made a shrug of half-concession. 'That's all Roger told you?' he asked, not answering my question.

'He said that was all he knew. In fact, he told me that he and Diane hadn't wanted to know any more about me. He said they hadn't wanted the "baggage",' I finished with a false-hood, as it had been Diane, not Roger, who had once used that expression.

I expected Dr Murdo to react to this, to make a show of sympathy or disgust. He didn't: he just kept a very straight face as he said, 'Under the circumstances I think that's perfectly understandable.'

'How's that, then?'

'I mean that if you were taking on a life, as you do when you adopt someone, you might wish to feel you were starting at the beginning.' He paused. 'To use a clumsy analogy: a computer with a blank hard drive, with no one else's data on it.'

'Apart from their genes,' I objected.

'Everyone has their own stamp, Georgia. Of course they do. But I think it's only natural and human for parents preparing for adoption to feel they're embarking on their journey . . . afresh, for want of a better word.'

I said nothing.

Now it was Dr Murdo who was persisting. 'Well, don't you?'

'I suppose so.'

Suddenly there was a long silence, really long. So long that I thought the session might end without either of us saying anything more. To begin with I was cool. Then that hot, prickly sensation started to creep up on me, like a cat creeps up on a bird, slow but sure. In the end the silence literally forced the words out of my mouth.

'Perhaps I'm not meant to find out anything more about them,' I blurted.

'Perhaps not,' Dr Murdo repeated, nodding like one of those animals you see in the back of some people's cars. And then he said, so quiet I almost couldn't hear, 'Try and describe how you would feel if it turned out your quest *was* over. That the knowledge you had unearthed now . . . well, that was the limit of what you were ever going to know.'

I didn't answer for some time. I didn't want to. Of course, the possibility of finding out no more had occurred to me before: Heather Cross's baby-in-a-basket syndrome. But that wasn't how it was for me. I hadn't reached the end of the road. I don't know how I knew, but I did. There was more to come: much more. But neither did I know how honest I could afford to be with Dr Murdo about this. Not with a place like Faversham House hanging over me, like the Sword of Damocles. There was a square of sunlight on the floor between us. Sitting with my legs crossed, I could get the foot that was hanging in the air to move in and out of the light, or hold it there, the shoe dark, the toe bright. I may not have been prepared to admit that I had been using, but I did know that I needed help.

'I just feel them all around me,' I whispered, and I was flicking my fingers open and closed, exactly like Drew does when he's pushing away the spirits. 'They're there.'

Dr Murdo is quick to repeat anything big you say. 'You can feel them all around you. That they're there.'

'They're in my hair – they're in my space. I hear them, I see them. They're everywhere.'

'Georgia: I have to ask you again. Have you been taking drugs?'

'No, I haven't, Dr Murdo, not since last year,' I answered him, barefaced.

'So what do you mean, they're everywhere?'

'They're in my dreams, and when I wake up they're still there.'

Dr Murdo sat back. 'I see,' was all he said.

'Is that so unusual?'

Dr Murdo made an expression a bit like the one I saw a gondolier make in Venice, when Roger complained about how much our half-hour up and down the canals had cost.

'No, it's not unusual. We all dream, daydream, fantasize. It's the engagement with these realities that concerns our work here. That's why you must be completely honest with me, Georgia. Not only about drugs ... but about everything. Last year when you were admitted to Faversham House you were psychotic – you were responding to hallucinations.'

'I know. I'm trying to be honest.'

'Good. So let's come back to the subject of your search for knowledge. Yes?'

'Yes.'

'Suppose you really weren't going to find out any more. You knew that the information was out there, but you also knew there was no way to it. Suppose you had been left in a foundling wheel.'

'What's a foundling wheel?'

Dr Murdo is always careful not to sound patronizing, but he was genuinely surprised. 'You don't know what a foundling wheel is?'

I shook my head.

Dr Murdo was staring at my shoes, not at me, as he explained. 'Many societies, most particularly in medieval times in Europe, made provision for mothers who were unable to bring up their own children, in response, I imagine, to the number of babies found abandoned. In the case of the foundling wheel it was usually attached to a convent, literally a large wheel bearing a small compartment in which a baby could be placed. And a bell for the mother to ring. Once the nuns were alerted by the sound of the ringing bell, they would turn the wheel to deliver the baby.'

'Bloody hell!' I couldn't help exclaiming.

'And in the context of our discussions here this morning,' Dr Murdo went on, 'I use the word "deliver" advisedly. Here is a life, brought into the world a second time, but this time with no history, background, pedigree, no clue to its origin whatsoever.'

I couldn't say anything in the next silence. It seemed amazing that, me being adopted, no one had told me about this wheel business, that I had never stumbled across it on-line when I was genning up on all the information I needed to start making my own enquiries. In my mind's eye I could see a little old lady in black turning an iron handle.

'Do you think it would have been any easier if you had been born this way?' Dr Murdo asked eventually.

Of course, it was too soon to answer a question as big as this, in spite of the fact it was pretty much exactly the same thing as Heather Cross's baby-in-a-basket-on-hospital-steps scenario. I knew perfectly well what Dr Murdo was driving at, though. If there were no birth certificates, no letters locked away in safes, no NORCAPs, no letterbox contacts, no matrons in the hospital to speak to, even, then perhaps stuff would be a whole lot easier. But the thought of this still petrified me. 'It wouldn't stop me wondering,' I said.

Dr Murdo was pushing me, just like Heather Cross had pushed me the first time we'd met at Faversham House, but he wasn't bullying me.

'Deep down, though, you would have accepted that you would never discover who your real parents were,' he said. 'That your coming into the world, or at any rate into the hands of the people who were going to adopt you, had come about as a result of such an extraordinary and . . . random event.'

I didn't reply for quite a while, before I said, without thinking, 'If you believe in random events.'

'Don't you?' Dr Murdo probed, his eyebrows high on his forehead.

'Not really.'

'How so?'

'Well, everything comes about as a result of something else. In which case how can anything be random?'

Dr Murdo smiled, but not in a condescending way. I smiled back.

Seeing Dr Murdo only once every two months instead of every day, as when I was an inpatient at Faversham House, it takes time to get back to how we once were – easy with each other, more like friends, really. Now, for a moment, the ice was broken, and I was grateful for the opportunity of steering the conversation away from the thought of opening a compartment and finding a baby without any history. So I was able to sidetrack him in a teasing sort of way: 'You don't believe things can be random, do you?'

'I do, actually.'

'Really?'

'Yes, really – and only this morning they were giving quite a good example on the radio.'

'Oh?'

'Would you like to hear about it?'

'Okay.'

'It was a discussion about the dangers of giving your credit-card details over the Internet,' Dr Murdo went on slowly, and you could see his eyes moving as he got the story right in his mind. 'A man was explaining how these details are encrypted, encoded, made impossible to decipher by criminals. He likened it to an imaginary scenario where you lock fifty people into a squash court, blindfold them and get them to mill about. One of them has got an envelope in his hand. As he bumps into the person next to him he passes the envelope, which then continues to get passed from one person to another for a full twenty minutes. He was saying that this epitomized the essence of randomness. No

one, but no one, could tell you who had the envelope at the end
of this experiment.'

I was laughing again when I said: 'Except a psychic.'

Dr Murdo was looking at me sideways on, suspicious although
still playful, mischievous. 'I forgot. You believe in that as well,
don't you?'

'You know I do.'

'Then perhaps you could tell me who's going to win the FA
Cup this year.'

We laughed for a few seconds more, then Dr Murdo raised
his hand by way of saying we should come back to the point.
'Okay, we've only got a few minutes left. Perhaps we should try
and understand what you *do* mean by psychic. We've talked about
this before, I know – but I think it's quite important, Georgia.'

'I just think we're all connected, nothing more than that,'
I answered, careful again with my words.

'Connected?'

'In psychology we learnt about the collective unconscious:
there was a definition for it – "the reservoir of the experiences of
our species".'

'That's only one theory, you know, Georgia. Other schools
of thought have it that the unconscious belongs solely to the
individual.'

'I don't go along with that.'

'You sound very sure.'

'It's my intuition, that's all.'

As Dr Murdo didn't comment immediately, I went on, 'Surely
you must believe that deep, deep down, in the dream world, we're
all connected?'

Again Dr Murdo looked like that gondolier. 'In many ways
I do,' he replied. 'It goes without saying that there is a very

well-developed relationship between the universe and all the parts that go to make it up. But I don't believe a psychic plane exists. To return to the analogy of the computer: I would go as far as to say that we are all networked to a server of sorts and that everywhere we go on the net we may leave a footprint – but I don't believe we have access to each other's hard drives.'

'What about synchronicity?' I objected.

'What about synchronicity?'

'An uncanny coincidence, a startling serendipity,' I answered, running off the definitions we had been made to learn by heart. 'You know – when you think about someone you haven't seen for years and then there they are on the bus.'

'There are counter-theories to that, too.'

'What kind of counter-theories?'

'Well, that in the course of a day – and in our dreams also – we think and see much more than we know or remember or care to remember, and that it's only through the law of probability that we experience what you call "uncanny coincidences" where the person we've thought or dreamt about coincides with a meeting or sighting of that person.'

'I'm not so sure,' I said.

And that coincided with our hour being up.

*

It took less than twenty minutes to track my mother down. I started with '"Elizabeth Florence Dunne" Horses Leicester', and when that didn't return any hits, just gradually opened it up: '"Elizabeth Dunne" Horses Leicester'; 'Dunne Horses Leicester'.

For some reason I ended up with Dunne Equestrian Leicester. And there it was on the third page of images: a thumbnail of the head of a horse with the words underneath: *Lumb Lane Equestrian Centre.*

The horse was the stallion I had seen in Hepstall Park. Simple as. Only it was completely calm, its plum eye coal-black and as still as a lake, its mane immaculately combed and glistening with a bar of straight light. I hung the cursor over the link for what seemed like hours, my heart thumping in my chest, as if there was a drummer inside me hammering a double pedal. Was this how Bluebeard's wife had felt as she pushed the key into its lock?

TWELVE

We were in the snug for the National. I was sitting on a beanbag, leaning against the front of the sofa, with Fudge stretched out at my feet, chin on paws, facing diagonally away from the TV. Roger had twisted the venetian blinds mostly closed and the half-light that filled the room was as thin as water. When I come to think about it now the whole vibe had that submerged, removed feeling – even the sound of the crowds at Aintree was exactly like the murmur you get when surf unfolds on a gravelly shore.

Roger was trying to get it on with Diane (this was their lucky sofa, wasn't it?). He had his hand behind where she was sitting, trying to pull her shirt out of her skirt so he could push his fingers up her bare back.

'Roger, *don't*!' Diane breathed, a sort of 'do but don't' breath.

'Can if I want to.'

'Oh, yes? Who said?'

'Clergyman said.'

I turned to look up at Diane. Her expression was cracked – there is no better way to describe it. Her eyes had a pretend warmth when she was looking at Roger, a sort of teasing, play-ground warmth, not a real warmth, because when she glanced back at me I could see them cold, as cold as the secret we shared.

Little consequence, as Roger would say. I was much too pre-occupied with the Lumb Lane Equestrian Centre, reliving over and over the moment my eyes had settled on the thumbnail of that horse, with its twisted neck and pointed ears, reliving that fractured second of recognition when I got to know – just *know* – that I had arrived. Quite often when you're tripping you get given knowledge, truths, like it's been slid under the door. It hadn't been like that because I hadn't been tripping. This was reality.

And everywhere I had gone in the website – from the homepage with its picture of a show-jumping hurdle, the posts and cross-bars in blue and white with the word WELCOME above in the same colours, to the aerial view of the whole centre, all green and brown, with the caption underneath – 'Lumb Lane Equestrian Centre has a large (55m x 35m) outdoor school which is ideal for show-jumping as well as flat-work training. We also have a recently resurfaced indoor school (40m x 20m) which provides a safe enclosed training facility' – that knowledge was reinforced to the point it was quite literally irrefutable. Well before I reached 'Photo Album' and found a picture of 'Proprietors, Jim Hayes and Elisa Dunne', standing in front of a stone house with a large shed (presumably the indoor school) sloping away to one side. Then more pictures of Elisa: her in front of the main gate; another of her in a tack room; more of her standing in a field with kids on horseback, their straw-coloured hair up in the wind, cantering around her, like satellites in orbit.

The sun was out at Aintree, but it looked cold, very cold, with clouds scudding overhead. The cameraman seemed to be more interested in the punters, especially the women, who were wearing hats like meringue puddings and high heels that punctured turf so soft it could have been the skin of a hot-air balloon.

Looking back on it now, I'm pretty sure the better part of me knew perfectly well that the Elisa Dunne I had found in Leicester wasn't my birth mother. 'Viewed in the cold light of day', it would hardly be likely, would it? But that didn't seem to matter. What seemed to matter was me believing in something. A that-will-do-for-now type of believing.

But the really confusing thing was that another part of me had to concede that there *was* a chance this Elisa Dunne was my mother: I could well have found her by magic, been led to her by the spirits, been shown where she was by the *aya*. And this part of me wouldn't stop chattering: 'Look at her hair, look at her eyes, look at the way she stands.' And what was scary, a bit like when you're being pulled out to sea by the ocean's undercurrents and you know what's happening but there's not much you can do about it, was that the more I let that voice have its say the more the down-to-earth part of me had to admit it would be just as wrong to discount the possibility that this person was my mother as it would be wrong to assume I had found her through some weird act of divination.

What I think I liked most of all about having the fantasy was that I could take some of the power back. Up until now Elizabeth Florence Dunne had had all the calls: she had given me away, she had made it plain that she didn't want me knocking on her door – she had become a totally unapproachable figure in my mind, a person full of silence and secrets. Now that I had seen a photograph of her in the real world, checked where she lived, how she earned a living, who she was hanging with – here were some important practical questions answered. Now it was up to me, not her, whether I introduced myself to her or not: the decision was entirely mine.

Still Diane was pretending to squirm. 'Do stop it!'

'It's good luck to touch you,' I heard Roger whisper.

'Lucky for whom?'

'For us all, of course.'

In the end I had to turn around to remind them that they were not alone in the room. Roger was like a teenager, embarrassed and flushed red. He winked at me and made a funny face, as if he was a clown in a circus. Then he pointed in an over-the-top way at the screen. 'That's your filly, Georgia: Solway Firth.'

Solway Firth was a beautiful chestnut, with a white star on her forehead and white socks. Her jockey, who had a big nose and sunken eyes, was in pink and cream. As she passed the camera she snorted and dropped her head and her flanks rippled and flashed silver in the air. I found myself staring at her in an absent, trance-like way, the way you stare into nothingness when you wake in your bed and you try to get back into your dream, connect with the characters and places once again.

'Come in from sixteen to one to twelve to one,' Roger was saying, whatever that meant. 'She's well fancied, Georgia.'

She was nothing like the wild horses I had seen in Hepstall Park, she did not resemble any of the horses in Lumb Lane's 'Photo Album', she was like no horse I had ever seen before – not that I had seen too many. But there was a connection to make, no question about it: her presence was just too strong and powerful. It was something you couldn't avoid, like you can't avoid smelling a smell. And yet it was too elusive, shadow-like, to grasp. I kept focusing, focusing on her big brown shape, willing her energy to flow into me in sort of Bluetooth waves, until finally, as the camera closed in on her a second time, I really did feel something, a bright tingling in my forearms.

'And here is Solway Firth, owned and trained by Terry Morgan, who told me earlier that he had woken this morning with a certain premonition. Although he wouldn't be drawn on this. Premonitions are quite often best kept to oneself, isn't that right, Gary?'

'Quite right.'

'She's in perfect condition, George.' Roger nudged me. 'Do you know, I think you're in with a shout?'

I said nothing. I wasn't listening to Roger or checking what he and Diane were up to on the sofa, because I, too, was having a premonition. A premonition that this horse would do something spectacular. If I blinked a couple of times I could actually see people milling about her, waving, looking up, looking down, everything centred around Solway Firth. And then it was obvious: this spectacular thing she was going to do would be a sort of message to me, some kind of indication, pointer.

They were massing behind the starting tape, coming forwards in a pack, a great cloud. I was totally into the race by now. It was nothing to do with winning, it was to see what would happen next, what I was going to be told.

'They're off!'

I felt Roger sit forward, and the volume go up as he pointed the remote at the screen like he was waving an invisible stick.

'They're all over that one safely.'

The cameras were tucked in behind the fences so that you could see the soft bellies of the horses as they flew through the air along with great clods of earth. The sound of the gallop that now filled the room was like a hundred drummer boys all playing at once. For a second I was back in Hepstall Park, with Fudge between my feet, the loose horses thundering past me. Like shutting a door on someone you didn't want to come into your house, I had to delete these images from my mind's eye.

By the time they were on their second circuit of the track, most of the horses had fallen or refused or unseated their riders, melted away, like they were the soldiers Roger used to tell me about who climbed out of trenches in France and walked towards a firing enemy. But Solway Firth was still standing. All the time I had never let her out of my sight. She was in the second pack, on the outside and not on the rails, which apparently was a good thing. And all the time I had been holding my breath, not daring to breathe in case it invited not exactly bad luck but somehow affected the balance of the race. Roger's horse, Marked Card, had fallen at a fence called the Chair. Diane's horse, Balinrobe, was in eighth position. By now I was so convinced that Solway Firth was going to win, I was already wondering what her winning might mean.

'Go on, Solway Firth, go on, you beauty,' Roger whispered, and that felt good too: that he was rooting for my selection and not Diane's.

'Here, Georgia, take the betting slip, pinch it tightly, like this – it's good luck.'

But no sooner had I taken the slip and pinched it, than a jockeyless horse crossed Solway Firth's path, making her lose her rhythm. At the next jump she took it sort of sideways on and almost from a standing position. She didn't reach the other side.

'Solway Firth has unseated his rider,' the commentator announced, getting her sex wrong.

I couldn't believe my eyes.

'Ooooh *dear*, George!' Roger groaned, putting his hand on my shoulder. 'What a shame! But *what* a surprise!'

'Can't the jockey get back on?'

''Fraid not.'

I had no interest at all in the race now. It was like the end of a good gig when the lights have come up and everyone's just wandering around, wondering what to do next. I sank back against the sofa. I was angry with myself for having a premonition; I was perplexed, irritated at the anticlimax of it all; and this irritation was compounded by the fact . . . surprise, surprise . . . that Diane's horse passed the line first.

'Hooray!' Roger shouted.

'Oh, my God!' Diane shrieked.

'How *did* you choose that horse? And at thirty-three to one!'

'I just liked the name.'

'Diane,' Roger pronounced, taking this opportunity to take her hand and place it in his lap, 'you're a genius!'

Fudge hadn't flinched. He was looking up at all three of us, his eyes passing from one to another without moving. I leant forward and stroked the crown of his head, watching the fur spring up from beneath my fingers. A hush had filled the room; there was a definite hiccup in the celebrations or congratulations or whatever it is they do at the end of a big race. I glanced up at the screen. A bunch of course officials was building an enclosure from green plastic right there on the track. 'What are they doing?' I asked Roger, who looked grim, and you could tell by his expression that he wasn't going to answer immediately.

'What are they doing?' I asked him a second time.

And Diane said: 'Georgia, don't look!'

Of course I looked. The camera angle was slightly from above and you could see over the side of the wall the officials had formed from their sheeting to where a horse was lying on the turf. I knew it was Solway Firth before the commentator came on.

'*Distressing images here at Aintree . . . Solway Firth brought down three from home. A tragic end to a very courageous effort.*'

And then the officials seemed to scatter, as if they were fleeing an explosive device that was about to be detonated, each of them crawling from underneath the green plastic, pushing aside the curtained entrance. Seconds later Solway Firth rose. Her back was covered with sweat the colour and texture of cuckoo spit. She reared her strong neck, then crashed it down before stumbling through one side of the green tent. And now everyone could see her injury, her leg broken just above the first joint, so badly broken that her hoof was just hanging there, like a lead weight. She stumbled and limped on, careful not to touch the ground with her broken leg; but it seemed she couldn't avoid this and every time her hoof scraped the turf she threw her head back in agony and her flanks flashed a shimmering silver, just as they had thirty minutes before in the paddock.

'*Distressing images here at Aintree.*'

'I really don't think we should be watching this,' Roger said, pinching the remote.

The room was silent now. And it was weird. There was all this stuff going off in Liverpool, only eighty miles away, and here we were, part of it but not part of it at the same time. I was trying to control my thoughts, actually picturing myself with my hand on a big switch that I could throw and which would take all the bad images away. I tried to focus on the Lumb Lane Equestrian Centre, but even the thought of that could not eradicate the suffering we had witnessed.

As usual it was Diane who had the last word on the matter. 'Do you think they'll have to destroy her?' she said, not expecting an answer.

*

I went straight round to Sula's. Something was up. It took me a few seconds to work out exactly what it was. But once you saw it, it was unmistakable.

'Sula! What's happened to your lip?'

'Nothing's happened to my lip.'

I had moved towards her and was trying to stare up into her face. 'It's bleeding,' I said. 'Sula, your lip's bleeding! What's happened?'

Sula retreated from me. She had been in the middle of doing the washing, but she had made much more mess than she needed to. There were piles of clothes everywhere, stacked on the work surfaces, heaped on the floor. The whole of Christine's kitchen had a topsy-turvy energy. I picked my way through the piles of laundry to stand before her a second time. She had filled up and I saw her clench her jaw as she swallowed. For some minutes she just looked at me, from one eye to the other, a silent pendulum.

'What's happened? Sula, please tell me!' With one finger I was very gently stroking her bottom lip, where there was a straight cut just left of the place where your lips can open up of their own accord in winter when they get dry. All around the cut there was a faint bruising, which had been difficult to distinguish from a distance on account of Sula's colouring.

'Please tell me.'

Sula tried to smile. 'That fella I've been seeing,' she whispered.

I couldn't believe what I was hearing. 'Tell me you're joking.'

The tears were streaming down Sula's beautiful apricot cheeks by now.

'Tell me you're joking,' I repeated, feeling an energy grow in my arms like I was ready for a fight.

Sula was shaking her head to say, no, she wasn't joking. Finally her mouth unbuttoned: 'I fought like a tigress, Georgie.'

I was hugging Sula, both arms wrapped around her, and smoothing the back of her neck where the vertebrae stood out like stepping-stones. First I was clinging to her. Then she was clinging to me. A minute of this and I felt her melt into me with one great sob. 'Oh, Georgie, it was terrible,' she cried. 'You don't believe it can happen until it does.'

'What happened?'

'I went back to his house – and there was another man, waiting there.'

'Do you know who they are?'

'Hazel knows who they are.'

'Have you reported it?'

'Like I say, nothing happened.'

'Sula! My lovely, lovely Sula!' And I hugged her again for all I was worth. Once more I heard her sob, quietly to start with, then louder.

She pulled away from me a little. Enough for me to see the good I had done her. 'Georgie, thank you,' she whispered, 'thank you.'

'Sula, I love you.'

'I love you, too.'

Now Sula stroked my lip, very, very gently on the line where the lip becomes skin, her eyes following her finger. Then she looked at me, through me, past me, as if to another me far off. I knew she was going to kiss me before she did. A dry kiss to begin with, just a peck; then her lips stayed on my lips longer, until I could not help but try to find her tongue with mine. Before we knew it we were snogging, really snogging. It wasn't a horny snog, but it had, in that split second, made me hungry, really hungry.

THIRTEEN

Lumb Lane Equestrian Centre is split in two by Lumb Lane. On one side there is the large indoor school I had seen photos of on the website, and beyond that a jumping paddock or manège, if that's the right word for it. On the other side lies a long, low building of old stone, which you can tell are stables even before you see the doors split in two, with those big heads cut off at the neck like they're in one of those mix 'n' match books.

About fifty metres beyond, with a dense wood of trees behind it, stood the house – I knew without knowing – in which John Hayes and Elisa Dunne lived.

I had checked the centre out on Google Earth – zoomed right in to see a line of buckets waiting to have food poured into them in the stabling area; checked the horses that were grazing in a field beyond the paddock, all of them with a thin shadow lying next to them, like a stocking; and of course I had checked Jim and Elisa's house, where the washing was up on a line in the garden, bunting-style, and a small greenhouse was crammed full of dark green plants. So I hadn't really needed to go to Leicester: I had seen all there was to see. But I *had* gone to Leicester. It had taken a train, two buses and a taxi, more than forty pounds.

For about twenty minutes I hung around the junction where Lumb Lane meets the dual carriageway, next to a sign: 'Leicester 6'. It had never occurred to me what I was going to do once I reached the centre: pretend it was kit I was after in the shop; hang out in the café I had also seen images of on the Internet; try to steal a glimpse of the woman who might or might not have been my mother? Along the dual carriageway, as far as the eye could see, cherry trees were spilling their blossom into the gutter, and against the double yellow lines, as thick as enamel, and the grey of the tarmac, the pink petals looked out of place. For a moment I wasn't sure if I was getting a flashback. And sure enough, right on cue, the fear came up to stalk me, like a jaguar trying to fix me with its golden eyes. It took a bit of shooing away.

Me doing the shooing – Drew's zoooh, zoooh – had attracted the attention of a girl who was making her way back from the paddock with a bridle draped over her shoulder. She waved. I half waved back. She gestured, as if to say: 'Can I help?' I shrugged and shook my head to indicate I was a stranger, but I was okay, thank you, and moved on. But still I wasn't ready to go into the centre. So I 'bought time', walked up the hill, away from the entrance with its motif of a hurdle in blue and white.

The road up into the woods was twisting and steep and seemed to be sunk into the earth, with high walls of black stone on either side keeping back the forest. Grandma Myers was not in such a forgiving mood today.

'You always did do as you pleased, didn't you?' she started, out of nowhere.

'What do you mean?'

'Remember that time at Filey?'

Grandma Myers was referring to our famous row, when I went out to swim on a Lilo and was pulled miles from the shore by the ocean's undertow. 'I remember.'

'You just went off when I said you shouldn't . . . and we ended up getting the coast guards. You could have drowned.'

'But I didn't.'

'No consideration for the feelings of others.'

'I've already said I'm sorry . . . hundreds of times.'

'And now look what you're doing.'

'What am I doing?'

'You know perfectly well! And I think you're making a grave mistake, a grave mistake.'

I didn't like the way Grandma Myers had used the word 'grave' twice like that. It reminded me of her funeral, and for a moment I saw the fingers of roots hanging from the black earth, and wondered whether by now they had closed and meshed over her – now that she had been lying on top of Grandpa Myers for more than a year.

'You never did have much time for other people's feelings,' Grandma Myers repeated.

So I turned her off, just like you do a telly.

I had got to the top of the hill. Ahead was a small cricket ground with a pavilion at one end and a pub at the other. A group of young boys was in the centre of the pitch. There was the usual banter going off.

'Hey, you, gay boy!'

'Come again and I'll batter you.'

I sat on a bench, against a metal plaque with an inscription – *In memory of Emma Lodge, 1937–2006, who loved this place* – and tried to centre myself. Immediately I felt calmer. The energy was much better here: light, open, the opposite of claustrophobic. Emma Lodge must have been a good woman.

For a moment Grandma Myers came back on and actually started talking to Emma Lodge.

'She's not a bad girl, really.'

'I can tell.'

And I had to switch her off again.

There seemed to be a constant stream of aeroplanes passing overhead, perhaps on their way to East Midlands airport (where Diane had had a panic attack when I was about ten and we had missed our flight to Paxos). Normally it's only dubs and sounds that take me places, but just the sight of the tiny silver aircraft, pushing and probing noiselessly at the sky, was enough for parts of me to feel that they were being pulled up and away, sucked in behind the glassy slipstream. Maybe these planes were hexing me, I thought, trying to draw away the strength Emma Lodge was bestowing on me, and the more I dwelt on this the more paranoid I got.

So I stood and began to retrace my steps on the road that led back down into the forest, back into the tunnel of trees, cave-like, mine-like, dark, dripping and bottomless. This was it! Make-your-mind-up time! No question about it! And even though the trees seemed to be waving me back, I wasn't going to hesitate. To help me on my way I became Judy Garland, hopping and skipping to keep the spirits at bay. It worked: just the thought of her and Toto in a basket had me looking straight at the trees and saying aloud, 'Don't bother trying to catch me, I'm too fly'; and to my mother, 'I'm sorry, but here I am.'

I got through the gates of the Lumb Lane Equestrian Centre and right into Reception without stopping.

The same girl whom I had seen walking across the paddock was sitting at what looked like a kitchen table. She glanced up at

me and smiled. I smiled back. This wasn't anything like the recep-
tions I was used to in doctors' surgeries and schools: it was more
like the front room of a house, with sofas, rugs on the floor, lamps
on tables. All over the walls, in neat, crowded rows like stamps in
an album, were pictures of horses and under most of these were
pinned rosettes, red, blue and yellow.

'I'm Rebecca,' the girl said. 'Can I help?'

My mouth was bone dry, but I managed to ask: 'What do I do
if I want to have a ride?'

'Have you been here before?'

'No.'

'Have you been riding before?'

'Only once or twice.'

'Did you want to ride today?'

'Is that possible?'

'Certainly it's possible. But you have to register first.'

I must have frowned.

'Just your details,' Rebecca explained. 'Date of birth, address.
Miss Dunne will need to see it before we start you off.'

'Miss Dunne?'

'Elisa Dunne is the owner of the stables.'

She took a form from a drawer, pinned it on to a clipboard, and
handed me a biro.

I sat on the sofa nearest the door, sideways on, my back half
turned to Rebecca at her table, and pretended to read the form,
which was exactly like one of those questionnaires you have to
fill in before you go on a school trip (so that when you end up
dead in a river the school can say they weren't to blame) with
all the usual questions: name, DOB, telephone numbers, email
address, next of kin, etc., etc. I heard myself swallow: a silence had
come down in that room like a curtain – or, rather, like a curtain

going up. And there I was suddenly: on stage, with no lines, no fellow players to speak of, no cues. Shit! I had no intention of registering or climbing on to a horse. I should walk straight out of there, I knew. But I also knew that having spent all day getting to Leicester, I needed to stay, check the energy, listen to it, taste it. To know. I needed to be quick, though.

I might have been pretending to fill in the form, but in reality I was letting the print swim out of focus, and having blurred everything on the page, I was trying to look through the mess of meaningless words and phrases. It wasn't easy, like looking through two keyholes at once: you had to get them in line. If this was my mother's home, the place where she went about her business, lived her life, then surely I would be able to connect with her. Surely I would be able to feel her. Sense her. But there was nothing. Absolutely nothing. Only the dull, all-pervading stench of leather. I tried again, and again. With the same result.

A wave of impatience, more anger, really, washed over me. I could feel it down my neck, all over my back, just like when you get dressed after swimming in the sea and your shirt tears at the dried salt. I hated this place now that it meant nothing to me, with its pair of antlers over the door I had walked through, and its stuffed fish in a glass case behind where Rebecca was sitting, an ugly fish, with a deep belly, hooked lower jaw and skin the colour of a stagnant pond. Why had I been so stupid as to come here?

I felt like bursting into tears – literally spilling my frustration and heartache all over the floor – and there seemed only one way to quell them: by writing. My birthday, my address, my next of kin. Neatly and slowly, paying attention to my handwriting. This was how I'd let off steam, make some gesture to justify the days of obsessive fantasizing, the finding and then the loss. It wasn't Georgia Myers I gave as my name, it was Lily Rose Dunne. And next of kin: not Roger and Diane Myers, of Moortown Road, LS17 6HG, but Elisa Dunne of Lumb Lane Equestrian Centre, Leicester LC14 5TK. I sat back, the anger on my neck gone.

'Are you done?' Rebecca asked me, with her smile.

'Nearly,' I replied.

Just then there was the sound of a door being thrown open in another room, a crying child, or two crying children, and a grown-up. At once the energy in the room changed. I glanced at Rebecca. I saw that she, too, had sat up, as if to attention. As she saw me looking at her she lowered her eyes. You could tell that something was going to happen.

'Do that again and you'll regret it,' came a voice. 'Do you hear me?'

No reply, just sobbing, a sort of heartrending sob, a bit like the way Sula had sobbed in my arms two days before.

'You won't be allowed over here. You'll have to stay in the house. Do you hear?'

A second time I glanced at Rebecca, who wouldn't look back at me. My eyes were darting everywhere; I was on the very edge of my seat. Because it seemed to me I knew that voice: I just knew it. Not from the real world, but from somewhere else. I could hear it in my solar plexus, right there in the corner of my ribcage. My mouth had gone completely dry now.

And then the person whose voice this was pushed into Reception. She wasn't able to open the door with her hands, as she was dragging two children. I saw her like you do when you get an impression of someone in a photograph: medium height, mouse-coloured hair in a ponytail, dungarees and lilac T-shirt. And in her hands . . . twins! Identical twins, with straw-white hair high on their foreheads, snotty noses and watery hazel eyes.

'Now sit there,' she told them, pushing them both to the sofa opposite where I was now standing. 'Who's this?' she asked of Rebecca, gesturing at me.

'She's just registering.'

Elisa Dunne came straight over to me and took the clipboard from my hand. I did try to resist initially, but it turned out that the better part of me was willing to surrender it. I watched as she read what I had written. My breath was high in my chest. Was this the moment? The moment of reunion? Was she suddenly going to throw down the clipboard and hug me? Not at all. She took what seemed like an age staring at the registration form before she looked back up and fixed me square in the eyes. There was another silence before she whispered: 'Is this some kind of a joke?'

I could not reply.

'You're written that you live here,' she went on, 'and that I'm your next of kin. Is this some kind of joke?'

I was indignant now. 'No.'

'Well, if it isn't a joke, what is it? You've said that I'm your next of kin.'

I could feel Rebecca's eyes trained on me so I moved a step to the side to put her behind Elisa Dunne, to stop at least one pair of eyes staring at me, before I answered. 'Because you are,' I said.

'And how do you explain that?'

I didn't know what I was going to say next.

'How can I be your next of kin?' Elisa Dunne demanded.

'Because you're my mother!'

The first thing Elisa Dunne did was look at her twins, and in her turned head I saw a serious expression of fright. Of course, now I can see that as a natural reaction, but then I saw it as flight, as if she was trying to close down really quickly.

'And my father is Ralph Peddar,' I went on, thinking I had gained some ground.

Elisa Dunne had turned to look me square on again, her head tilted to one side. There was the look of a bitch in her pursed lips, the look of a slammed-shut door. 'Never heard of him,' she said.

'And I was born in Pond House, London.'

'You need help.'

I tried to reach out to touch Elisa Dunne, but she stepped quickly back. The sight of her doing this, physically avoiding me this time, made things much worse. 'Please!' I begged. 'Please!'

'Rebecca, call the police,' Elisa Dunne barked.

'Don't,' I implored. 'Just talk to me.'

'The police, Rebecca. Now.'

And so I just ran out of the Lumb Lane Equestrian Centre and did not stop until I had the pink petals of cherry blossom under my feet, around my ankles.

*

Sometimes things in life just have to change. Otherwise the pressure gets too great. A bit like when I was eleven and I wanted Fudge so bad. Or I had a crush on that boy in Blackburn, and he didn't text for days and days . . . and then he did. A sort of feeling like you don't know what you're going to do next if the energy doesn't shift.

And things did change that night. Big-style. I got into the house late: there was only the hall light on; all the other windows were as black as wells. After hugging Fudge and breathing his damp, doggy smell, I looked up and saw on the piano an envelope addressed to me in unfamiliar writing. I opened it without thinking . . . to find the letter I had written to Pond House . . . with the words WHO WANTS TO KNOW? scrawled in biro at the bottom.

FOURTEEN

WHO WANTS TO KNOW? So there I had it: a hand-written note in biro from my mother. The writing wasn't neat or straight and the question mark was bigger than it should have been and looked a bit punky and out of place. And there were the splodges you get with ballpoint pens all over the page and the back of it too, as if my mother had been turning the letter backwards and forwards in her hands, wondering whether she should send it or not. But she had.

Again I had that feeling of getting some of the power back. For what seemed like hours I held the piece of A4 between my fingers, offered it up to the light, smelt it, ran my finger over the writing. A picture kept coming to me of a great crowd of people crossing a bridge. And there was my mother in the middle of the crowd, buried in a sea of people. With me just a few yards behind. And, like a shadow, I wasn't going to let her go – this time I wasn't going to lose her

Part of me wanted to get the train to King's Cross there and then, with its homeless people and everyone coming and going, get on the tube and turn up on the doorstep of Pond House. But the bigger part of me knew better. After Lumb Lane (which I suppose was like a practice run), how was I going to cope when the door swung open and a woman whose appearance I hadn't had a chance to get familiar with said: 'Yeah? Who?' Admittedly that meeting at the centre had been a farce – the delusion had exploded just like one of those bubbles you blow as a child, which wobble and shine colours at you before spitting wetness on your knees – but the one thing I was being told time and time again was that, really, anything went off where this stuff was involved, and quite often it was the last thing you expected on the list.

I didn't want to scan and email the note I had written to Heather Cross. I wanted to show it to her, for her to feel the power of the ink, and to see it blue, not black. Don't ask me why. More importantly, I didn't want to have to wait for a reply: it was time for action. So I took the train over to Huddersfield the next morning.

This time the whole energy was different. The sky was open and blue and full of great meringue clouds that resembled enormous armchairs for the gods to sit in. It didn't take much for me to imagine myself clambering up into those clouds and joining the gods, from where I could stare down at all the people and cars going about their business, ant-like. There was something very comforting about this view: a sort of there's-more-to-life-than-just-what's-going-on-in-mine type of feeling, a knowledge that if things didn't work out there was loads of stuff out there I could become part of. So I was quite chilled, and I remember thinking that maybe I was being prepared for something.

There were changes going on in the Sunsets. I saw that as soon as I turned the corner and started to climb the hill. And the activity was concentrated around number fourteen. I stopped for a moment to take it all in. A removal van was reversed into

Heather Cross's drive, facing uphill. Allan was making his way backwards and forwards to the rear of the van with boxes piled high in a wheelbarrow. There didn't seem to be anyone helping him. Heather Cross was at the front door. She was wearing jeans and a white shirt, not tucked in. She didn't look anything like she had looked on the occasions when we had met before. And she was speaking very loudly to her husband, almost shouting, although he didn't seem to be taking a blind bit of notice.

'Allan, those ones go in last – they're not coming with us, they're going into storage, so leave them to one side,' she was saying, pointing in the same way Diane does when she's determined to have her way.

I hesitated a second longer. All was not well between them, you could tell that from their body language: the way Heather Cross was talking to her husband, and the way he paid no attention, just kept pushing his wheelbarrow with a stony expression. But if I looked hard enough the light around them seem to pulsate. A bit like when you see an atom bomb going off on telly and everything bleaches white for a moment and then it's black. For a moment I actually connected with their space – and it wasn't good.

I waited until Allan had gone into the bungalow before I stepped forward.

You could have knocked Heather Cross down with a feather. 'Georgia, what are you doing here?'

'I should have rung first,' I said.

'Well, yes . . . As you can see, we're finally moving. Is everything okay, love?'

'It's fine,' I stammered.

'So why have you come to see me?'

Just then Allan came out of the front door. He stopped, looked from his wife to me (without even a nod of acknowledgement), before placing the box he was carrying in the bottom of the wheelbarrow. There was a darkness about his eyes; he looked like he had been in a fight.

'Allan, let's have a break,' Heather Cross said to him. 'I have a visitor, Georgia here, who has, as you can see, just dropped in to see me.'

She led me into the bungalow. It was pretty much empty – of furniture, pictures, curtains and ornaments. Even the carpet was up. Whoever had painted the skirting-boards hadn't been fussed if the paint got on the floor, where you could see each of the brush strokes over the pebbly concrete. We stopped in the middle of the sitting-room, the emptiness of our footsteps still ringing between the walls, trying to get out.

'I should have rung first,' I muttered a second time, handing over the letter I had been holding in my jacket pocket.

'You may not have got through,' Heather Cross answered. 'We disconnected the phone last Friday.' She shook open the page. 'You were lucky to get us at all: we'd have been gone by teatime. But I'm pleased to see you again, Georgia. Now, what's this?' she asked, beginning to read.

'I wrote to the address in London,' I explained. 'And this is the answer I got.'

Heather Cross read the letter like you see politicians reading stuff on *News at Ten*, with their index finger going along the lines and down.

'When did you get this?' she asked, fixing me with that look.

'Just yesterday.'

'*Yesterday?*' she repeated, then said nothing; and in the silent seconds that followed I watched her expression begin to dissolve. The look she had now, she could have been behind a net curtain. 'How strange,' she murmured at last. 'How very strange.'

'What's strange?'

'The night before last I dreamt exactly this. Well, not exactly this, but you came to me with a letter.'

This completely wrong-footed me.

Heather Cross laughed and touched my arm. 'Don't look so worried. I'm always dreaming about my work. If anything, it's a good sign.'

This wasn't the time or the place to be discussing dreams. I pointed at the letter she was still holding. 'What does it mean?'

'Not so fast. Let me read it again.'

'Does it mean my mother has been living at Pond House all this time? Under a different name?'

She frowned. 'I can't think of any other possibility,' she said eventually. 'Can you?'

I didn't like the way she had asked my opinion. Surely this was her 'field of expertise'. 'So what do I do?' I asked her straight up, looking from the packing boxes all around us (in one there was the pair of shears with the yellow wooden handles) back to her in an impatient sort of way.

'What do you want to do?' Heather Cross asked me. 'Or what would you like *me* to do?' she added, quieter.

That threw me again. 'Well . . . will you write to her?'

'I could, Georgia; of course I could. But your mother has made it clear she doesn't want contact.'

'I don't want *contact*,' I said, sort of spitting the word out. 'I just want to meet her, that's all.'

'My love, meeting her is contact.'

I took the letter from Heather Cross. I could feel myself becoming what Diane calls the petulant child. 'I'm sorry to have bothered you. I shouldn't have come.'

'Georgia, wait a minute.'

I had filled up.

'Georgia, let me keep the letter. I shall write to Pond House. I'll say that we know about the no-contact request and explain that notwithstanding this you, Georgia, are eager for some form of contact. We could ask her to reconsider her position. We could ask if she might entertain the idea of letterbox contact, however limited. Perhaps she has some photographs that she would be prepared to let you have. Maybe just send you one letter. What do you think?'

I couldn't speak: it was as if someone had me by the throat.

'And just as soon as I've had a reply – because I think we will get a reply – I'll email you. Okay?'

'Okay.'

'I would have told you about our move before now but as it's turned out things have happened that much quicker than we thought. We're moving to Spain in July.'

'To *Spain*.'

'But not until July, Georgia. Until then we're going to live with Allan's sister in Goole. Only an hour and a half from here. But, Georgia, I want you to know this: I will be contactable twenty-four hours through adoptionsearch.com. If ever you need to speak to me you have only to email me there.'

'Okay,' I whispered.

I let Heather Cross pull the sheet of A4 from my fingers, with the now very smudged biro words: WHO WANTS TO KNOW?

'I'll be in touch just as soon as I've had an answer to this,' she said, fixing me once again with her stare.

*

That night I dreamt I was in Filey with Grandma Myers. Dreams are so weird, the details. We had just had an enormous fish-and-chip dinner and were climbing the stairs to the flat when Grandma

Myers turned around. She was breathing very heavily and her lips were blue. 'Georgia, I think I'm going to die,' she whispered, and her words were sharp, like glasses chinking against one another.

'But you *are* dead, Grandma.'

'You know you shouldn't call me that.'

'I don't. Why not?'

'Because I'm not your grandma.'

I play-acted affronted. 'That's not a very nice thing to say, is it?'

'Orlando can call me "Grandma", but not you.' And there was something very childish about the way these words were pronounced. 'Anyway, as I said, I think I'm going to die.'

'But you *are* dead.'

'Okay. I'll die again, then.'

'Grandma, don't . . .'

Grandma Myers began to sob. 'I just want to die,' she kept saying over and over again. 'Is that too much to ask?'

I woke up with a start. For an instant I thought I *was* in Filey, in the spare room with the bed that creaked every time you turned over in it. I stared into the darkness, trying to make out where the chest of drawers should have been, and the slice of light, as thin as a Rizla, under the door that was the light in the hall if Grandma had remembered to leave it on. And I still couldn't get my bearings. I knew I was in my room at home, but the distance between the walls felt different, as if they had been stretched, like you can stretch shapes on a computer. In the corner furthest from the window the half-light was fizzing. I remember thinking that if Drew had been there he would have said it was a spirit, so I spoke.

'Who's there?'

'It's only me, Georgia . . . again.'

'Grandma Myers!'

'I didn't mean to frighten you.'

'You didn't . . . but you weren't being very nice a minute ago.'

'Everyone has moments they live to regret. I'm afraid life's like that.'

'Grandma Myers, what's all this about?'

'I don't follow you.'

'Are you haunting me?'

'No, looking over you.'

'Looking over me?'

'Yes, making sure you're okay. And I can tell you it's a pretty full-time job.'

That seemed a reasonable response, so I said, 'Okay, then: what have you got to tell me?'

And Grandma Myers came straight out with it, as bold as brass. 'I've been talking to your father . . . and he's a little concerned.'

I don't think I've ever been as frightened as I was at that minute. It was as if someone had thrown a bucket of ice-cold water over me. It was all very well talking to Grandma Myers in the sort of make-believe, casual manner we had adopted over time, which was no more than me talking to myself, really. But my father: that was 'quite a different matter'. Straight away I had sat up in bed, the wall behind me cold on my shoulders.

I could only repeat Grandma Myers's words, exchanging 'I've' for 'you've' and 'your' for 'my'. 'You've been speaking to my father?'

'Yes,' Grandma Myers replied, in that matter-of-fact way she has, 'and he says that you're better off not knowing about any of them.'

'He *is* dead, then?'

'Alas, yes.'

'How did he die?'

'Georgia!'

'That's not too much to ask, is it?'

'No, I don't suppose it is. He died of a disease.'

'A disease?'

'That's all I'm allowed to tell you about that. But what I can tell you, in fact what he has asked that I tell you, is that ultimately no great benefit will come out of discovering anything about Lizzie and how you came to be . . . you know.'

'Lizzie? Is that her name?'

'Yes, Georgia. It is.'

As soon as I sat up Grandma Myers was gone. I listened very carefully for her, but all I could hear was the faintest sound of Roger snoring. And now I could see the shape of my bedroom, which was once more the correct proportion.

FIFTEEN

A week later it was Uncle Rob's fiftieth. Insisting that I come for lunch at the castle was a set-up, though. I should have smelt a rat in the car.

'And Orlando's got a new girlfriend,' Diane said, as we rumbled over the cattle grid into what Aunt Yvette now called the deer park.

'A new girlfriend?' I repeated, half asleep but half alert at the same time.

'She's a bit older than you, but by all accounts she's very nice. She's called Charlotte.'

'Oh, really?'

'Yes, really.'

We pulled up in the courtyard, the gravel popping and crunching beneath our tyres.

'Look!' Roger said, half under his breath. 'They've got the flag flying for us.'

And there was that very slight edge of sarcasm you sometimes hear in Roger's voice when it comes to discussing Uncle Rob: a subtle way of making fun of him, which is really a way of saying he isn't bothered that Uncle Rob is fifty and he, Roger, is forty-six, and that was why the castle belonged to Uncle Rob, with its 'deep cellar' and 'overdraft to match'. But today the edge was edgier. It dawned on me then that perhaps Roger knew about Diane and Uncle Rob, and that he was half okay about 'sharing' her in a weird, brotherly, posh sort of way – but at the same time he wasn't really okay about it at all (and why should he be?).

We got out of the car. It was such a wild day the flag was pretty much horizontal and every now and again it would clap and slap in the wind. The wire that's used to hoist it up into the air was also banging against the flagpole, which made a ringing, empty sound. If you closed your eyes you could have been on board a yacht, slamming into waves, the surf flying past you.

Roger said something to Uncle Rob along the lines of 'over the hill'; and Uncle Rob said 'still nifty at fifty'. Then Aunt Yvette introduced me to Charlotte.

'Georgia, this is Charlotte.'

'I've heard so much about you,' Charlotte said.

'You have?'

Charlotte's handshake was firm, like an adult's. 'Only nice things.'

All through lunch I wondered what she could know. Had Orlando told her I'd given him a hand job (which I hadn't) in the shack in the woods where the gamekeeper keeps his pellets for the pheasants? Or had Uncle Rob and Aunt Yvette been discussing me at last night's dinner, explaining that I was a bit of a handful; that I had been sacked from Holland & Barrett for having my hand in the till; that I was into the rave scene (which I most certainly wasn't); that I had been in Faversham House? I didn't get to discover what it was until we found ourselves alone in the hot tub after lunch. I was in the astronaut lounger (as Uncle Rob calls it, because he's obsessed with rockets and the moon landing) and Charlotte was in one of the underwater chairs facing me. The water was furious and hot.

'You and me have got something in common,' she said, just like that.

'We have?'

'Both adopted.'

I found myself trying to sit up, which wasn't easy given the shape of the moulded bed I was lying in. 'You're joking!'

'Not.'

I didn't say anything for a bit. I was indignant that this stranger had had the nerve to think she could be so familiar with me, but at the same time I was anxious to know exactly how much she had been told. Did she know that I had been trying to make contact with my birth mother, but had had the door slammed in my face? Surely not; Roger and Diane wouldn't have gone that far, would they? And then I was just curious full stop. Apart from a gawky kid at school called Peter, who'd never said anything much at the best of times, I had never met anybody else who had been swapped from one set of parents to another after they were born. Because Heather Cross was a foundling, she didn't really count.

My eyes were just above the level of the water. A thousand prisms stood in front of everything I saw: I was looking at Charlotte through a cut-glass chandelier. 'It's weird, isn't it?' I said, dead casual, not knowing, or that fussed, whether my words could be heard over the gurgling of the tub.

But Charlotte had heard exactly what I'd said. 'What's weird?'

'Not growing up with the people who brought you into this world.'

'I used to think it was weird. Now I don't.'

'So what changed?'

'When I found out about them.'

I sat up properly this time, the water boiling about my shoulders, and scrubbed my eyes to get a better picture of the girl who was sitting opposite me.

'You found out about them?'

'Just as soon as I was eighteen.'

So Roger and Diane *had* been talking about me to Uncle Rob and Aunt Yvette. It was obvious now: and they must have all come to the conclusion that this lucky coincidence of stubby-fingered Orlando having a new girlfriend who was also adopted should be 'exploited to the full'. Her shining example, her perfect ponytail, her exactly painted fingernails, would sustain me through the confusion. I was pissed off, but I was intrigued as well.

'So what did you find out?' I asked her.

'I found out that I was perfectly happy where I was.'

'Meaning?'

'My mother has psychiatric problems, Georgia. She's been in and out of institutions all her life. No one knew who my father was – maybe a neighbour.'

'Did you meet her?'

Charlotte looked down into the foaming water. 'I went to see her once but she couldn't really understand who I was.'

I felt sorry for Charlotte now, not the sorry I would have been if I had been at my mother's bedside and she wasn't able to understand who I was, but the sorry you feel when someone else has been hurt. 'That must have been very hard,' I said, and when I heard my words coming back at me it was as if suddenly Charlotte and I had bonded, clicked.

'It *was* hard. But I was determined to meet her. Nothing was going to stop me. Is that how it is for you?'

I didn't answer immediately. I had sunk into the cauldron once more, almost letting the water fill my eyes. 'I suppose it is,' I replied eventually.

'My only advice would be not to let your expectations get too high.' Charlotte nodded.

I nodded back: it seemed like good advice.

'You can't afford to have preconceptions. But getting to meet my mother stopped all the other stuff,' Charlotte finished.

'What other stuff?'

'You know, the fantasies: that I had brothers and sisters; that my parents were rich and famous; that they were only waiting for me to make the first move. You must know what I mean.'

I did know what she meant – of course I did – and I was nodding some more. Perhaps it wasn't such a bad thing I was having this conversation after all, I was thinking: in fact, it was 'just what the doctor ordered'. But as usual me thinking the positive side of something turned out to be tempting Fate – because the bigger part of me didn't want to hear what Charlotte had to say next.

'I even had a fantasy that I was a twin,' she went on, 'and that *I* had been given away but my sister hadn't. That part of me was living a sort of parallel life. My twin used to talk to me. At night. Try to make me feel better by saying that I was well out of it, because where she was there was a lot of arguing, rows, fights, even violence. Incredible, I know! Of course I didn't really believe it, but when you're young you're not so sure what you believe and what you don't.'

I was trying to sink further into my seat to hush the words and blur Charlotte's face, but it wasn't working. If anything, her features appeared sharper than in real life, haloed by the rainbow chandelier, and her words were coming at me clearer.

'And then I had it the other way round: that I had a twin and the story was that we had both been given up for adoption, but in actual fact it was only my sister who had been adopted. I was still with my biological parents. But because my mother and father felt so guilty about my sister being given away they felt they had to pretend that I, too, had been adopted. And I was never going to be able to get them to admit that they were my real parents.'

'Gosh,' I murmured, half hoping that Charlotte had heard the irony in my word: not even I had thought this one up.

'Not a day went by when I wasn't fantasizing that I was going to meet my twin. You know, in a cinema queue or a shopping mall, in a library or a swimming-pool. I mean, we could meet here today – just as we are now, and we could be sisters without knowing it. Couldn't we?'

I didn't answer. The air was suddenly colder, as if a massive cloud had eclipsed the sun; instinctively I began hunting around to see where my towel was.

Then she asked me straight up: 'Are you using a counsellor?'

'A counsellor?'

'An intermediary.'

'Yes, I am, actually.'

Charlotte didn't say anything further. Since she was staring up at the sky, her head tilted right back, the nape of her neck on the mosaic edge of the hot tub, there was plenty of time to take a good look at her. From the boiling-water level, her jaw appeared lantern-shaped, angular, beautiful, a bit like Fudge's when he lifts his head to have his chin scratched. And now her hair was soaked it was much darker than before, a sort of mahogany red. Through the white foam and prisms I watched as gradually her features began to morph, a bit like Drew's had that night in the Wigton a month back. It wasn't anything so dramatic as to be worrying, but I could definitely see what appeared to be different aspects of Charlotte, distant relations, ancestors, people who had lived before. Each of them perfectly calm and still.

'Is it Heather Cross?' she asked me then, just like that, without even moving.

Had I really heard her right? I might have told Roger and Diane about adoptionsearch.com, but certainly I had not mentioned the names of any of the people who worked there.

'What?' I stammered.

'I said, is her name Heather Cross?'

'How did you . . . know that?'

'I just knew.'

To reassure myself I was in the here and now, to prove I was not dreaming, I glanced over to where Uncle Rob, Aunt Yvette, Roger, Diane and Orlando were still sitting at the long table on the patio, eating *al fresco*, as Uncle Rob called it, but really beneath two of those mushroom gas heaters they have outside pubs. Aunt Yvette was telling a joke and you could see everyone was getting ready to laugh.

But when I looked back to Charlotte . . . Fuck! There, sitting right next to her, *was* Heather Cross. As clear as day, *absolutely* no mistaking it. They were seated so close to each other, they looked like they were crammed together on a bus. Heather Cross was wearing a brown one-piece swimsuit. Her hair was up at the back with pins.

'Heather!' I gasped.

'Georgia, I didn't mean to frighten you.'

I was amazed I could even answer. 'You did, actually.'

'I'm sorry for that. And I'm sorry I'm late. I missed the train at Goole: I didn't realize you had to go over the bridge. All the time I was waiting on the wrong platform.'

I wasn't in the least bit interested in Charlotte now. 'Have you heard anything?' I demanded of Heather Cross.

'Heard anything what?'

'From Pond House.'

Heather Cross grimly shook her head. 'Nothing, I'm afraid.'

'Nothing?'

'It's only been a week, Georgia. You must be patient. These things can take time.' She gestured to her right. 'Anyway, you've met Charlotte, I see.'

'Yes, I have,' I answered, hearing my words like they were in a dream.

But when I looked at Charlotte I came right back into the present. Because sitting there, every bit as clear as Heather Cross was sitting there, was the girl I had met at the Wigton, the girl with the crater-scar on her right temple, the leather map necklace of Africa around her neck with its cowrie shell, the strap dark in places where it had got wet. My identical twin, in other words. Her eyes had the same pale zombie-like silvery light shining from them, deep, penetrating but impossible to see into. I hadn't touched any drugs since the Wigton so I knew I wasn't properly hallucinating. Okay, okay, I was saying to myself, this is just a flashback – but it was a flashback of the highest order.

'*Fucking* hell!' I swore.

'That's twenty pence in the swear tin!' Heather Cross and my sister said in unison.

I tried to scrabble out of the hot tub, but my feet kept slipping on the plastic step. In fact my efforts succeeded only in sinking me deeper and deeper into the water. Heather Cross and my sister didn't seem bothered that I was virtually drowning: they were too busy talking among themselves. I ended up with one ear in the water, the other just out of it, listening to their conversation.

'How are you, Heather?'

'Fraught.'

'And Allan?'

'Not so good.'

'I'm sure when you get to Spain things will work out better.'

'I pray to God so,' Heather Cross pronounced, with force. 'Because as things stand something's got to give.'

'Hmmm.'

'Secrets: they fester and inflame.'

'That's right, they do.'

'Not that Allan has a secret. Just guilt.'

'Guilt festers and inflames,' my sister said, repeating Heather Cross's words.

I found I was suddenly cold to my bones. Not cold from the April afternoon, as I was almost completely immersed in the steaming hot tub, but chilled from inside out. And with this wash of coldness came a fear like an electric current, swamping my veins. I could feel it in my temples, in the bottom of my spine, in my soul, a dreadful darkness. And it was obvious where it was coming from: the two ghosts who sat facing me. I was unable to clamber out of the hot tub, but I knew I had to push their darkness away: 'under no circumstances' could I afford to let it take hold.

So I began to blow, hiss through the white water. 'Zooooh, zzoooh . . . zooooh, zzoooh.' Playfully to start with, as a small part of me was still conscious that the spirits might be imaginary and that I might have to explain myself later. In which case I could say I was fooling. But then I had to use more force, as something or someone was telling me I was only going to succeed if I used every last ounce of my strength. And so I totally gave myself up to the job. And it did seem to work. The harder I blew, the more determinedly I pushed away my twin and Heather Cross's energy, the more I could get them to melt in the tangle of prisms. Then, once I found my feet, I began to splash the water away from me like you do in a swimming-pool, with the heel of your hand. The water was going everywhere. I must have looked like a windmill.

There is no way of knowing how long this went on for, but when I stopped and opened my eyes my twin and Heather were gone. And I was alone in the hot tub. Only now everyone had come over from the lunch table and they were standing around and above me, all of them with their mouths hanging open.

Charlotte was standing next to Diane, her shoulders all scrunched up, half pointing at me, like she was telling on me. She was sobbing – although what she had to sob about I don't know.

'Georgia, get out of there now!' Diane growled.

Seeing Charlotte in such a mess started me off.

Diane barked the order this time: 'Do as I say. Come out of there at once.'

Out of the corner of my eye I saw Roger bend to pick up a towel from one of the loungers, which he held up for me, just like he used to do when I was a toddler at bathtime ('Pat a cake, pat a cake, baker's man'). I clambered out at his side of the tub and, because everyone was staring at me in that gormless way, I buried my face in Roger's shoulder. I had hoped he might say something; he didn't, though. A second later and Diane had me by the wrist. 'Get changed, we're going home,' she said, leading me over the patio, my footsteps wet on the stone.

What was weird was how calm I felt behind the locked door of the castle's cloakroom. When doctors talk about episodes, they're not so far off the mark. Episodes can last days, weeks, months, and they can also last just a few minutes. One moment you can be in the eye of the storm, not knowing which way you're pointed, the next everything is so quiet, as silent as a wood with all the trees covered in snow. I could sense Diane waiting for me on the other side of the door, but I took my time. I found myself staring at my reflection in the mirror, smiling, even. Okay, I knew I had made a fool of myself, but I also knew I had won a battle. There *had* been a darkness in the hot tub and I had managed to successfully push it away: I had prevailed.

Just as Diane had said, we got straight into the car.

'I'm ringing Dr Murdo the minute we get in,' she said to Roger – for my benefit too – as we rumbled over the cattle grid a second time.

'Perhaps calm, quiet and rest might be called for,' Roger murmured.

'I'm ringing Dr Murdo just as soon as we get in,' Diane repeated.

I could see Roger looking at me in his mirror, an envelope of the top of his face. Although his mouth wasn't in the frame, his eyes were warm, smiling and wet. I think maybe he had been crying, too.

'We should consider having a break, a weekend away,' he said, in his brave voice.

'I'm phoning Dr Murdo,' Diane said, staccato.

'I think you're right, we *should* call Dr Murdo,' Roger conceded, firmly now, his fists at twelve o'clock on the steering-wheel, which is a habit he has when he gets impatient in traffic. 'But we should also keep an open mind about having a weekend away, maybe a city break.'

'Let's wait and see, shall we?' Diane whispered but, once again loud enough for me to hear, added: 'We may find that Dr Murdo readmits her to Faversham House.'

SIXTEEN

The one thing you don't do to someone who has been in Faversham House is to threaten them with Faversham House. Just as soon as Diane picked up the receiver to make her call to Dr Murdo, I crammed some clothes into a bag and went AWOL, straight round to Drew's.

'Can I stay for a couple of days?' I blurted on the doorstep.

'Only if you don't molest me,' he said, leading the way, barefoot, upstairs.

I didn't want to talk about what had happened at the castle: I'd had enough of post-mortems. It was only the future I was interested in now. Drew knew all about the letter I had written to Pond House, which had been returned: WHO WANTS TO KNOW?

'Why hasn't she written back?' I kept asking him. 'She's had the letter ten days. Do you reckon Heather Cross has written something that's put her off? Why won't she write? She wrote before.'

Drew was looking at me very carefully when he said: 'I think we should go down and take a look for ourselves.'

'To London, you mean?'

'If it had been me, it's the first thing I would have done.'

I hadn't told anyone about my trip to Leicester and the Lumb Lane Equestrian Centre. Not even Drew (Drew is the last person I would have told): it had been both such a big deal and such a non-event, impossible and embarrassing to describe. This time, for good reason, I was scared, properly scared.

Drew could see the fear in my eyes. 'All we do is have a look, nothing more,' he said. 'We won't go knocking on any doors.'

'What good can come of just having a look?'

'You'll get a feel for it by being there.'

'What do you mean a "feel for it"?'

'Trust me, Georgia, you'll see.'

'What if I recognize my mother? In the street?'

'What if she recognizes you?'

'Shit, Drew!'

'Georgia, you need to go. You owe it to yourself.'

So we went. The following night. Got the overnight bus. (Eight pounds return.) It was hollow black, moonless, as black as a coal mine, when we set off. But by the time we reached Luton the sky had begun to lighten and the air to hum, like it does when the backlights come up and gently reveal the stage of a vast auditorium. Okay, we were just going to check out an address, I kept telling myself, nothing more – but I knew I had to be careful here, as there was a distinct possibility that, as had been the case in Leicester, the curtains would go up and there I would be with no lines, no director, no idea of the other players on the stage, just me ad-libbing. I snuggled up to Drew, and he put his arm around my shoulder. There was nothing sexual between us, I just needed him – badly.

We came off the M1 and headed into central London, through miles and miles of that type of semi you see up in Yorkshire: two storeys, bay windows, garage, hedge. I had only smoked a bit of weed at Drew's, yet still I was seeing things. Some of it you could suggest to yourself: the lines of buildings, for instance, which you could imagine resembled those regiments of old clay soldiers they discovered buried in China, line upon line of silent men bearing arms, with a stony determination in their bulbous, blind eyes. And some of it which came from outside of you: superimposed over the low buildings the silhouette of a face, the back of someone's head, flashes of random images, as if a series of movie stills was being held up for you to study before being snatched away. On my own I might have been scared, but with Drew I felt safe, almost relishing the task of trying to suss out the significance of these brief pictures; until, without warning, they'd be gone, scattered like you see fish flash away from you when your shadow slides over a pool.

It was only ten to seven by the time we reached the bus station at Victoria, but the capital had come alive big-time, with the streets full of traffic, drivers honking their horns, people walking with that straight-ahead look they have when all they know is that they've got to reach a place and they'll think about other stuff once they're there. We headed towards the Underground, where we were literally swallowed up by the earth.

I was amazed at Drew's knowledge of the tube. We went down one escalator, turned left, down another, kept right, stopped for *one second* in front of a map, which looked like strings of coloured toothpaste, and then we were on the right platform, heading north towards Belsize Park. If it had been me I would still have been at street level, hassling someone in a uniform, squinting at the map.

'You've been here before, haven't you, Drew?'

'Never in my life.'

'How come you know this is the right platform?'

'Because, Georgia,' he winked, 'I'm on the vibe.'

Our train exploded out of the tunnel. People spilt out through the sliding doors, and we pushed our way into a carriage. Then we were off, twisting and turning through the blackness, a noise of screaming steel all around us, what Roger would have called a veritable cacophony of sound. You could hear every dub-plate that had ever been recorded in that endless crescendo, the pounding of a thousand bass guitars, the sip-sipping of a million high hats.

But then, after only three stops, the train came to a standstill between stations. And now it was the silence that was deafening. This didn't seem to bother the other travellers, who didn't even glance up from what they were reading, but I didn't like it. Where could I look? Not at Drew, who was sitting bolt upright in what he calls his Buddha pose. Not out of the window to my left, which if I stared hard enough became a bottomless pit teeming with creatures, some so small you could barely see them, others so big it took ages to work out you were staring at just a toenail or a scaly knuckle. And not at the other people in the carriage, who resembled those waxworks they have at Madame Tussaud's, pretending to be real, but lacking the spark of life. I could hear the hiss-hiss of someone's iPod and tried to chain myself to the beat. But this was techno rubbish, thin and watery, and only seemed to make matters worse.

'Don't be nervous, Georgia,' Drew said, taking my hand. 'You've got nothing to lose. Believe me. You'll be cool.' And I did believe him.

*

We didn't break hands until we stopped at the head of Fitzroy Avenue, a wide road literally a mile long, with parked cars lining both sides and massive trees planted in squares of earth where the pavement should have been. My immediate thought was that Elizabeth Dunne had duped us all: Heather Cross, me, even Mr Auty, who had filled in and signed my birth certificate. There was no way this was a place where you would find a block of flats. This was a posh street for posh people.

But again Drew did not hesitate. 'This way.'

And sure enough, just before Fitzroy Avenue reached a parade of shops, at the top of an incline, set back a little from the road, there was a square, red-bricked building, with POND HOUSE 1902 carved in stone above a set of black doors you reached by climbing some steps from the pavement. It wasn't the skyscraper I'd had in my mind's eye: it was no taller than the icing-fronted houses we had just walked past, but it was squatter, wider.

This was it!

'Shit,' I said.

Drew tried to stop me, but I had walked on, leaving him alone to stand in front of the black doors. This was way too much, way too soon: I needed time to observe this place from a distance. So I walked to the top of the rise, where there was a health-food shop called Top Banana, before I even so much as looked back.

When I did I was amazed at how calm I felt. The fact of the matter was that the building meant absolutely nothing to me, nothing at all. If you had asked me whether I had darkened those doors as a babe in arms, I would have bet my life that I hadn't, that this was the first time I had ever clapped eyes on the place. Yet the moment one half of the black doors opened and a man stepped out and took the steps to street level two at a time, I almost turned and ran.

And when I looked back the second time, now I wasn't so positive. It's weird how the longer you think about stuff the more unsure you get. Because, on the face of it, how could I be sure? Perhaps at that very moment in time my mother *was* somewhere inside Pond House, I couldn't help thinking, and that suddenly, without knowing why, she had sat up and was listening – just like Fudge does with his head down on one side – aware that something had changed, and that something was me and my energy existing just a hundred metres away.

I watched Drew turn and walk back to where I was waiting. 'What do you think?' he asked me.

I told him I hadn't got anything off the place – no connection with it at all.

'That's because this is the first time you've been here, Georgia. You never came here and your mother never lived here.'

'Really?'

'Yes, really!'

'So why did she put this address on my birth certificate?'

'Maybe a friend lived here. Or maybe your mother stayed here once. I don't know yet.'

'You're talking rubbish. Someone replied to my letter, didn't they?'

Drew had turned his back on me to stare at Pond House once more. 'I know they did,' he muttered. 'Come on, let's take a proper look.'

'I'm staying here.'

'Give me something of yours, then.'

'Like what?'

'Something out of your pocket.'

The first thing that came to hand was a top-up card for my mobile.

'Not that.'

Then my Lipsyl.

'Good. Okay. You wait here.'

Drew went back to the exact spot where he had been before. He was holding my Lipsyl end to end, away from his body, and moving it from side to side, just like he does when he's using the set of dowsing rods he keeps in his kitchen drawer. To be honest, it was hilarious, and I had to pinch myself not to laugh. But just as I was thinking it wasn't so heavy after all, this coming to London and trying to spy on my biological mother, and even if it was heavy at least I had someone like Drew to put it into perspective, the doors to Pond House swung open a second time and an old lady came out with one of those shopping baskets on wheels. Drew stepped forwards to make a fuss of helping her, then carried on up the steps. Because the doors were on a damper, the type that close in slow motion, he had a foot inside the building before they were even half shut. He gestured for me to join him. I turned my back by way of response.

He was in there, behind those windows, swallowed up by the stone, for what seemed like hours. And now I wasn't smiling. Not at all. In spite of the fact that twenty minutes before I had complained of the sun and taken off my coat, now I was cold, freezing cold. I tried walking about, but going around in circles only made me feel self-conscious: it seemed that everyone who drove past was staring at me, checking what I was doing. I marched back to the top of the rise and stood in front of Top Banana's window, pretending to read the adverts ('Shamanic Homeopath available', 'Reiki Healer, good rates') when really I was staring at the reflection of the doors to Pond House.

Finally Drew re-emerged on the steps. Again he waved at me to join him. And again I declined, just like I had seen Roger decline an auctioneer when the painting he was planning on buying had exceeded his limit. Drew disappeared inside again for a couple of minutes; then he came out with a pile of phone directories, which he used as a doorstop. He started walking towards me – I met him halfway.

'Georgia, I need you in there. You've got to come with me.'

I was shaking my head.

'There's absolutely no one there, not a soul. I promise you. We'll just be two minutes.'

'Drew . . .'

'Trust me – please. Georgia: you need to do this. You owe it to yourself.'

'What happens if we meet someone?'

Drew was leading me by the hand. 'If we meet someone let me do the talking. We won't, though.'

I can see the inside of Pond House now, all brick and stone: bare-brick walls, stone window frames, concrete ceilings with a stone staircase that went round and round and up four floors. Each level seemed to be identical to the ground floor, which had three flats leading off a narrow landing, the doors painted a crimson red. The stairs also went down to what wasn't exactly a basement but was half beneath the ground. Once again Drew was holding my Lipsyl between two fingers, end to end, like it was a battery; with the fingers of his other hand, he was touching my shoulder. I had seen him do this before, what he calls closing the circuit. For a few seconds we both stood staring down into the gloom, before he murmured, 'Not here.'

We climbed the next flight of steps. With no stairwell light, just a small window on each of the half-landings where the staircase turned back on itself, it was just as gloomy upstairs as it was down in Pond House. I paused a second to look on to the street. I could see exactly where I had been waiting next to Top Banana. And then suddenly I began to feel weird. It was as if a bit of me was still standing on the street. If I tried hard enough I fancied I could see myself, not me but the colours of me: the blue of my jacket, a smudge of ginger red, which could have been my hair, the brown of my shoes. I might have been okay on the bus and on the tube but now I was beginning to lose my nerve. Just as I was about to turn and go back down to street level, Drew called to me from the top landing.

'Georgia, here . . .'

I was silent.

By leaning right over the balustrade Drew could just see me. 'I think I've found it,' he whispered, his eyes bright and wide.

'Well done. Let's go.'

'And it's empty.'

That stopped me. 'Empty?'

'There's nothing in there at all. It's bare.'

'Bare?'

'Georgia, I need you here.'

I looked out on to the street once more, perhaps searching for the excuse that would get me out of this place. There was no sign of me outside Top Banana now.

'Georgia, come on!'

I knew deep down I hadn't come all the way to London to bottle out at the last moment, so I took the steps to the top floor two at a time. Drew was waiting for me with an open hand. He led me to the door furthest from the head of the stairs.

'This is it,' he whispered again. 'There.' And turning me around to face him, he pinned my shoulders backwards so that they were actually touching the woodwork of number ten. 'Now, tell me, what do you feel?'

I was breathing too hard to feel anything. All I could hear was blood streaming through my temples.

'Come on, relax,' Drew drawled, and with his forefinger and thumb he did that thing you do to people who have just died when you bring down their eyelids like blinds. I caught my breath, terrified of what I might see once my eyes were shut – Charlotte, Heather Cross, my mother, those shapes, masks and creatures, teeming in the pit. But actually what I saw was nothing. Literally nothing. Just miles and miles of what looked like ice.

'I see nothing, Drew.'

'Nothing?'

'Just a blanket, white like snow.'

'And what do you feel?'

I opened my eyes. I was emphatic: 'Absolutely nothing.'

'Okay. No problem. Now take a look. Go on.'

As soon as I bent down and squinted through the letterbox, beneath the numerals '10' screwed to the crimson panels above, a draught of cold air filled my eyes, making them flood with water. For a moment it was as if I was snorkelling without a mask. Here goes, I'm getting something, I thought, but almost immediately I realized that in the 'cold light of day' I wasn't. Nothing at all.

The flat – or what could be seen of it from the front door anyway – was basically as Drew had described it: empty. There weren't any pictures, carpet, furniture; and where the room at the end of the corridor turned L-shaped and out of view, those walls were bare, too. There weren't any windows on to the street, just a glow of light from panels of frosty glass above each of the passage's crammed-together doorways, all the doors shut fast. The floor was stone and, just like in Heather Cross's bungalow, whoever had glossed the skirting-boards hadn't been fussed where paint went. Forget about getting a connection with the person who had brought me into this world and then in her wisdom decided to give me away, my only random thought was, how come I was visiting all these places where people were moving out of all of a sudden?

'So this is it, huh?'

You could tell Drew was disappointed. 'Don't you get anything?'

No, I told him, nothing. And there was impatience in my voice. Why should I believe him when he said this was the flat – hadn't he told me half an hour since that my mother had never lived in Pond House? That this was the first time I had been here?

'Your mother had a connection with this building, Georgia, that's what I said. She never lived here, but she visited often.' He was running his fingers over the letterbox. 'Can't you feel her? I can. Try again.'

I didn't like the way Drew had referred to my mother as 'her'. All it did was to make me even more positive. 'Believe me, this place means absolutely nothing to me, Drew,' I pronounced.

'Take your time. Have another look.'

Maybe it was me being determined not to make a connection, I half conceded to myself, so I bent down to look a second time. But no: still nothing. The only thing that had escaped my notice before was the heap of newspapers and mail shots just the other side of the door. There was a calendar in the pile, the type that had a page for each month. Again my vision was blurred by the dry, dusty draughts that were pouring through the letterbox, and try as I might I couldn't see which month was face up: the harder I looked the more smudged and out-of-focus my vision became. Eventually I stood up. To find that Drew was gone. He had left me there. I didn't like the silence of Pond House and the silence of number ten, so I turned to follow him down the stairwell.

But on the second floor something stopped me in my tracks, as unmistakably and firmly as if a policeman had placed a hand on my shoulder, barring the way ahead. It wasn't frightening: it was how it was, that sensation you get in a trip of being shown a truth, something that exists but you hadn't clocked before. It was the doorway to number eight. I had seen that doorway before – that much I knew at once – not the woodwork, the door frame, or the doormat but that 'opening', that doorway into 'somewhere else'. I had my hand on the rail, gripping the clammy steel. Forget about nerves and what-if-someone-appeared-on-the-stairs-who-might-be-my-mother, I was concentrating like you concentrate on trying to remember something that may or may not have been in a dream, its connection is so vague and remote. And then I had it – in my grasp. The second time I had taken *aya* in Rochdale I had gone down, down, to a place where there appeared to be recesses, shaped like compartments within a honeycomb, a place full of gloom and sadness. It had been here where I had first seen and spoken to my mother. This was it – the same place. This doorway had the same energy.

'Georgia,' Drew whispered up the staircase.

'One minute,' I whispered back.

'Georgia!' Drew hissed again.

'What?'

'Come here.'

I hesitated a few seconds longer, then tiptoed down to the ground floor. Drew was standing next to a table just inside the doors of Pond House, this, too, covered with mail shots. In one hand he had a letter. As soon as I got close enough I could see to whom it was addressed: Elizabeth Florence Dunne. And on the reverse side the name and address of the sender: Heather Cross, PO Box 148, HU10 2NP.

'Where did you find that?'

'In among this lot.'

SEVENTEEN

Two queues – twelve pounds at the door, ten pounds for advance tickets – were already snaked to the top of Mexborough Avenue. Queues of students mainly, as this was the first Saturday of the summer term. The air was buzzing with eagerness and anticipation, since not only was Ozymandias playing it was also the night of the annual skanking competition. Last year the hall had been filled well beyond capacity.

For more than two hours I had been standing just inside the doors of the Methley, waiting for Sula to show, blindly watching the students dribble through (the one thing you never do is rush a queue), exchange their money for an inky stamp of the lion's head on the back of the hand, 'proof of payment'. . . all the time knowing it was useless. I was willing myself to see her, shutting my eyes, then opening them again. For some reason I kept imagining her in khaki or the fatigues she sometimes wears. Her hair was less clear: it could have been piled up through a scarf or pleated into locks. She may even have had it straightened. It didn't matter, just so long as she showed. But it wasn't going to be. I knew that from earlier.

*

All the way back from London on the bus I had been singing, 'As soon as I see Sula, everything will be okay, okay,' as if it was a dub. She wouldn't have had any more answers than Drew and I had had about why Heather Cross's letter had been lying unopened among a sheaf of junk mail . . . none apart from her faint smile, the corner of her mouth creased and lifted as if by an invisible thread. But once in her arms, breathing her scent, my lips dry then wet on hers, my stomach hollow and tight at the same time, the questions would just melt away.

It was so cruel. There she was . . . packing.

'Where are you going?' I demanded of her, in that one instant feeling the exhaustion of the whole day on my shoulders, like one of Grandma Myers's counterpanes.

At first Sula wasn't going to answer.

'Come on, Sula . . .'

Nothing.

'Sula, please.'

'I need to get away for a bit . . .'

'Away? Why?'

'Because I need to.'

'Where?'

Now she could tell me: 'I'm going to Jamaica.'

'To *Jamaica*?'

'To Miami first . . . then Kingston.'

I was so shocked I had to look down at the floor to check it was still there. And then I felt as if I'd been dunked in a pond and was doggy-paddling about, scratching at the bank. It shows where I was at. 'What about me?' I blurted.

No answer.

I had my hand over my mouth. 'What about me?'

Sula looked impatient and guilty at the same time. 'What about you, Georgia?'

I was so shocked by this, I couldn't say anything: I was frozen, like a statue.

'Georgie, I didn't mean that,' Sula half cried, immediately taking me in her arms.

'But why?' I managed, pointing at her holdall, the same holdall we shared whenever we stopped over after gigs. 'Why?'

'I want to be a proper musician, around proper people.'

I pulled back to stare into Sula's face. Now that the bruising on her lip had gone, her apricot skin seemed to glow pinker, as if to spite the pain she had weathered. 'What do you mean?'

'My father's cousin has a recording studio in the hills outside Kingston,' she explained, in a whisper. 'I want to learn how to be an engineer, learn about production, be around real musicians. I need to do it, Georgia.'

'It's what's happened, isn't it?' I interrupted her, trying to touch her bottom lip with the point of my finger.

She gently pushed it back. 'Yes and no,' she answered. 'To be honest, I've been feeling this way for some time. I just don't enjoy the scene any more. It's not for real.'

'You know that's not true.'

'It is – everyone's so wasted. I don't want to perform for those kids for ever. It's been fun, Georgie, but I need to move on. I want to be around real people, people with soul,' she repeated.

I couldn't look into Sula's eyes any longer. Instead I was staring at the sculpture on a low shelf beside the fireplace, a tall African woman in ebony with both arms up balancing an urn on top of her head. She had big lips, a blind expression and long, bony toes. I had never liked this figurine: it had always seemed to be the antithesis of Sula's beauty and elegance.

The pain was coming at me now in waves. 'But you said you'd be there for me.'

It looked for a moment as if Sula was going to cry, too. 'You'll be fine, you'll see.'

'I won't . . . I won't . . .'

'You *will*, Georgia. And perhaps one day you'll be able to come and visit me . . .'

'Visit you?'

'In Jamaica.'

'But what about the band? What about Barrett and Ben?' I spluttered.

No answer.

'You haven't told them, have you?'

'Georgia, I don't owe anybody anything.'

That was what she said!

*

Ten o'clock and she still hadn't shown. By now I think Barrett knew something was up. But not Ben. He was starting to panic. 'Where is she?' he kept asking.

'She'll come when she's ready,' Barrett answered, in his Barrett-like way.

For another hour we waited there, watching the punters stream through the foyer, push into the hall proper. Each time the doors opened the bass came up strong, unrestrained, that all-enveloping *phat* sound, like a dragon roaring from the entrance of its den. Waves of impatience and anger were beginning to bubble up inside me. Okay, Sula didn't owe anybody anything, but was this the way you treated people, your friends, your fans, the people who loved you? She could at least have been up front about what she was doing. But this was hardly fair: I had not been home myself for three days; my mobile was full of missed calls and messages from Roger and Diane.

Britta had finished setting up the nitrous stall, laying out the balloons, hanging her sign that read, '£1 ONLY' around the neck of the gas cylinder. 'What are you doing tonight?' she asked me.

I knew she was talking about drugs. 'I'm doing nothing.'

'That's unlike you.'

'I'm through with that stuff.'

And I was. Dr Murdo was right. Roger and Diane were right. Even Barrett with his 'smoke a bit of weed every now and again' was right. Drugs distorted your view of stuff. All they did was make things more complicated. Besides, something was telling me I had to hold myself together.

*

By one the Methley was completely packed, heaving. The MC had made his announcement some time ago. 'Brethren gathered, there is some things in life beyond our control, believe me. Nevertheless we must apologize: we're sorry, people, there is going to be no live music this night. The skanking competition will still be held though . . . and trust me when I tell you we're gonna be KICKING it up tonight. Most high Jah, Rastafari!'

In the Drum 'N' Bass room all you could see was a seething mass of rolling heads, just like when water breaks into a boil. Condensation was drip-drip-dripping off the ceilings. Thinking back on it now, it was obvious that something was going to go off: just too many people had been crammed in. I had carved out a place for myself in the main hall next to the barriers they place around the amp rack, my back to the wall, but even this was tight. And to make everything more intense, the selector was dropping some serious dub-plates. Forget about pills, you could go anywhere with those plunging bass lines, so low they made your teeth rattle. In fact, everyone had that smile you have when your top lip is quivering, as if you've heard something really profound and beautiful and are on the verge of tears.

Someone tapped my elbow. At first softly, then more firmly. I turned, half knowing it was Drew before I saw him. He was totally wasted, just like I had seen him so many times before, his eyes burning silver, looking far beyond mine, his face bathed in glistening, oily sweat.

'Georgia,' he mouthed, then cupped both hands to my ear and shouted, 'I've got to talk to you.'

I didn't want to speak to Drew, but he was so excitable, insistent, urgent. As he dragged me out of the hall, I saw my precious space taken, filled like you see treacle fill a baking tray. We stood at what was the end of the queue to the toilets.

'Georgia, Georgia,' he kept repeating.

'What?'

'He's in there.'

'Who's in there?'

'Don Frederico.'

'Who the fuck's Don Frederico?'

'Don Frederico, the *curandero*.'

'Give us a break, will you?' I hissed, trying to unclasp Drew's fingers from my arm.

'Don Frederico, the shaman from Iquitos. He's over by the bar, smoking a *mapacho*.'

'What's a *mapacho*?'

'A sacred cigar.'

This was funny. 'Hasn't he heard about the smoking ban?'

'Georgia, he says the answer is there for you now.'

'Oh, yes?'

'He's had to travel far, through many realms, but he's sorted it. You will know soon.'

'Okay, fine!'

'But he says you must prepare yourself, Georgia. If you don't feel ready then you must delay.'

I managed to shake off Drew's hold. 'Tell him thanks a lot.'

By the time I got back into the main hall, selection for the skanking competition was just finishing. Still people were raising their hands, but Chessy was waving, enough was enough: he had finished dividing the contestants up into eight groups of three. The MC didn't need to explain the procedure, but he did. Each group must report on stage 'without delay' when called up; the selector would start the dub; and the contestants then had exactly two minutes to do their skank. Applause of the crowd would decide who was the best dancer, with this winner going through to the next round, until ultimately there was a champion.

'Let's do it,' the MC drawled. 'Let battle commence.'

And that Aggrovators dub, a sort of dub anthem, fizzed the floor like it was mattress of leaves.

> *King Solomon was a black man*
> *King David was a black man . . .*

I had been looking forward to this competition as much as everyone else and I pushed forward into the crowd. The first three contestants consisted of Froggie, the plumber friend of

Ben's; a girl in a beige, hooded top; and a student with wiry hair. The student was useless, completely out of his depth, and to make matters worse he had this stupid grin on his face, like he was sharing an exclusive joke with the mates who had dared him to enter the competition. The girl was better: she stalked about the stage, hood up, like she was a character out of a Grimm's fairy story, her shoulders going lower and lower as if she was going down some basement steps, sinking into the ground.

King Moses he was a black man
From Africa, yaaay . . .

Froggie was by far and away the best. Tall, thin, bony, angular, his locks trembling in a woollen hat of red, gold and green, he had the natty dread poise of a proper skanker.

The dub stopped as abruptly as it had begun.

'And now the time of reckoning,' the MC announced, half patois, half Yorkshire. 'If you want to vote for number one . . . MAKE SOME NOISE! If you want to vote for number two . . . MAKE SOME NOISE. And if want to vote for number three . . .'

Froggie, in other words.

'MAKE SOME NOISE. . .'

Applause and sea-lion barks rose to the dripping ceiling and filled every corner of the hall.

'But wait a minute. . .' the MC was trying to sound confused '. . . which one's number one?'

As the contestants got their applause a second time, I began to look around the dance-floor. So far that night I had been cool, but now I was beginning to get that anxious, raft-without-an-oar feeling. Don Frederico wasn't in *my* Methley, I kept telling myself, he was in Drew's, but that didn't seem to stop me searching through the crowds to make 100 per cent sure. Many times Drew had shown me photographs of the Amazonian shamans, with their weird headdresses and necklaces of stones and parrot feathers, at their feet the plastic bottles of *ayahuasca*, between their fingers the magic tobacco, the tobacco that summoned and placated the spirits of the jungle. I couldn't help it: part of me was daring myself to catch sight of one of these travellers from the other side, to taste the iron of fear in my mouth. The other part of me was desperately pushing away, like I was in a canoe using my paddle to prevent a collision with the bank.

'Next three, please. Hurry now! I said, "without delay".'

> *King Solomon was a black man*
> *King David was a black man . . .*

As the contestants started their skank, the crowd pressing forward, I felt my mobile ring in my pocket. I was getting to feel quite bad about Roger and Diane – more Roger, it goes without saying, whose messages were kind and loving, than Diane, whose last text had just been a repeat of her previous ones: *we need 2 spk 2 u call asa u get this.* And so, out of a sense of needling guilt, I unlocked my phone to check which of them had rung. No one had. It turned out I had a message. And the message was from Heather Cross.

For some minutes I just stared at the screen, too shocked, amazed and scared basically to look up. For nearly two weeks I had been waiting for Heather Cross to get back in touch, and now, hours after I had seen her letter lying unopened on a table in a hallway of a block of flats two hundred miles away, she was contacting me. That was bad enough. But the worst of it was how come a text had arrived just half an hour after Drew had said it would?

I needed to open the message alone, in a place where there was more space. And it was only then, as I turned to make my way back towards the foyer, that I realized the area behind me, which had been empty just a few minutes before, was now completely jammed with all the people who had crowded through from the other room. I was only ten metres from the swing doors, yet in terms of actually getting there I was nowhere. So I opened the message anyway. Heather Cross had written: *I have news. Please phone me. Kind regards.*

I definitely needed to be alone now – perhaps I even needed to be at home, I was thinking. But when I tried to move . . . no way, I couldn't, not even half an inch: I was literally locked into position, locked on to a moving, living mass, so solid that when it turned and surged it took you with it, irrespective of which way your feet were pointing. My first concern was for my cash and keys. Then, when I felt the cheek of the girl standing next to me brush against mine, my next was for my safety.

Things started to happen very quickly after that. There was a short guy in front with spectacles crooked over his eyes, yelling, 'Get back, stop fucking pushing me, man . . . you're crushing me.' There was a black girl trying to climb on top of everyone, pushing people's heads down, like you do in a swimming-pool. There was another girl, her shoulders scrunched up to her chin, her mouth round with shock and terror.

As the crowd surged towards the stage, this time my feet lifted from the floor. I tried to focus on the faces of the people who looked unperturbed, but there were fewer of these now: pretty much everyone had that expression in their eyes you see when there's a loud bang in an aeroplane and for a second everyone's convinced they're staring death in the face.

'Stop fucking pushing, man,' the short bloke was screaming, his spectacles now gone.

Then the crowd heaved in one great melded whoosh. For a moment when it stopped there was a deathly silence, and in that silence you could actually hear the crush, the pressure of people all around you. That was when I realized there was no music and the lights had come up. Then the screaming started. I caught sight of Barrett, who was standing out of danger up on the stage. When I saw the alarm in his eyes I knew things were really bad.

'Don't go down, Georgia,' he was shouting, 'don't go down.'

But I did. And then someone else went down on top of me.

It was weirdly calm there, so close to death. Again I could actually hear the pressure, a long, constant hum. I remember thinking a lot of random stuff, meaningless stuff. I wouldn't have said my life flashed in front of my eyes but, crystal clear, my main concern revealed itself. After all I had been through, were the people who had brought me into this world never going to meet their daughter?

*

I came round flat out on the pavement, my arse in a puddle, my head in Barrett's lap.

'Go easy,' he whispered to me, as I tried to sit up.

To my left there were two ambulances, blue lights twisting in the night sky, and down the side of the Methley people slumped against the wall, all of them staring at their knees, as if they were drunk or asleep.

Barrett's grip on my shoulder was firm. With his other hand he was gently stroking the back of my neck.

'What the fuck happened?' I asked him.

'Crush,' was all he answered.

'Crush?'

'Big crush, sister. We have to thank God no one was properly hurt.'

EIGHTEEN

I thought I was early for our appointment, but when I got to Hepstall Park Heather Cross was already waiting in the picnic area between the car park and the tennis courts. This is where the chavs hang out of an evening, smoking spliff. Sometimes you see whole families seated at those tables, with their newspapers of fish and chips spread over the wet-black wood spattered white with bird shit. I didn't want to have this meeting anywhere near those benches.

'Georgia!' Heather Cross half exclaimed, trying to look surprised, and I could see immediately by the type of smile she was wearing that this was going to be bad news or, in any event, news I wasn't prepared for.

'I got here a little before time. Shall we sit here? Or walk on?'

'Prefer to walk on.'

'We'll go that way, shall we?'

It seemed strange that I should be told which way to go – this was my park, wasn't it? We walked in silence for a couple of minutes, out of view of the car-park area. I remember there were a lot of people out, playing frisbee, walking dogs, and that there were literally dozens of magpies about that morning, more than I had ever seen before in one place in all my life (the only creature that Noah did *not* invite on to his Ark, as Roger had once told me). Every now and then Heather Cross turned to look at me, as if she was a doctor, just like the first time we met at Faversham House. I made a point of not speaking first.

'So, Georgia, how are you?' she asked.

'I'm okay.'

'You're sure?' she persisted, staring right into me.

'I look okay, don't I?' And I held her eye, like I was saying to her: 'Go on, tell me what you've found out. I can handle it.'

We had reached the entrance to the woods. Once inside, we could either go left or right. Without thinking about it we both turned right – the against-the-grain way. It was dark in the woods, like we were suddenly backstage.

'So, Georgia, as you know, I have some news. I've had a reply to the letter I sent to Pond House. And I want to tell you about it.'

I almost sounded sarcastic when I said, 'Thank you.'

'And it's not what we were expecting.'

Pause.

'The reply didn't come from your birth mother, Georgia,' Heather Cross said quite quietly, bending a little to try to catch my eye again. 'I had a phone call in response to the letter from someone called Phoebe Evans.' She reached out to touch my forearm, as if to stop me stumbling.

'Phoebe Evans was a friend of your mother's from school days,' she went on. 'Your mother and Phoebe were best, best friends. The flat at Pond House belonged and belongs to Phoebe Evans. Your mother never lived there.'

'And?'

I remember Heather Cross saying: 'Georgia, there don't seem to be many ways of telling you this . . .'

But I don't remember the exact words she used when she told me that both my parents were dead.

'I'm very sorry,' she finished, so softly I couldn't be sure she had spoken.

I said nothing. I felt as if I had been plunged into a trip and it wasn't Heather Cross who had been talking: it had been a tree that had given me this information, the words slipping in and out of the branches. There seemed to be no way of knowing whether I had heard what I was being told, or whether I had heard something else and had got it wrong.

'Your father died more than six years ago . . . overseas.'

And then she told me that 'in point of fact' my mother had died just this last year.

Now I was in the present. We had both stopped on the path.

'Last year? She died last year?'

'That's what Phoebe Evans has told me.'

'Died what from?'

'Georgia, we didn't speak for long. I didn't ask and Phoebe Evans didn't say.'

'Last year, last year,' I kept repeating, over and over, completely lucid now. 'But what about the no-contact request? How come she wrote that if she was dead?'

'The no-contact request was dated August 2008: I checked on this before I came out to see you this morning. She must have died after that.'

I began to feel weird again, like the air was being pushed out from the bottom of my chest, exactly like the sub-bass you can't even hear at a gig that can leave you gasping for breath.

'And what about my father?'

'At the moment all we know is that he died six years ago, overseas.'

'What do you mean, "overseas"?'

'Abroad.'

'Where abroad?'

'In Malaysia.'

I was staring ahead to where the gravel path finished at a gate at the far end of the wood, then became a tarmac one. I remember having a flash of calmness, detachment. This was it. There was no need for more information: I had reached the end of the road.

'Phoebe told me your mother was the most wonderful person she had ever been friends with,' Heather Cross went on, in a sort of automatic way. 'Beautiful, with dark red hair, energetic, intelligent, with a warm, generous heart. When I described you to her – your dark eyebrows and green eyes – she said you sounded exactly like your mother.'

'But how did she die?' I couldn't help asking again.

'Georgia, Phoebe Evans didn't feel she wanted to say on the telephone. She told me that receiving first your letter and then mine had been a great shock and that she needed time to collect her thoughts. She wants to provide details, but she needs time.'

This was Heather Cross again with her weird use of the English language.

'Your mother and Phoebe shared a lot together. They had been a big part of each other's lives. Georgia, she does want to tell you about the past – I know she does – but she needs time to get everything right in her mind first. I think that's perfectly reasonable . . . don't you?'

I shrugged.

'She said that she would very much like to meet you one day . . . but that maybe, at this point in time, rather than to meet face to face, it might be easier if she wrote down the sequence of events as she perceives them. To my mind, that does seem to be quite a sensible way forward. In fact, it's something I have tried to encourage with other clients.' Heather Cross nodded, as if she was now talking to someone else. 'The written word is there – the person writing it can come back to it, revise it. And for the person reading it, it can't be . . . misinterpreted, can it?'

'So when's she going to do this?'

'Just as soon as we tell her that's what we'd like her to do.'

I gave Heather Cross what Roger would call a quizzical look.

'Because at this point, Georgia, we have to be sure that you want to know more.'

'Why wouldn't I?'

'Well, now that we have established, very sadly, that you will never have the opportunity of meeting your birth parents, things are a little different.'

I did not reply.

'I think you will agree?' Heather Cross prompted.

'Are they?'

'Well, yes. Forgive my clumsiness in using this as an example, but last week my lovely chinchilla died, just like that, out of the blue.'

Heather Cross paused long enough for me to say how sorry I was – I didn't, though.

'I was all for having a post-mortem, but Allan wouldn't hear of it. "What good can come of knowing, Heather?" he kept asking me. "What's happened has happened." And he was right, you know.'

I was adamant. 'I need to know.'

Heather Cross took a deep breath. 'We could spend some time working on this. I could come to see you again.'

'I need to know.'

'That is your prerogative, Georgia, and it is my job to support you in that. I only ask that you listen very carefully to your feelings.'

'How do you mean?'

'Be honest with yourself. If your feelings change, honour them. In other words, don't do anything lightly.' Heather Cross frowned before continuing. 'This isn't easy to explain, Georgia, but I know from my own experience and from working with all the people we've helped at adoptionsearch.com that at some point there will come a time when you're going to say to yourself, "Enough is enough." There is knowledge out there,' she waved at the branches in front of us, 'of course there is, but when all's said and done, what good, what real use, is that knowledge? It can inform us but it won't change us, won't have any real, material effect on our lives. All I am trying to say is that deep down there will be a part of you that doesn't want or need to know of your parents' deaths, will be perfectly content not knowing. Just don't be deaf to that voice, is all I'm saying.'

I said nothing.

'And that moment can come when you least expect it. Perhaps it would help if I gave you an example?'

'Feel free.'

'Two years ago I was working with a young man. We found his mother on the Isle of Wight, and through her we were able to track down his father to a village in Hertfordshire. This young man told me afterwards that he had *known* that meeting his biological mother was enough. And yet he felt compelled to go on, thinking he needed to meet his father, too. Against my advice he refused to write first. Instead, he drove to the village, and parked up outside his house. He sat there at the bottom of his father's drive for more than two hours. He told me the lights were on in the house, the windows were open, and there was the sound of jazz coming from inside. But in the end he just drove away. "I just thought I didn't need to know any more," he told me. "There was a whole lot of stuff I was better off not knowing."'

'But I need to,' I said.

*

I went straight round to Drew's. 'Both dead,' I told him.

Drew wouldn't say anything: he just stared at the floor between us.

'Both dead,' I repeated, determined to get a response.

'I know,' he eventually said.

'You *know*?'

No answer.

I had sat down and had my head in my hands. The tears were plip-plip-plipping on to the yellow wood of the laminate floor.

Drew sat beside me. 'How? What happened?' he asked.

So I told Drew about Heather Cross getting a phone call from someone called Phoebe Evans in Pond House, and how Phoebe Evans was my mother's best friend and how she was going to write everything down – if I wanted her to. But that I was paranoid about what Phoebe Evans had told Heather Cross, because now Heather Cross was saying I knew enough. 'And you were right about my mother never living in Pond House,' I finished. 'The flat belongs to this Phoebe Evans woman.'

'I know,' Drew said again.

Even I was surprised by the bitterness in my voice: 'You know a whole lot of stuff, don't you, Drew?'

'You know what it's like. I had a sense, Georgia,' he replied, unfazed.

Again there was cynicism on my tongue: 'So what sense do you have now?'

Drew paused before answering. 'My intuition is that maybe Heather Cross is right. You should think very carefully about what you do next. Both your parents are dead, Georgia. That's it. You can't go any further.'

'Except find out how they died.'

'What's that going to tell you?'

'Maybe it'll tell me why they gave me away.'

Drew shrugged.

'That's what I want to know, isn't it?'

'Maybe. Maybe not.'

'What do you mean?'

Drew didn't answer my question. 'And you would be relying on someone else to tell you what happened. It would be this Phoebe Evans's story – not your mother's or father's,' he said instead. 'It might not be true.'

'So I should just walk away?'

Drew was almost looking through me. 'I think so.' He nodded.

'But up until now you were always telling me to go for it. That the truth was out there and the sooner I "dealt with the energy" the better, that I needed "to embrace it to sort it". Those were your exact words.'

'I know they were.'

'So how come this change?'

Drew glanced away from me. 'Remember what I told you in the Methley?'

I had sat back with a huff. 'About Don Frederico, you mean?'

'Yes, Don Frederico.'

'Who told you he had been over "many realms".'

Now Drew was looking at me square on. 'Okay, forget it.'

The sky was a blanket of white through the Velux window. It could have been a mile away or right there on top of us. I didn't speak again for a long time, so when I did it sounded ridiculous, me asking, in a high-pitched, little-girl's voice, 'Please tell me what Don Frederico said.'

Drew had risen. 'He didn't actually *say* anything.'

'So how come you told me he did?'

'He was holding both my hands: there was a vision flowing into me.'

'A vision of what?'

'It was all to do with a lake.'

'A *lake?*'

You could tell by the way Drew's eyes had softened and distanced that he was back in his trip. It hadn't taken much, so it must have been just below the surface. 'You and I were going to go fishing in this lake,' he began. 'There was a boat we were going to use, tied up to the bank. But the lake was dark . . . so dark. Maybe it was because it was night-time or maybe it was the hills that surrounded it which made the water so black. There were inlets, promontories, and there was an island. We were going to get into the boat and fish behind the island. But then we were both given a picture, like it was a television picture – a flash, you know what it's like – of what we were going to catch, and it was such an ugly fish, with one evil, squashed-up eye on the side of its head, a yellow belly and a hooked jaw. Right then, at that very moment in time, together, we both felt so alone, so in danger . . .'

'In danger of what?'

'A hex. A hit. We didn't need to get into the boat, Georgia. We were safe where we were.'

'And?'

'That's it.'

'That's it?'

'Don Frederico was warning you. Catch the fish, okay – but be careful, you have to deal with its . . .' Drew looked like he was literally going to throw up '. . . its ugliness.'

I hadn't got the time for this. 'I need to know, Drew. We've been here before.'

'I know we have, and I think I may have been wrong to say you could handle it on your own. This is too big, Georgia.'

'So what do I do?'

Drew spoke over me. 'You could come to Peru.'

Two invitations to exotic locations in just two days! 'You're off your head!'

'I'm an apprentice, nothing more, you know that, Georgia . . . but the *curanderos*, they deal with this kind of stuff all the time.'

'How would they help me?'

'You could purge all this darkness in the jungle. The shamans would guide you, heal you.'

The thought of this darkness, a lake of sadness, brought more tears plip-plipping on to the laminate flooring.

Drew sat beside me a second time. 'Sometimes in life we come across stuff which is too large for us to deal with on our own. A splinter you can remove by yourself with a pair of tweezers. Something embedded in your body you need a surgeon.'

I was amazed by my next question, but I suppose it had been bubbling away in the background, unanswered, ever since that morning in London. 'When we were in the Underground, and you knew which train to take and how to get to Fitzroy Avenue, how did you know all that?'

An embarrassed smile flickered over Drew's lips, a smile of apology.

'How did you know?' I pressed him. 'Was it by clairvoyance?'

'Well, no. Actually I checked on-line,' he admitted.

Immediately I stood. 'On Multimap, you mean?'

'Yes.'

'So you weren't on the vibe at all?'

'Not exactly,' he answered. 'But that's different, Georgia.'

'It isn't,' I said, and stormed out of the flat, taking the stairs two at a time until I reached the street, where I pulled shut the door on Drew's house – for the last time, as it turned out.

NINETEEN

The double doors to Pond House were jammed open, one side with a table, the other with an armchair. It looked like yet another person was moving house.

I went straight up the steps, into the hallway, and didn't stop until I reached the first-floor landing. Here was the window I had stood in front of only three days before, when I'd thought I had seen myself, or bits of myself, outside Top Banana. It was amazing how different I felt now: although the blood was hammering through my veins, it was running cold, which made me focused and bold, like I was going to have a fight with someone and wasn't going to stop until I got them by the throat. I wouldn't have felt that way if it had been my mother I was going to meet – 'to make myself acquainted' with Phoebe Evans was a different matter.

But by the time I reached where I was headed – the flat on the penultimate landing, the one I had been *told* belonged to Mother – I had lost pretty much all of my momentum. I stood maybe three feet back from the door, staring at the red paint, trying to connect with it again. As much as I tried visualizing the entrance I had seen in Rochdale, I couldn't get it to stick. It was the same deal as trying to get back into a dream: you thought you could, but it turned out you couldn't. I tiptoed forwards and bent to peer through the letterbox.

This flat, or as much as I could see of it, most certainly was not empty. Everywhere there were books, shelves, boxes, pictures, clothing hanging from the walls. And that was before you saw the aquarium, with its tiny multi-coloured fish hanging, as if in mid-air, the exercise bicycle with a black plastic seat, the dead plant in its pot on top of a pile of magazines. The book lying on the floor just the other side of the door, which looked as if it had been literally chucked there, was a book Diane has at home: *Alan Carr's Easy Way To Stop Smoking.*

I stood back and knocked.

Nothing.

And knocked again.

Not a sound.

I bent to peer through the letterbox again. The only light was in the hood of the aquarium, which made the red and blue of the tiny tropical fish brighter than it should have been. This time I could smell tobacco.

The possibility that Phoebe Evans wouldn't be in had occurred to me. I had been half expecting it: most people go out to work, don't they? But it didn't make it any easier. Now that I had time to kill, what was I going to do? Walk up and down Fitzroy Avenue? Wait there on the landing, my back to the door of number eight until teatime? I felt myself start to boil over with frustration: as usual, I was doing stuff on other people's terms. But also I was getting a growing feeling, a gut feeling, of the pointlessness of it all.

It shows how focused I must have been as it was only then, as I was hunting around in my head, wondering what to do, where to wait, that I became aware of the sound of reggae, a John McLean song Sula likes to sing on her own, just her and a guitar.

If I gave you my heart
What would you do with it?

And guess where it was coming from? The top floor, street-side: the flat, in other words, that Drew had assured me was the one we had come to London to find three days before.

Would you tear it apart?
Or would you look after it?

I found myself being drawn up the remaining flight of stairs, as if by a magnet.

Would you tear it apart?
Or would you treasure it?

The first I saw of Phoebe Evans, as I climbed the last of the stone steps, was her bare ankles and sandals; then the blue of her boiler suit; then her hair, wrapped roughly in a scarf. Framed by the open doorway of number ten, she still hadn't noticed me. I took a look at her as you might a portrait in an art gallery. She was short, round, maybe thirty-five years old, hippie-looking. In her right hand she held a paintbrush, in the other a black roller tray, so far tipped over that the paint could have slopped out of it. She was dancing while she was painting. But as soon as she saw me she stopped. We both stood there, still as statues.

About half a minute passed before she dropped the paintbrush, covered her mouth with her free hand, and whispered: 'Christ!'

Although I hadn't lost all of my boldness, I couldn't get any words out. What could you say, really, under the circumstances?

'Christ!' she hissed again, much louder.

That second a girl came out of the L-shaped room at the far end of the passage. She was barefoot, wore tight blue jeans and a T-shirt of red, gold and green beneath the word 'Strummerville'. She was someone Barratt would have called *simpatico* – someone you knew instinctively you could be friends with – but there was an expression of real alarm in her eyes. She bent to turn off the CD at the wall.

'What is it, Phoe? Who is this?'

By now the paint tray had fallen out of Phoebe Evans's other hand.

'Lizzie!' Phoebe Evans gasped. Then: 'Lizzie . . . Lily!'

'Phoe, who is this?'

'Lily!'

'No, Georgia,' I corrected Phoebe Evans, cool as a cucumber, perhaps on account of it being two against one now.

'It can't be true!'

I had found my tongue. 'I am Georgia Myers, Elizabeth Dunne's daughter,' I said. 'Please don't ask me to go away.'

'Who is this?' the young girl kept repeating, tugging Phoebe Evans by her elbow.

Being tugged seemed to pull Phoebe Evans out of her shock. She came towards me where I was standing in the doorway, looking at me from one eye to the other, her stare like a pendulum. Then she took both of my hands in hers; her fingers were wet with paint.

'My God, Lily,' she whispered again.

'I'm not Lily, I'm Georgia.'

'Of course you are, of course you are. I know you are.'

And she took me in her arms.

I didn't like the smell of Phoebe Evans. In actual fact, she stank: of BO, tobacco and perfume. And she was shorter than me, which made everything more difficult somehow. I found myself staring at the young girl, who was starting to look a bit awkward, a bit like Fudge does when you pay too much attention to another dog. I was getting to be awkward, too: the last thing I had been expecting was hugging.

Eventually Phoebe Evans stepped back, though she still held me by the fingers. 'You know who I am, don't you? I am Phoebe Evans, your mother's best and oldest friend.'

I was nodding.

'And this, Georgia, is my daughter, Scarlett.'

As Phoebe Evans let go of me, Scarlett stepped up to stand beside her mother.

'Scarlett is five months older than you, Georgia,' Phoebe Evans went on, and you could see by the way she was swallowing that she was fighting to get her voice under control. 'You were born in February, Scarlett in the previous September.'

I was taken by surprise. 'You know my birthday?' I stammered.

'Yes, Georgia, I do.'

'How?'

'How? Because your mother was staying here until a few weeks before you were born.'

We were in the sitting room by now, with its view over the street and branches full of leaf. It came to me like a hundred bolts of lightning all at once: I was walking over the very floor my mother had walked over; I was staring out of the window she had stared out of; these walls had heard her voice, her cries, her laughter.

I was definitely getting a connection now. I can't remember how long I stood there, taking everything in, but when I finally looked back to Phoebe Evans, I could see she had composed herself. And, sure enough, there was something brittle and business-like in her voice when she turned and said: 'Scarlett, darling, can you leave us a minute?'

Once we were alone, with the door half pulled to, Phoebe Evans took both of my hands in hers a second time. 'I spoke with someone over the phone the day before yesterday,' she began. 'Someone called Heather Cross. Did you know that?'

I told Phoebe Evans I had seen Heather Cross in Leeds the day before.

'And she informed you . . .?' Phoebe Evans asked, not finishing her sentence.

'She told me both my parents were dead.'

I saw Phoebe Evans flinch as I said the word 'dead', and I lost contact with her eyes for a second. When she looked back to me she still wasn't *looking* at me. 'Who is Heather Cross? I couldn't quite understand. Is she a counsellor?'

And so I explained how Heather Cross was helping me to track down my parents, that I had been searching for them since the day I was eighteen but she hadn't been all that brilliant, actually. It had been me who had first written to Pond House. We hadn't got a reply to the second letter, though. Everything came out muddled, in a bit of a rush, yet my voice sounded good in the room, and I felt a bond was forming between Phoebe Evans and me. But when I stopped talking and waited for a response, maybe another hug, another tear, I could see that she had withdrawn into herself again, like you see a sea anemone tuck its arms into its body when there's danger.

'I didn't reply to the second letter because we were away. We only got back from France the day before yesterday. Did Heather Cross explain to you what I was going to do?'

'Sort of.'

'That I needed time to gather my thoughts, so that I could get everything straight . . . and that I was going to write to you, if that's what you wanted me to do?'

Phoebe was looking carefully into my eyes. I was filling up. When I swallowed the whole room seemed to crackle.

'Oh, darling!' Phoebe Evans sobbed, flicking out of cautious mode, like she had dropped a stitch in her knitting, and taking me in her arms a second time.

My tears were hot and soaking. It sounds corny but I could feel something melting inside me. 'I just want to know what she was like,' I cried.

'She was beautiful, Georgia. What more can I tell you? She was beautiful, warm, innocent, intelligent . . .'

'Then why did she give me away?'

Phoebe Evans would not answer.

'Why didn't she love me?'

'She did love you, Lily.'

I didn't need to correct her and she didn't need to apologize for getting my name wrong again.

'Lily, she did love you!' she repeated, her lips clamped shut and crinkly like a clam's. 'She never stopped thinking about you!'

'Then how come there was a no-contact request?'

A blank look had come over Phoebe Evans's eyes. And so I had to explain about NORCAP, the stinking register of people's wishes and non-wishes. As I did so, I could see the cautious expression stiffen her eyes, only it was more pronounced this time. 'Georgia, my love, I think we're going to have to draw a line in the sand there.'

'Why?'

Phoebe Evans had a hand at her forehead. 'Because everything . . . happened such a long time ago. I have to get it straight in my mind.'

'But what happened? Why did she give me away?'

'Because . . . there was trouble,' Phoebe Evans answered finally.

Believe it or not, the possibility of 'trouble' hadn't occurred to me (although, of course, it must have done). 'Trouble?'

'Yes, Georgia, your parents got into trouble. It was just so . . . terribly . . . sad.'

'What happened?'

But there was no way she was going to tell me. 'It would be very wrong of me to try and explain here and now,' she said.

And the fact she had got my name right this time made me realize I wasn't going to get any further.

'I do want to give you the facts, the proper facts,' she finished, 'but in the right order, not just bits and pieces here and there. Do you understand?'

I did understand actually, and I expect I said as much.

I don't remember how we parted; I can't even remember saying goodbye.

*

Once when I was about nine at the castle, Orlando and I had gone to play in the haystacks and farm buildings at the top of the lane. We had gone into a barn and up some wooden steps into a long, low loft, with window frames empty of glass, and pigeons cooing in the eaves. There was a door at the far end, set in the whitewashed stone. Which I had opened. And nearly fallen out of. In fact, if it hadn't been for Orlando I would have fallen: he had grabbed me by the belt.

Going back up to Yorkshire I was having the same feeling: a feeling of crystal-clear vertigo on my naked shoulders, of being on the brink of something that was going to change everything for ever. When I had opened the loft door, it hadn't been like looking down a mineshaft, when you can't see how far there is to fall – I had seen the ground right there underneath me, with grass growing through the cobbles, puddles staring back at the sky. I had known immediately that if I had fallen I would have broken bones – I might even have died. Of course I didn't know what Phoebe Evans was going to write if I told her to go ahead and write it. I only knew that things would never be the same again.

The whole way back on the train it was as if there were two dub DJs at war inside me: one who wanted to know every last detail of my birth parents' history; the other who knew enough, perhaps too much, already. And as this battle was going on – bass lines endlessly inventing new ways of holding the tempo, high hats sip-sipping, guitar strokes echoing as they reinforced, then broke down the melody – I was also getting a feeling of homesickness like I had never experienced before. In all the confusion of the last five days I had hardly thought of Roger once. And yet it seemed to me now it was he who was holding me by the belt, it was he who was going stop me falling. I had to see him immediately I got off the train – but what if what I didn't yet know had already poisoned our relationship, what if the ground I had been standing on had splintered and was drifting away from the mainland, with Roger, Fudge, everyone I loved receding into the distance?

Thank God Diane's car wasn't in the drive. As soon as my key turned in the lock Roger was there, right in front of me. 'Georgia! Thank heavens!'

We went straight into the sitting room. Fudge came too and lay on the floor in front of us, chin on paws, staring up into my eyes. His ears weren't properly pricked, but you could tell he was listening very closely.

'Georgia, where have you been? What's happened?'

So I told Roger everything. About the letters that had been sent to Pond House; what Heather Cross had advised and how I hadn't taken that advice; what Phoebe Evans had and hadn't told me in London. How it had all messed with my head, but how I was getting myself together. I knew what I was doing now. 'Because I don't want to know any more,' I told Roger. 'They're dead, they're gone. In a way I'm glad they're dead.'

'Georgia!'

'I wish I'd never bothered.' And I started to cry, a deep cry right from the bottom of my guts. 'I'm just so sorry,' I couldn't help moaning.

'Darling, what have you got to be sorry about?'

'Everything – everything I've put you through.'

'You haven't put us through anything.'

'I have.'

'And even if you have, so what? You're home, you're safe, you're here. Please, please don't cry.'

'Roger, do you still love me?'

'What a thing to ask! No one loves you more . . . than I,' he whispered, and for a fraction of a second he looked guilty, because he was going to say or he had meant to say 'Diane and I', but he hadn't.

'Promise me you haven't called Dr Murdo,' I begged.

'We did speak to him on Tuesday . . .'

I tried to stand, but Roger had a hand on my shoulder.

'Darling, Georgia, you never replied to our messages. We were so worried we nearly went to the police.' There was still no tone of reproach in his voice as he said: 'My love, you could have phoned.'

'I just couldn't.'

'Well, I can understand that, too.'

'Swear that you won't make me go back to Faversham House.'

'Faversham House is not on the menu.'

'Really?'

'Really!' He smiled, squeezing my hand so tightly I almost cried out. 'In fact, if you'd like to and you think it'd help, we could go away. I don't know about you but I think it would do us all a power of good.'

I must have looked perplexed.

'That hotel in Barcelona Uncle Rob is always talking about – you know, the one with snow-cured ham for breakfast. I'm on if you are. Would you like me to see whether there are any rooms?'

TWENTY

I'm standing in front of Drew's lake. I know it's the same one: no one need tell me. All around there is a high ridge of hills, not rolling into one another but flat at the top, as flat as a tabletop. Which means that everything below is dark: the air, the water, the trees. You can even smell the darkness. Drew hadn't told me there was a boathouse, but there is. It has a wind vane and a tiled roof. The windows are painted the kind of green they use at Wimbledon. It looks well maintained, it could almost be occupied, but this place has a dark energy too, really dark.

The door opens and Grandma Myers steps out. In her left hand she is dragging a dead fish, as long as an eel. It's the ugliest, dirtiest, most revolting thing I have ever seen in my life, bone-thin with a massive head, a yellow-green underbelly and the one saucer eye Drew has described to me. Even though I am twenty yards away, I can smell its stench. It's more its stench than its ugliness that stops me looking away.

Grandma Myers has closed the distance between us. She stops and throws the fish at my feet. 'There you are,' she says. 'Go on, then, take it.'

I bend, pick it up by the tail and chuck it back at her. Before I can stop myself I have wiped my hand on my jeans below the knee: the stink of rotting fish makes me gag. 'I don't want it,' I say to Grandma Myers.

'You do, you do,' Grandma Myers insists. 'You do want it.' And she chucks it back at me.

When the fish is on the ground before me this time, it has landed on its head, and because the flesh is so rotten, the skin has broken. Inside, it is a putrid grey-white. I am able to pick it up by the tail, and throw it back to Grandma Myers, but it falls apart midway, literally into a million little pieces. All over the ground is this stinking, rotting mess.

Grandma Myers turns, climbs the two steps into the boathouse, closes the door and is gone.

'Grandma Myers, I know you're in there. Come out – do as I say,' I yell (and what's weird is that I sound exactly like Grandma Myers in one of her tempers).

But all I hear is a thumping. Bang, bang, bang. It's the sort of noise you hear when those chefs are making pastry on the telly and talking at the same time.

'Grandma Myers!'

Bang, bang, bang.

*

I open my eyes. Light is seeping around the edges of the curtains; the drone of traffic, too. Bang, bang, bang. The sound of this banging is coming from below.

*

I don't get to see what's making this noise until we're having breakfast in the restaurant area next to Reception. It's a man with a sullen expression, who is whacking the filter part of the espresso machine against a wooden box to loosen the damp, compressed wedge of ground beans.

'You know, that man woke me up,' Roger murmured, his eyes as blurred as if they were behind a net curtain.

'Me, too.'

'Perhaps the banging is part of the coffee experience,' he tried to joke, which was his way of getting over the irritation. 'Sets them off, like Pavlov's dogs.'

But it was something I couldn't get over. The banging, thumping, whacking had worked its way into my brain, as regular and as relentless as a metronome. It was with me in my dreams, with me in the taxi, and with me on the open-air glass escalator that drops you right there at the entrance to the Park Güell, where you look down on Hansel and Gretel houses, their roofs dripping icing, their gingerbread walls studded with mosaics of weird stone. And with the banging, hand in hand, came the stench of rotting fish.

It was so hot my shirt was stuck to my shoulders. The sun was bright in my eyes. Everywhere you looked there was just a glare. Diane and I were standing in front of a stall selling fans of peacock feathers, each of them with a dozen eyes, eyes that seemed to follow you everywhere, concealed in that shimmering green you see on a duck's neck. Roger was still at the bottom of the escalator, choosing postcards. Grandma Myers had really got under my skin. Every time I heard the thumping, I saw her and smelt her.

I suddenly turned on Diane. What I said sounded so casual it was like I was commenting on the weather. 'So when are you going to tell Roger about you and Uncle Rob?'

Diane gawped at me, her mouth hanging open. 'Excuse me?'

'I said: "When are you going to tell Roger about you and Uncle

Rob?"' In a fleeting second I saw Diane glance away, as if she was trying to catch or follow her reply, of the possibility of her reply. I also saw my words escaping. I was committed now. 'Or are you never going to tell him?'

Once she found her tongue her words came out real fast. 'Tell him what exactly?'

'That you're shagging his brother.'

Diane's eyes were round with fury. 'For your information, I'm not *shagging his brother*, as you so elegantly put it.'

'Of course you aren't!'

Even though Roger still hadn't begun his ascent on the escalator, Diane took me roughly by the wrist, and led me to a place under the wall, beneath a tree that had spat globules of resin on to the pavement. 'Here and now, you tell me exactly what you mean.'

'Just that I know what you're up to, that's all.'

Narrow eyes. 'Which is what exactly?'

'I saw you with Uncle Rob.'

'You *saw* me with Uncle Rob?'

'Making out.'

Silence.

'In his car.'

'I don't have to listen to this!'

'I saw you – in his car.'

'Saw what, for Christ's sake?'

Roger was rising up the escalator by now. Standing so straight, motionless, but lifting up into the air he could have been a saint going back to heaven. He made a show of stepping off the last stair and began to make his way towards us. There were three bottles of water dangling from between his fingers, just like I'd seen him squeeze shotgun cartridges between them when he was shooting – at Uncle Rob's, of course.

Diane took me by the wrist again, really roughly this time. With her other hand she made a sign for Roger to stop where he was and wait for us. She was white now. 'Okay, Georgia, tell me exactly what you saw.'

'I saw you in the Tong Road Tennis Club car park in Uncle Rob's Porsche, and you were all over him.'

'Are you *mad*?'

'Last autumn. You were in his car.'

Diane had her head back, shaking it slowly from side to side. 'Watch my lips, young lady,' she hissed. 'I've never been in Uncle Rob's Porsche. Ever.'

I spat my words out: 'You're a fucking liar.'

Diane's nails were digging into my wrist. 'And you're off your stupid little fucking head,' she spat back. 'Look at you! A fucking mess!'

'At least I don't spend my time deceiving people.'

'Deceiving people – deceiving people?'

'You were in his car, and you saw me, Diane. We saw one another. You know perfectly well what I'm talking about.'

'Georgia, I'm very sorry to say this but you need help.'

I was crying now. 'But I *saw* you.'

'You've been seeing a lot of things this last year. Why do you think you were in Faversham House?'

Roger was on his way over to where we were standing. His expression was long and grey. 'What is this?' he asked. 'What's going on?'

By now some other tourists had stopped to look at us. We were a spectacle. Normally this would have stopped Diane – not this time.

'We appear to have a problem,' she told Roger. 'Georgia, per-haps you would like to repeat what you've just said to me.'

255

I couldn't.

'Lost your tongue?'

Roger had raised his hand; he looked like a boxing-match referee. 'Okay, wait a minute . . .'

Then suddenly Diane did one great sob. It shocked all of us, her included. 'I know I'm not perfect . . . I know that, I know that,' she cried, and her breath came in stuttering stops and starts. 'And that it was because of me that we got you, Georgia. But I've tried. Honest to God, I have. I *always* wanted you, Georgia. Roger has been better, better at it than me, but that didn't mean I didn't love you, want the best for you, and you never let me love you.'

That was what she said.

*

It's four o'clock in the afternoon and still there is banging. Not so much, but just when you think it's stopped for good it starts again. I can picture the bloke with the sullen expression. Every time he does a whack his top lip lifts a fraction in boredom and disdain.

I don't know what to think about Diane. I'm going over and over the seconds I walked past the bonnet of that Porsche. But it's over a year ago now and how can I be sure? I can't. But I saw her clock me, I keep reminding myself, and I saw that expression of hardness in her eyes, unmistakably Diane's.

Since meeting Phoebe Evans and learning that both my parents were dead, I was positive I didn't want to know any more about Lizzie Dunne and Ralph Peddar. But now I'm not so sure about that either. I try to push them to one side. I can't, though. It's because they're actually living inside me, two people breathing, thinking, talking. The whole time. And because of this, because they're around me 24/7, of course I need to know everything about them. I'm dreading Phoebe Evans's story. Because even though I'm going to get to learn a whole lot of stuff, I know that even that may not be enough. It's what Roger would call a no-win situation.

There's a knock on my door. It's Roger. He comes over to my bed and sits by my feet. His hand looks for mine, and when I give it to him a smile brightens his eyes. He strokes my wrist, side to side, slowly, deliberately, just like he used to do at bedtime when I was a little girl.

Everything is intense. If I close my eyes, the pit is swarming with what look like black beetles. If I open them I'm being bombarded by tiny meteorites of shining light, which is worse than the beetles.

'Are you okay?' Roger whispers, his words low and rounded.

'Not really.'

'Perhaps coming here wasn't such a good idea after all,' he says, with his brave expression. 'Would you like to go home? I can easily arrange it.'

'I want to go to Jamaica,' I answer.

TWENTY-ONE

The usual stuff is going on in the quadrangle: a bloke of forty-something on a pair of wooden crutches, the old-fashioned type with leather pads for under the arms, smoking a cigarette; two women seated on a bench, one perched forward, the other leaning back and to one side, as if she might not be listening. The hospital is going on all around us, that much is obvious, but at least we're in Dr Murdo's George Street office and not in Faversham House, where all the 'service users' are mad.

'Now then, Georgia,' Dr Murdo says, even though we've been sitting there in silence for more than ten minutes. 'How are you?'

'I'm okay.'

'You sure?'

'I'm sure.'

In the middle of the quadrangle there is a rectangular bed of flowers, and in the middle of that a stone fountain. Even though the windows are only open a fraction I can just hear the sound of breaking water.

'So: shall we open the package?' Dr Murdo pauses before he finishes, with a smile, 'I can't wait to see what's inside.'

I wouldn't have let anyone other than Dr Murdo get away with a remark like that. But the fact is, he's said it. To be honest, it helps.

Phoebe Evans has sent her account in a Jiffy-bag, the flap Sellotaped over and over. I tear at the tape with my nails. When it finally comes off, so does some of the envelope, and a little puff of the filling, dry and dusty, escapes and tries to form a cloud before settling on the floor.

'And the office was cleaned only this morning.' Dr Murdo tuts.

Inside the Jiffy-bag there is another envelope and a single sheet of A4 paper. I take out the single page and read it, at first to myself, then aloud:

My dear Georgia

Meeting you has awakened so many memories, some of them fine, others not so fine.

It is a great responsibility of mine to tell you the story of your parents and how you came to be adopted.

I have come to the conclusion that it is not up to me to decide how much or how little I tell you. This, then, is the extent of what I know to be true.

I can see I've written too much, but I would rather that than write one page only.

With my love
Phoebe Evans

I remove the envelope. Again, Phoebe Evans has used Sellotape to seal the flap. This time it comes off without any problem.

There's about fifteen pages of A4 inside, closely typed. The top page reads: 'For Georgia'. I put this to the back, like you do with a pack of cards, and stare at the first line of the first page: 'I met your mother at Mrs Selkirk's, a crammer off the Gloucester Road, West London. We were both sixteen.'

And try to read it aloud, but find I can't. 'I met your mother . . .' comes out high-pitched and then gets literally stuck in my throat.

'Are you okay?' Dr Murdo asks.

'I can't,' I tell him.

Dr Murdo sits forward; for a moment he looks a little worried. 'Shall I read it?' he offers.

I hand him the pages and turn my chair towards the window, so that I can't watch his eyes as they go backwards and forwards on the page, so that I can't see his lips moving. The guy on crutches hasn't budged: every time he puffs his cigarette the smoke is pulled upwards and then to one side, away and then gone. I find one of Fudge's hairs on my jeans, a coarse one from the back of his neck, and rotate it between my thumb and forefinger.

Dr Murdo has already started to read.

This, then, is what Phoebe Evans has written for me. It's what Roger would call a statement:

> I met your mother at Mrs Selkirk's, a crammer off the Gloucester Road, West London. We were both sixteen. Lizzie had been expelled from a posh boarding-school in Bedfordshire for smoking dope. I had been at what was known then as a progressive comprehensive and needed to get my act together if I was going to pass any exams.
>
> We became friends straight away.

We were both living at home, Lizzie in a house in Redcliffe Gardens, off the King's Road, me with my mum and dad in Paddington.

Lizzie's parents, your grandparents, were conventional, but they were the kind of people around whom there was a sort of static electricity. My parents, professionals from Bristol, keen to get on, seemed dull by comparison. Which they were. Nothing much happened in our house. But in Redcliffe Gardens you felt anything was possible and, what was more, it could happen at any time. It had an unsettled, crackling energy. To be honest, I was more than a little envious of this element of unpredictability.

Mr and Mrs Dunne were both Names in Lloyds, underwriting insurance risks in syndicates where it was possible to lose everything, down to the clothes you were standing in, if things went against you. Which they pretty much did for the Dunnes. The second occasion I met them was on Lizzie's seventeenth birthday, the day her parents learnt of the full extent of the disaster that had been stalking them for months, like a predator. Jack, your uncle, met us in the hallway of Redcliffe Gardens.

'It's a fucking disaster,' he growled.

'I like that: not even a "happy birthday",' was all Lizzie said, as she brushed past her brother and climbed the stairs. 'It's always the same with you, isn't it? Money. Money.'

'That girl just has no concept,' Jack hissed at me. 'Not even *that* much.'

I could tell something serious had happened as soon as we got into the upstairs drawing room. Mrs Dunne was sitting bolt upright on a chair next to the fireplace. Lizzie's father was beside her, like a soldier standing to attention. His face was ashen. They looked like they were in a painting everything was so still around them.

'Difficult times,' was all Mr Dunne said.

We had Lizzie's birthday dinner in Pizza Express in Notting Hill Gate. There was a sombre atmosphere, but also that edge of anticipation, the type of buzz you get when people are making plans, looking into the future, however bleak. And the Dunne edge, I can see now in hindsight.

'The one thing this will not change is your education, Lizzie,' I remember Mr Dunne kept saying. 'Your grandmother has made provision for this and whatever happens over the next months and years, whatever comes to pass, it will have no bearing on your completing university, whenever that may be.'

Lizzie was staring at her plate, arms folded. She might have turned seventeen but she was still a child. That's not to say she wasn't a young woman too, and an extremely beautiful young woman. That much anyone would have told you. There was a faint smile on her lips and a steely light in her eyes. It was obvious to everyone but the Dunnes that she had no intention of going to Oxford or Cambridge or one of the 'better places', as they were known, even in those days. It was the University of Life that she was after. And then Mr Dunne started talking about their own circumstances, his and Mrs Dunne's.

'We'll have to sell Redcliffe Gardens – that goes without saying. But perhaps we'll be able to have a flat in

London *and* a small house in the country. Who knows? We'll have to see. Didn't we always say we wanted somewhere near Amesbury? It may not be Queen Anne, but it will have a roof!'

'David, don't!'

They held hands for a second, and you could tell when Mr Dunne was squeezing his wife's fingers by the smile that flickered on and off their lips. All through the meal Jack had been nodding, his mouth buttoned up.

In fact, it was your uncle who really lost most. For the second time, as it turned out. A young trader straight from school (too impatient to go to university himself, but for different reasons), he had already lost heavily in the recession of the late seventies. A flat in Craven Gardens off the Bayswater Road, massive room after massive room. Gone. A share in a racehorse stabled near Newmarket. Sold. A Porsche Carrera, brown with a black top. Sold for cash. The irony of that recession was that it was man-made. The Lloyds Names, you felt, had had it coming to them. They had put their necks on the block in the way you only do when you feel you want to court danger. I don't know much about these things, though. Nor do I want to. I just believe certain things and not others.

But for Lizzie and me, what effect did it have on our lives? Absolutely none. It couldn't have done less to change anything. We just went on dancing, dancing. The acid-house scene was in its infancy and our heads had been turned, so turned that we couldn't see anything beyond the next party, our next foray into the country where we would watch the sun rise with 'an intimate gathering of like-minded people'.

Okay, we were kids but it *was* a big deal. Maybe not as big a deal as the sixties, but change was in the air. At a punk gig just a few years before you might have seen someone get set upon by a mob, glassed, and you would wonder how that person could get to their feet. The whole movement had such a violent energy buoying it. Now everyone was into love, empathy, sharing stuff with one another. At one of those warehouse parties in 1985 a big guy would push past you; he might look threatening but he would just go, 'Safe!' It was very seductive.

Then there was Ecstasy! Believe it or not, word was that MDMA could change you permanently for the better, make you less cynical, more tolerant and accepting, give you a better pair of eyes through which to view the world. And being in West London, we were in the vanguard of this new scene, riding the crest of the wave. We were the enlightened people!

We were all into drugs, of course we were. But for Lizzie something extra clicked. Your mother and I took our first Ecstasy tablet together at a party in Stockwell. It's difficult to describe what I witnessed, but it was as is if you could see Lizzie shrink a little, like air being released from a balloon, then she seemed to grow again, this time stronger, with more poise, purpose and elegance. And her smile. Her smile told it all. She had arrived. 'I want to feel like this for ever,' I remember her saying to me. 'In my house there's going to be a saucer of E, and everyone can just help themselves whenever they want to.'

To cut a long story short, I passed my A levels at Mrs Selkirk's but Lizzie failed hers. She was every bit as bright as me, brighter, really, but I had the facility of knowing how to answer questions, knowing what was required of me.

'I didn't want to pass them anyway. That's why I failed them,' was how Lizzie tried to explain it to herself. But I think she was disappointed, angry with herself. Mr and Mrs Dunne were disappointed, too. 'Sad and disappointed' – this was one of their catchphrases. There was a lot of pressure.

No longer being academic peers put pressure on our friendship as well. The idea had been for Lizzie and me to take a year off before university, travel for a few months, see a bit of the world. Maybe go west to Machu Picchu, east to the Khyber Pass, picking up work where we could. Now she had to stay on at Mrs Selkirk's (Mr and Mrs Dunne were insistent about this), return to Gloucester Road, with its grey traffic and Princess Di lookalikes in their Laura Ashley frocks and pumps, to study the same old stuff for another whole year.

'I'm not going to fucking do it,' she said.

'So what are you going to do? Marry someone and live in a council flat?' Jack goaded her. 'Is that the best you can do?'

'Fuck off, Jack! I don't want anything you've got.'

Which she didn't. She didn't want the Sloane life, which was in essence the equivalent of what her parents had had in their time. The bread-roll-throwing hoorays that Jack hung out with. The weekend house parties in the country with the green-wellie brigade, going to Goodwood or Ascot or Henley. Those long August holidays in the Highlands, watching your fiancé hook a salmon (again like that Princess Di photo of her, demure on the banks of the Dee). I've already told you Lizzie's mother's family had once been very wealthy and owned great tracts of land. She was no stranger to that side of life. But she knew it wasn't for her. She was a freer spirit. And I think she was right to feel that way, I might add for the record. The landed gentry enjoyed a renaissance in the eighties but, by God, they were dull! So what did Lizzie and I do? We went to Ibiza.

Now it was my head that was turned. What a place! What an atmosphere! I had my epiphany in a club called Amnesia (I'm not sure it doesn't still exist, the name at least), an outdoor club, just a series of terraces on a gentle incline, a few steps up into alcoves covered by vines and bougainvillaea. The night was powder-black, the stars pinpricks of light through heavy felt. You could smell jasmine, orange blossom and hash, deliciously scented hash. They were playing a Balearic beat, the type of stuff you heard right at the beginning. Everyone was on something. Smiling, smiling. Eyes burning with love, passion, acceptance. The warm night air felt like a second skin, joining you to the universe. You wanted this feeling to go on for ever and ever. And it did. The next night. And the night after that.

There was a black guy dancing in the shallow end of a pool, with shoulder-length locks swinging and swishing in the air. He was smoking an enormous joint, head back, baying at the moon like a wolf, puffing in time to the beat. He was called Pete.

Pete was my first love, the first man I would lie next to, pressed into every contour of his body, trying to work out the scent, so strange, thick and musky – and yet so completely right. Pete was from Nottingham. He had been in Ibiza for eighteen months, selling stuff on the beach, cheap jewellery, tie-dye sarongs and T-shirts, that kind of thing. Lizzie and I fell into the role of helping out. Literally just fell into it. After a week our hands were raw from bleach and dye. We moved in to stay in Pete's house and ate FOC, too. We had arrived! When the season came to a close and you began to see the boarding-houses and bars shuttered for the winter, there seemed nothing extraordinary about Pete's suggestion of moving on. To Goa. 'We'll be there right at the beginning,' was how he put it. 'We'll have the lion's share, the place to ourselves.'

We flew Iberia, reached Bombay on 5 November 1987. Not a difficult date to remember as it was then that Lizzie phoned home to tell her family she wasn't returning to London. She was going to put off her A levels for a year.

'And I could hear the fireworks exploding, Phoebe.'

'What did they say?'

'I only spoke to Jack.'

'What did he say?'

'He told me they were going to forfeit the fees at Mrs Selkirk's and that I was a fucking *loser.*'

Jack didn't have any qualms about making you feel bad. He could make anyone feel shitty if he thought about it long enough. And you could tell his words had got to her. But his approach (and don't forget he was really speaking for Mr and Mrs Dunne as well) only helped close the door. Okay, your mother was tethered by a sense of what was expected of her, loyalty to her family, her class, all that stuff. But she couldn't be corralled in that way. For a day or two I could see she was torn between what she wanted and what she 'knew she should do'. Then she seemed to let go of it – utterly. We were in Colaba, at the Gateway to the East.

'I don't think I've ever felt so free, Phoebe,' she said. 'I feel like I've shed a skin, a skin that had to be shed. I'm a new person.'

We travelled south by train through Karnataka, stopping in Bijapur (where there is a whispering gallery in an enormous hemispherical dome and Lizzie said, 'I love you,' and it came out as 'morning dew'), and in Hampi, the surreal landscape of golden boulders.

When we reached Goa we stopped in Panjim for a week or two, then stayed in the flea-market town of Anjuna. There were plenty of opportunities for Pete there, but our idea was to get as far away as we could from the conveyor-belt of backpackers (people just like ourselves, I can see now). A couple from South London who were wearing the DayGlo colours and the baseball caps, badges of the dance scene then, told us of a village in the very southernmost region of the province, only just accessible by road. We jumped on the first transport, travelling down in a lorry used for moving gravel and road-building materials.

Ralph – your father – and Pete hit it off immediately. You might have thought that because Pete had that acquisitive sparkle in his eye, Ralph would have seen him as a threat, a potential usurper in this, his very own fiefdom. And for that reason alone they might have fought like two bulls. But no. The opposite. From the start they made room for one another. And in time became virtual partners.

At the far end of the beach, which was sickle-shaped and gold, with the sea a foaming azure, Ralph had the beginnings of a little settlement, maybe four houses in the Goan style, built on stilts, facing the ocean, with walls of woven reeds.

Pete, Lizzie and I had climbed out of our transport, and were sharing a plate of food at a stall at a crossroads in the middle of the village when Ralph came by. It was almost as if he had been expecting us. 'If you need somewhere to stay,' he waved, 'follow me.'

As we walked down the beach I knew we were walking somewhere. So did Lizzie.

'Oh, God, Phoebe,' was all she could say as we reached the settlement, her eyes like two pieces of blotting paper. Ralph and she spent that very first night together.

There were few visitors to Palolem in 1987. For this reason there was only one proper boarding-house and three places to eat. Apart from Ralph's. Life is simple there. You watch the sun rise, a wash of pink and mauve and great brushstrokes of red, and give thanks for another day in paradise. Then you watch as it sinks into the meniscus of the horizon, where the silver ocean refracts the light and the hanging clouds glow every colour of the spectrum. I'm sure it doesn't seem that way to the Goans, who go to sea each and every inky night to provide for their families. Or who ride out into the country on their laden bicycles to till the land they have tamed on a temporary basis from the jungle. But at least there is no struggle for sustenance. For these reasons, the climate, the simplicity, the cheapness, hippies had long since wintered in Goa. But it was the dance scene that really brought it alive. If it hadn't been Ralph, any number of other people would have stepped in to take advantage of the times and of the place.

When we arrived that November, Ralph was in the process of building four new huts. By the following March he had a total of eight, each sleeping two to four people. Right in front of the sea there was a communal area where the guests could hang out, an open-sided space with a roof of leaves. At any time of the day or night you could order food there: fish, shellfish, rice, any vegetable you could think of, and fruit, great mountains of fruit. Ralph's had come of age. To say it hadn't taken long to establish itself would be an understatement. Everything, including dreams and aspirations, grows quickly in the tropics, as if nurtured by the sun. But of course it's down to labour. Even then it seemed Ralph had an army of people under his control. And there lay the seed of his undoing.

To be absolutely honest with you, I didn't like your father, I'm afraid. With me it's the intuition I get from someone in that split second of meeting them, that moment your eyes lock. On paper he was fine. A Sydney boy, master builder, he had been travelling through South East Asia, slowly, slowly, taking life one day at a time. He was good-looking in a big-boned sort of way,

271

and you could see that there was – as you can see the kid in people sometimes when they're not looking – kindness in his expression. But you could also see by the way he spoke to the Goans in his offhand, brittle fashion that he was ruthlessly ambitious, unforgiving, very determined. He had long, matted dreadlocks, and quite a swarthy appearance. Not my type at all. But there is no accounting for other people's taste. Least of all your friends', I have learnt. And the sex was good. That was obvious. You don't get a lot of privacy in those huts. Even though Ralph and I kept our distance, and I felt excluded to some extent, I was happy for your mother.

'That man makes things happen, that man's going to protect me,' I remember your mother telling me on Christmas Day as we floated in the sea, so salty you could sit upright just like you do in an armchair. 'I wish Jack could see me now!'

I think the villagers viewed Ralph as I did, with wariness, distrust, even. But he was bringing people to the place and people bring money. That was all that seemed to matter at the beginning.

One day rolled into another. Pete made a new jewellery connection in Dabolim. And a hash connection, too. Word on the circuit was that black dreads had the smoke, white dreads the pills.

I left Palolem in June. I was starting university that October and I knew I needed to re-acclimatize, be on my own for a while, like a diver in a decompression chamber. It wouldn't have been right to return to academic work straight from that coast, that Utopia. Anyway, it was the rainy season and Ralph, Pete and Lizzie had plans to go north to the foothills of the Himalayas – maybe even fly into Kathmandu.

'What do I say if they ask?' I said to Lizzie, the evening of my departure.

It was picture-postcard. A warm breeze was fingering the palms that fringed the beach. The sand, a spider's web of golden rivulets, gave and oozed between our toes as we walked through the shawls of draining surf.

'Not much.'

'If Jack gets in touch what do I say?' I pressed her.

'Tell him to put me on hold for a while.'

'Is that all?'

'Phoebe, I'm not going back to that, probably never.'

Deep down I didn't want to go home either, to leave Lizzie and Pete in this paradise. And there were tears, lots of them. It seemed to me that I was the adult, denying myself pleasure to make room for the future, while Lizzie was indulging herself, feasting on the present with all its riches, like a child. But there was something about Ralph that evening which wasn't quite right. His eyes were blank – not cold, they just had no expression at all. You couldn't see his pupils. And the way he lounged in the manner of the self-assured landlord, arrogantly barking orders, I thought then that he resembled that character out of the book *Heart of Darkness*, the one who loses himself because he has reached a place where there are no points of reference to hold him. Something was not *right*.

It haunted me on and off in England. But I had other things on my mind: Durham, meeting new people, getting to grips with my work, or not, as it turned out. Yet out of the blue I would have dreams, nightmares really, premonitions that something dreadful was going to happen in Palolem, that Lizzie was in some way in danger. It felt quite incongruous that this paradise had left such a dark smudge. But paradises are like that. There must always be darkness where there is light, and the stronger the light, the darker the dark.

The idea hadn't been to go back to Goa so soon. If ever, if I come to think about it again. But to say Lizzie's letters were effusive would be an understatement. She was having the time of her life, there could be no other way of describing it. 'Holy Heaven!' 'Eternal Love!' 'Thick Bliss!' I had asked that she should be honest when it came to Pete. Every night there were parties on the beach, people sitting around a fire of copra, the sound of house music filtering in and out of the ocean's roar. And there were girls, lots of girls. According to Lizzie, though, Pete was being faithful. So the following Easter I returned to Palolem for a fortnight.

And that was when I put two and two together and saw what it was in Ralph's expression that made him so brittle and offhand, gave his voice that tone so devoid of meaning.

Heroin.

There was a craze for chasing the dragon in London in the eighties, and although at that point I had never tried it I was no stranger to the rectangle of aluminium foil burnt brown-black. Once again it was the West London crowd who set the pace. But this time it was purely a demographic thing, nothing more, since the heroin had come to Britain on the back of a wave of Iranian refugees, fleeing the regime that had replaced the Shah. Well-heeled and educated, the immigrants headed for Marble Arch – those with drug problems supporting their habits by selling wraps of beige powder in Kensington Market.

The hut Lizzie shared with Ralph had the same aroma of almonds I knew from the Notting Hill Gate parties, a sort of smooth, butterscotch smell. There had been no effort to conceal the paraphernalia.

'Oh, Lizzie!' I said.

'It's nothing, Phoebe.'

'Why are you doing this?'

'We're not really doing it.'

'What's this, then?' I demanded, holding up a tube of foil, wet at one end with saliva and crystals of brown at the other.

'Ralph smokes a bit.'

'And not you?'

'Every now and again. It's not a problem. You should try it. Then you'd see.'

Which, with a great deal of trepidation, I did later that week. I can't think why now, because I was terrified. Would one taste be enough to leave an indelible mark? Awaken a desire that as yet did not exist, a desire and longing that would anchor itself in my mind and grow like a grotesque parasite? In my case, there was thankfully no basis for this fear. I didn't smoke the heroin, I snorted it. It wasn't acrid to taste, as I'd expected, rather warm, dull and oddly innocuous. But the effects were certainly powerful, and I studied them like a student in a laboratory. At first there was an overpowering sense of nausea. If I didn't lie down in the darkest spot I could find I was going to succumb to this poison, retch until my stomach turned inside-out. Then came the euphoria and anaesthesia. One moment you felt like the top of your head had been lopped off, like it was a boiled egg; the next you languished in a bath of warm milk. There is nothing about any sensation that is wrong when you take that stuff. To pass your finger through a candle flame would be exquisite. And exactly the right thing to do at exactly that moment in time. Then that deep, fathomless energy, a well of as yet undisclosed resources.

Until that afternoon I'd had images of the opium dens of old days, figures sprawled on wooden couches, held in the arms of Morpheus, their heads supported on what appeared to be stone pillows, attended by shadowy figures proffering nuggets of glowing charcoal. But this stuff in Palolem seemed to endow you with endless stamina: you could walk through the rainforest, hacking at the clinging undergrowth with your machete, oblivious to the effort and the sweat that coursed in torrents down your glowing body, you could talk all night (remembering little of it the following day), and yes, you could make love all night, too. Or you could stop what you were doing, roll yourself into a ball like a broad bean in its velvet pod, and just lie there gazing at the sky.

I was confused by the experience. But there was one thing I did know – this wasn't an experiment I was going to be repeating. It took three days for the taste of the drug to leave my mouth. Longer for me to shit and sweat every last remnant out of my system.

Not so for Lizzie. Watching her chasing the dragon, hunched over the flame, the puddle of brown hesitantly tracing up and down the foil like a globule of mercury, you could see that she was forcing herself through the zone of nausea, her stomach rising and falling like a dog's when it's eaten too much grass, her cheeks ballooning as if any second there would be an explosion of vomit. In order to reach the other side.

'This stuff makes me feel like I'm Queen of the World,' she whispered, a day or two later, glancing up and catching me studying her.

I shook my head. I wasn't being judgemental. I just couldn't comprehend the attraction.

'Phoebe, I promise you, as soon as I feel the faintest pull I'll stop it, never do it again,' was how she put it. What a thing to say! Wait until you hear the call of the sirens before you lash yourself to the mast. I don't think so! Drug addicts are deluded.

When I returned the following Christmas your mother had a proper habit. There was such an air of predictability about it. Sadness on my part, naturally. And now she was secretive about her drug use. Dishonest too.

'We've been clean for weeks,' she said, within an hour of my arrival. In response, I suppose, to my scrutiny – warranted scrutiny, since Lizzie had lost a great deal of weight. Although her complexion was clear, there was that treacherous smile on her lips, feather-soft but vacuous, the type of smile that might lead you to the doors of hell if you gave it the chance. There was no disguising the stamp of the drug.

By now Ralph's settlement was much larger. In twelve months he had really put Palolem on the map. There was buzz of euphoria about the place. In spite of their drug use he and Lizzie had a runaway success on their hands. Both were incredibly busy, Lizzie especially so. She was all things to all people: hotelier, fixer, confidante, raver. And, as a result, very, very popular. People flocked around her. But I'm afraid it was a sham: you could tell where the boundless energy was coming from.

We didn't get to spend much time together that January. Your mother was wary of me. I was avoided. Evidently my being there pricked her conscience. And now that she had been effectively poached from me, Palolem ceased to hold any attraction. When I was packing, getting ready to return to university, I knew then that I wouldn't be coming back to Goa. That was it, the dream was over.

Departure fosters frankness, and as we waited for my transport, your mother got to hear herself talk. 'Phoebe, what am I going to *do*?'

'You just stop,' I told her.

'I *wish* it was as simple as that . . .'

'Why isn't it?'

'Because when one person is strong the other is weak,' she replied, gesturing towards the bed, just a mattress on the floor, a tangle of sheets and clothing. The light had gone out of her expression. In fact, she resembled her mother that time I had seen her in Redcliffe Gardens, haunted, deflated, lost, inconsolable almost.

'Last month we went to Panjim and stayed clean for eleven days. Eleven days, for Christ's sake! But it just seemed we were waiting, waiting . . .'

'Waiting for what?'

'Waiting for the next time to score.' She frowned and the tears were bubbling down her cheeks. 'That, or it was waiting for us.'

'Lizzie, come back with me,' I implored her. Because I could see in her expression a real understanding of the dangers that lay ahead.

But the sound of the crashing surf held sway.

'There is nothing for me in London.' Lizzie was shaking her head, just like you do when you're confronted by a *fait accompli*, a locked door. 'I can't go back there. I just can't.'

All this was confirmed by Pete, who returned to England briefly the following summer. Pete and I were no longer lovers but we still corresponded. This was something I encouraged. I liked waking up to a postcard with its stamps burning foreign colours from the floor. We went for a walk on Parliament Hill.

'They're addicts, Phoebe,' was how he put it. 'They don't need to lie and steal out there. But if you brought them to London, they would be street junkies. Nothing better.'

'Does she look bad?'

'Maybe it's because they're smoking it, but she looks fine.'

'And is Ralph good to her?'

'Yes, but it's only the money he's interested in. They're

not in love. When you look at them it's like they're bonded together, stuck together – by brown, though.'

I didn't know what to do. In hindsight I was to think I had made a mistake in calling a meeting with Jack. Because I knew Jack would pass any information to his parents. But it didn't feel right, me doing nothing. I was in possession of the truth, I held its key. Maybe I was just being selfish (am I being selfish now in writing this?), but I didn't want it to fester in me. I wanted to be free of it, share it at least.

Jack was completely straight as far as drugs were concerned. I'll never forget the way he dragged the word out, his eyes wide with astonishment. 'Her-o-in? Heroin? Jesus, Phoebe! Tell me you're joking.'

'There are cures, you know.'

'Tell me who this fucking man is!'

I was summoned to a meeting with your grand-parents in Jack's Battersea flat. They were by now living in the country, in the Avon valley, just as Mr Dunne had said, but in very straitened circumstances, in the gate-house of the estate belonging to Mrs Dunne's frail old mother, the one whose family had once been fabulously wealthy.

Lizzie's mother was weeping, plangent almost. 'What have we done? Where did we go wrong?'

Mr Dunne was matter-of-fact, business-like, aloof. 'She's fallen in with the wrong crowd. That's all. But how to get her back? That's the question. Phoebe, only you can help us.'

It was 1989 by now. And just as only a few years before the craze for silver-paper tea parties had swept

London, now Narcotics Anonymous was on the tip of everyone's tongue. I had been with a friend to a couple of open meetings and had thought that a lot of what I heard made perfect sense.

'Lizzie's going to have to want to change,' I told her parents, using the language of the day. 'It's going to have to come from her.'

'We must have her back – back here at home where we can nurse her,' Mrs Dunne sobbed.

'You won't be able to make her do anything,' I warned them.

'Phoebe, please! Help us . . . please!'

It was an awful meeting, heartrending. Even Jack was moved. He looked like he had been punched in the stomach, winded. Perhaps he felt terrible guilt. Guilt that it had been he who had accelerated his sister's descent into depravity, as he called it, that it had been he who had put her in self-destruct mode, again his expression.

'Do what you can do to help us, please,' he said, as he saw me off at the tube. 'I beg you.'

I said I would write to Lizzie. Which I did. A simple, loving letter. But honest about what I had done, too. That was the whole point. At the end of the day, I had, of course, acted in Lizzie's best interests. I do now know that to be true.

A reply full of invective came boomeranging back. I was a traitor, a two-faced interfering bitch who had been motivated by jealousy and inadequacy. I had completely overstepped the mark and, as far as she was concerned, our friendship was over. She enclosed a photograph, which she asked I forward to her parents.

Whoever had taken it had probably had to swim out to sea, as Ralph and Lizzie were standing knee deep in the foaming surf with the golden beach behind them, Ralph with his arm around Lizzie's shoulders, Lizzie with both arms encircling Ralph's midriff. Ralph's locks were longer than I remembered them and a thick smile played on his lips. Lizzie was smiling, too. The photo had obviously been chosen to show how well they both looked. Which they did, I suppose. Although you could see how much weight Lizzie had lost by the shape of her collarbones.

I wrote back. And did not get a reply. Neither did I expect one.

Nothing for a year. Lizzie just vanished out of my life, my life which was having its own twists and turns. I had dropped out of university after the first year, had started a foundation course at St Martin's School of Art, and had found myself pregnant. All in ten months. Goa could not have been further from my mind.

Once again it was Pete who brought news. He had spent a season in Kovalam, at the very tip of southern India, and had made of point of passing through Palolem on his way back to Bombay. Where he had found Ralph and Lizzie gone. 'It was the weirdest thing, Phoebe. I got on to the beach where the fishing boats are, started to walk towards Ralph's and must have gone about five minutes before I realized it just wasn't there any more. It was like an oasis in reverse.'

There had been a fire. All the buildings at the far end of the beach had been destroyed. Word in Palolem was that it had been started by arsonists, locals who were determined to replicate Ralph's in their own name, larger and from scratch. Ralph and Lizzie had gone east, apparently.

'East?' I pressed Pete.

'That French boy, Pierre, he told me he'd had a card from Bangkok.'

So, effectively Lizzie had vanished. There were no leads. I couldn't bring myself to write to the Dunnes, but once again I passed on this information – a sort of hot potato – to Jack.

We met in a wine bar on the Fulham Road, next to the hospital. Jack had a small business renovating property (I have to give it to him, he was never short of ideas) and I remember his hair being powder-white with plaster dust, like a wig. He was shaking his head in bewilderment. 'Somewhere out there is my sister, Phoebe, somewhere. It's strange when it's your own flesh and blood.'

I was looking around the wine bar, thinking this was exactly the type of place Lizzie would have derided, not been seen dead in. 'She'll be back, I'm sure,' I tried to reassure Jack. And although this was easy to say I did know it to be true somehow. Of course I hadn't anticipated in what capacity.

My daughter, Scarlett, was born in September 1990. Since I was a single mother we went straight to the top of the list and were placed in Pond House by Camden Council later that summer. I was just so *happy*. I wasn't living with Scarlett's father, but I had everything: someone to love, a home, the beginnings of a career, something to give my life to.

Frankly I could have done without that knock on the door. It was past midnight and I had fallen asleep on the sofa. I literally couldn't tell whether I was still dreaming or not.

'Lizzie!'

'Phoebe!'

'Lizzie, is it really you?'

'Phoebe, you've got to help me. Help me!'

Your mother had one piece of luggage, a shoulder-strapped holdall, and a clutch of plastic bags. She had come straight from Heathrow. There were two things you could see about her straight away. One was that she looked dreadful, gaunt, haggard, almost yellow beneath her tropical tan. The other was that she was pregnant.

'Lizzie, are you okay?'

'Do I look okay?'

I shut the door to my flat with a sinking heart: I felt as if I should have been opening all the windows and doors to let out a cloying smell or presence.

Lizzie dropped the bags in the hallway and pushed into my sitting room. She didn't waste any time. 'I know what you're going to say, and you're right, Phoebe, and I am going to get myself together, I am, I am,' she said, breathing so hard you thought she might pass out. 'But *right now, right now* I need to use. I've *got* to use.' And she produced a ball of heroin about the size of a marble, wrapped tight in plastic and tied with a piece of thread.

The air of despair about your mother was almost palpable, humming like electricity. It was an urgent, terrible feeling, discordant, fragmented, wrong. Everything, even the question of whether I had any aluminium foil in my kitchen cupboards, was a matter of life and death. You could see it in her eyes, pure fear.

She smoked for a good twenty minutes without speaking. This heroin wasn't brown, it was an opaque, pinky colour. Finally she looked up and sat back a fraction. In the beginnings of that smile, in those eyelids, in the corners of her mouth, you could see the relief, the luxury, even, begin to express itself, just like you see an image take shape on a piece of photographic paper in the darkroom. Talk about Jekyll and Hyde! It was dreadful. After a few more minutes of slowly taking in her surroundings her eyes alighted on Scarlett's Babygros, which were hanging on the radiator.

'You've given birth,' she said.

'I have,' I replied, surprised by her turn of phrase.

'Same thing in store for you?'

Lizzie nodded. And then, with a flash of panic once again visible beneath the veneer of opium, she asked, 'Phoebe, can I stay here for a while?'

'Lizzie, I've got Scarlett now,' I answered her.

'I know, I know . . .'

I had to be firm. 'If you're clean you can stay for a while, if you're not, you can't.'

'Don't worry. I've *got* to get clean now.'

'What about Ralph?' I asked her.

'Ralph is not in the picture,' Lizzie whispered, staring at the funnel of foil in her hand. 'You won't see Ralph again.'

At that point the possibility of giving you up for adoption just hadn't occurred to Lizzie. I know it hadn't.

You were due at the end of February and that was that. Time would deliver, and what was delivered would be accommodated. It couldn't have been any simpler than that. It was the Dunnes, in particular old Mrs Dunne, who were adamant. But that was later. To begin with, we took everything a step at a time.

Our first port of call was the drug dependency unit in Harrow Road, where Lizzie was assessed and prescribed a heroin substitute. I sat with her in the waiting room and went in with her to see the doctor. The prognosis didn't seem that bad. Your mother had never injected drugs, she hadn't been on them as long as some of the people you could see hanging about outside, and she was determined to get clean, for herself and, more importantly, for you. The birth was still fourteen weeks away. If Lizzie could reduce to five milligrams of methadone linctus a day over the next six to eight weeks, the baby would be born virtually without a habit.

'I'm going to do better than that,' she said, as we walked up Sutherland Avenue, away from the unit. 'The baby will be born completely clean.'

And, to give credit where credit is due, things began well. Very well. I introduced Lizzie to my friend who used the Fellowship of Narcotics Anonymous, and she attended two meetings a day, well ahead of the schedule of 'ninety meetings in ninety days', which was considered a prerequisite to recovery. It wasn't easy, though, not at all. There were moments of euphoria, honeymoon moments, but mostly it was pain. You couldn't help but see what she was going through, in spite of the methadone. She was being pursued by demons, chased through the streets of hell. She couldn't keep still, couldn't stop yawning, stop rubbing her watery eyes or scratching at her pale, clammy, cold-turkey puckered flesh.

'I wish I could *sleep*,' she cried every morning. 'I'm so tired, so exhausted, I could sleep for a year. But I can't get comfortable. Every bit of me is on fire. I wish I was a baby . . . I wish I was dead. Oh, *Phoebe* . . .'

And I would say, 'Don't worry', 'It's going to get better', 'Let's ring so-and-so', 'Let's get ready to go to a meeting.' It wasn't a question of 'one day at a time', it was a question of taking a block of thirty minutes and getting through that.

The Dunnes were the last people who could help. The last. But who could blame them? Few parents confronted with a suffering child find they can exercise the special kind of restraint they aren't even aware is required of them. But this type of parent, the posh, come-along-now-pull-yourself-together type of parent, is probably the worst of the lot. The sound of Mrs Dunne's wailing down the telephone had been loud enough to fill the room. It was a thin, pathetic, self-piteous, reedy weeping.

'Phoebe, you've got to come with me,' Lizzie said. 'I won't be able to handle them on my own. I won't.'

Jack was there too. Once again he had been delegated the post of spokesman for his parents and researcher-conciliator. After an emotional reunion between the family in his sitting room (where there was an abundance of love and affection, you could physically feel it), he beckoned me out into the hallway of the house. We actually had this conversation in public, so to speak.

'What about the baby?' he whispered.

'What about the baby?'

'Well, has she said what's going to happen?'

'Normally when you're pregnant you—'

'Come on, Phoebe! After the baby's born. What are her intentions?'

I didn't answer.

'It's obviously too late for a termination. My parents are pretty much convinced it should be given up for adoption.'

Like I said, this possibility had never even occurred to me, us, at that point. I stared at Jack with an open mouth. I felt like I had to get back to Scarlett at once — that she was suddenly not safe with the childminder to whom I had entrusted her. A terrible panicky feeling. I pitied Lizzie then, and the pity came from the bottom of my stomach.

'Oh, no, Jack!'

Jack wouldn't stop firing questions at me, hissing at me like a snake. Even though I had my hands up to my ears I couldn't stop them coming.

'So what else do you suggest? That she has a bastard? And supports it on what exactly? Have you thought of that? Where's she going to live? In her druggie squat? Is that what you think?'

Jack was really shaking — you could see the blood thrumming in his neck.

'It doesn't make any odds to *you*, does it?' he spat. 'I can see that. And why should it? But it does to us. Why should *we* have this fucking man's blood in our family? What have we done to deserve it? Why has she done this to us?'

Judging by the way he wouldn't catch my eye as we took our leave, I think that Jack knew he had gone too far. I was in no two minds about my obligations, however. As we drove back to Pond House I recounted the conversation to Lizzie, word for word.

'He said that?'

'Lizzie, I think they've got plans.'

'Over my dead body!'

I didn't accompany Lizzie each time she saw her parents, it just wasn't practicable, but I remember well not being able to understand why she had to visit them so often when they were causing so much confusion. She would go straight to a meeting of Narcotics Anonymous afterwards and come back buoyed, but it wasn't enough to restore the balance. The situation was just too knife-edge, her mood swings too severe.

Finally the pressure overwhelmed her defences. And she relapsed. I returned from a day out with a friend and found her with that removed look in her eyes, scratching her arms, nodding forwards. 'I'm sorry, Phoebe . . . so sorry.'

'It's okay, Lizzie.'

She had a bag packed. 'I know the score,' she said. 'I'm going to move on.'

She had nowhere to go. 'Lizzie, you're not moving from this flat.'

Even though you could see the drug in the way she sat, index finger over the bridge of her nose to conceal those empty eyes with their pinprick pupils, we had a frank exchange. Ironically, it helped that she was high as it enabled us to talk over her situation in a reasoned, detached manner. 'I think maybe they're right.'

'You really think that?'

'My grandmother says I should turn around, like you do in the street, and never look back.'

'What does she know?'

'She's eighty-two, isn't she?'

'Why are they pushing you to do this?'

'Money. How am I going to bring up the baby if I haven't got any money?'

'I seem to manage okay.'

'And family honour.'

'Fuck honour! You've got a person inside you!'

'But I'm a drug addict.'

'Don't call yourself that!'

Your mother burst into tears. 'That's all I am, Phoebe. That's what Jack calls me – a snivelling junkie, a waste of space. Oh, Phoebe, I'm never going to get clean. I'm never going to get out of this. I hate myself, I wish I were dead . . .'

I was crying too. 'You were clean today, before you used.'

'It's hopeless. Jack's been in touch with an adoption agency.'

'He *hasn't*.'

'We're all going in tomorrow.'

When I got in from the park with Scarlett the following day, Lizzie was gone.

I sat for some minutes in the chair she had chosen as her chair, like you do when you're staying in someone else's house. The stillness and silence were extraordinary. To be honest, I was relieved. That tight knot of energy she had brought with her, an energy that had seemed to fill every corner of the flat, a Dunne energy to the power of ten, was gone now, exorcized. But of course I felt pangs of the most dreadful guilt. I had failed my best friend, hadn't I? Why hadn't we gone away somewhere together, anywhere? Why hadn't I intervened and stopped Lizzie seeing so much of her family? These are the questions I have asked myself endlessly since. And pointlessly. It's true when they say that there is only so much you can do for other people. The bottom line is you've got to let them get on with their own lives. And it went without saying that I had plenty to get on with in my own.

But when I rang Jack to let him know Lizzie had vanished and heard him say, 'She's with us now,' I only just managed to get the receiver down before my own sobbing filled the room.

I didn't see Lizzie for two years. I was in my final year at St Martin's, preparing for my degree show. That spring there had been a show of Kokoschka's paintings at the Heywood Gallery. It was his pale oils of bridges, thin limbs over water, which had moved me, and to which I was paying homage. I had set up my easel on the pavement, the north side of the Thames, by Lambeth Bridge. Lizzie came from behind, tapped me on the shoulder. 'Phoebe!'

'My God, Lizzie!'

We met at a sandwich shop that lunchtime, sat at a counter overlooking the street. Lizzie was clean. You could tell that straight away. Her skin and eyes were clear. She was wearing trousers, which was unlike her, and a scarf in her hair. She almost had that Sloaney Princess Di appearance we had both found so risible only five years before. As soon as we touched on the baby her eyes filled with tears.

'It was the right thing then,' she said. 'I was in such a mess. It was the right thing then.'

'But not now,' I couldn't help saying.

Lizzie was going to reply, but stopped herself. She turned to face me and put her hand next to mine. Tears were silently flowing down her cheeks and splashing on the bar in front of us. I grasped her across the breadth of her knuckles. 'I think of her every day,' she whispered.

'Her?'

'Lily Rose.'

'Lily Rose?'

'I named her after my two favourite aunts.'

It was a dreadful lunch. More than once I interrupted your mother and told her that she needn't go through it all for me, I could imagine the chain of events. But she insisted. It was cathartic to speak about what had happened, she said, especially with someone who was familiar with the background against which the drama had been enacted.

As it turned out, there wasn't that much to explain, really. Events had conspired to persuade her that giving up her child for adoption was the right thing for all concerned, Lily Rose included. After she'd left Pond House that afternoon, she explained, she had spent a week on the streets, hustling drugs, getting by. 'If Jack hadn't been there to take my call, I would have had no one. Literally.'

She was driven straight to her parents' home near Amesbury, where she stayed the remaining weeks leading up to the birth. The baby was delivered in Salisbury hospital and had been born dependent on opiates – for that reason mother and daughter had been transferred to a specialist ward in a West London hospital, where they had been together for five long weeks.

'I bonded with Lily Rose in that time, Phoebe. Of course I did.'

Baby Lily was registered in London. Lizzie didn't tell me that afternoon she had used my address on the birth certificate. In fact, she never told me. The first I knew of this was when you came to see me, Georgia. I can only imagine that she thought Pond House was a stepping-stone as far as I was concerned, temporary accommodation, and that soon I would move on. She knew nothing of the 'right to buy scheme' Mrs Thatcher had got under way in the late eighties. Why should she?

'It was just awful, dreadful, just the most terrible thing in the world,' she whispered, exhaling through her nose, her midriff rising as if to contain the pain. 'I went in one door with Lily: there were forms to sign. There was a little suitcase next to the desk. Inside there was a knitted shawl, socks, a hat. They thought me seeing all this would help. Then there was the last kiss and cuddle . . . I held her to my stomach, and then she was gone, gone through another door . . . to new parents. They told me they had found a couple who weren't exactly . . . but who were of a similar class and background. I walked out into the street. How can I describe it? I was empty-headed, empty-handed, just empty, empty – a part of me had gone, surgically removed. These NA meetings I go to have been my saviour,' she finished. 'They've helped me to get clean and they help me on an ongoing basis, a daily basis, to deal with this.'

'My darling Lizzie!'

There was a long silence between us.

She wasn't looking at me when she said, by way almost of qualification, 'There's always someone worse off than oneself.'

'That doesn't make it any less difficult.'

'It does, actually. It makes me feel grateful.'

'Grateful?'

'Okay, some people who come into recovery get off lightly. Some not so lightly. People with HIV, for instance. It puts it into perspective.'

Lizzie was very Narcotics Anonymous (they're big on gratitude) and her speech was punctuated with expressions and slogans you knew could only have come from the meetings. 'One day at a time'; 'Keep it simple'; 'Let go, let God.' She told me she was completely immersed in the programme, was secretary of a meeting in Marylebone, treasurer of another in Lisson Grove, had sponsees – fellow addicts in whose early recovery you took a close and personal interest.

'But I think of Lily every day,' she said again, without prompting and without tears this time. 'I sit there wondering what she's doing. Which nursery school? Which part of the country? Does she have brothers and sisters?

Is she smiling? Is she happy? What are her friends like? It's strange when there's someone somewhere out there, your flesh and blood.'

And it was strange, too – or perhaps not so strange – that Jack had used these exact words some two years before.

'And Ralph?'

Lambeth Bridge was just visible from where we were sitting. I could see Lizzie's eyes move from one shore to the other, just as mine had been doing all morning. 'No news of Ralph,' she whispered. 'There won't be either.'

The story of your adoption was as sad and heartbreaking as I had known it would be. But I was pleased for Lizzie. I was happy that she was at least alive, and had redeemed what she could from the tragedy and confusion of her situation. There were plenty of casualties from Lizzie's peer group who weren't so fortunate: you saw them in the papers, high-profile toffs, 'heirs and disgraces', as they were known – the Marquess of Blandford, Lord Jermyn, Lady Camilla So-and-so. Most of them never got clean. A good number had died. But Lizzie had survived. And she was healthy, beautiful – really beautiful. I hoped she would meet someone, settle down, have another baby, put everything behind her (I sound a bit like old Mrs Dunne now). That was the obvious way forward.

I saw her face in the papers quite often after that meeting on the Thames. It turned out she was a PR officer for a charity. Not landmines, but something connected to the damage wrought by war, which was fitting, as her own circumstances had resembled a conflict and her ongoing battle to keep her head above the waves was a sort of war of attrition.

Although there was a completeness about the story of your adoption, I had an intuition, the intuition of a mother, that there was more.

And I was right.

Lizzie just turned up on my doorstep about four years later. No letter, no phone call: she just turned up. 'Phoebe, I've got to talk to you.'

We sat opposite each other in my sitting room. Lizzie had both hands cupped over her heart.

She was staring at the floor, unable to speak. A good ten minutes must have passed.

'Is it Lily?' I prompted her.

'Have you seen Pete?' she fired back.

'No.'

'What has he told you?'

'My love, I haven't seen Pete in years.'

By now Lizzie had looked up. Her eyes were deep, old, imploring. 'Phoebe, I've got to share something with you. Can I?'

'Of course you can. But why me?' I asked, as I knew there was no shortage of people within her support network to whom she could have spoken in confidence.

'Because you were there. Because – I don't know why – it's *you* I've got to tell.'

'Tell me, then.'

'Only promise me it will stay between us. Promise me you'll not repeat it to anyone.'

'I promise.'

And this is what she told me, Georgia.

We have to go back to Palolem. To the time there had been a fire at the far end of the beach. It was just as Pete had said. Trouble had been brewing for some time, resentment about money, the heavy-handed way in which Ralph ran his interests, the fact that in the eyes of the village elders he was attracting the wrong type of visitor. The fire ripped through the settlement in a matter of minutes and had been seen by the fishermen two miles out at sea. Everything was lost. Money, possessions, their *raison d'être,* their livelihood, the facility that enabled Ralph and Lizzie to live like king and queen in this, their fools' paradise. They had left Palolem in pretty much the clothes in which they were standing. The dream was over.

They hitched north to Bombay, where they spent the next three months. By now they had heavy heroin habits, especially Ralph. The only way to fund their addiction was to sell drugs to the backpackers who congregated about the waterfront in Colaba, making commission on pieces of hash, packets of brown, passing phials of dust to those too young and naïve to know better. I've seen that area in Colaba myself, Georgia. Of all the places to end up on the street, fighting for a place in the pecking order of destitution, this was it, a dog-eat-dog world within a dog-eat-dog world. The Australian, Italian, German hippies-turned-junkies know no moral code – their only motivation for living is the poppy. You see them collecting empty water bottles to earn a fraction of a rupee, then you see them injecting in alleyways.

It's dangerous there, really dangerous. Death is never far away. And when you die who is going to miss you?

Your mother was acutely aware of how far and how quickly they had sunk. Much more so than Ralph, who was in a sense worldly-wise.

'And I didn't even love Ralph. We were just together. I can't describe it any better than that. I was sort of *stuck* to him, but we managed to get out.'

'Getting out' involved a robbery. Two thousand US dollars stolen from the room of a tourist hotel off Marine Drive. It had been a premeditated act and there had been violence.

'It was terrifying, Phoebe. It was yet another step down the ladder. But what a step! I knew then I no longer had any control over my destiny. Not one bit. And now there was another dimension. I was frightened of Ralph. But we just *had* to get out. It had been the only way.'

There were tears, tears of fear or the vestige of fear.

'We flew to Bangkok and then on, with the last of the money, to Penang. When we got off the plane, everything green and flat and different around us, I may have been oceans away geographically but I was exactly the same person who had got on that flight in Bombay.'

Your mother paused and shook her head. She had a faraway look in her eyes, the type of look that suggested she was the listener rather than the narrator, that she was hearing this story for the first time. She was smoking a cigarette, blowing the smoke in forced clouds towards the floor.

'Against even our own best expectations we got clean,' she went on, with an empty laugh. 'Strange, I know.

Ironic. And, of course, it goes without saying that just as soon as we got clean things improved dramatically. Ralph got back into money-making mode. It was extraordinary, crazy, really. Like King Midas, everything he touched turned to gold.

'We pretty much carbon-copied what we'd had in Palolem: the deserted beach a few miles off the beaten track, the huts, the parties, the scene. Simple as that. Before long we had got back everything we'd lost in Goa. Respect, money, and the kudos money brings. It was unearthly in Penang, so quiet, almost ghostly it was so tranquil. The quality of life was just as good in Malaysia as it had been in India, only the police seemed to be much more interested in our activities. We took this to be just a difference in the culture. Ralph handled it. "It's only money they're after," he told me. "They're like kids – you just have to tell them enough is enough."'

'That was Ralph's big shortcoming. He was arrogant.

'Something in me had changed, though. There had been a fundamental shift. My conscience wouldn't leave me alone. Bombay had been a real eye-opener. Even though I was thousands of miles from the Fulham Road, I hadn't lost sight of the middle-class girl from central London who had had every advantage. Maybe she was in better focus for being so far away. In Colaba I had peered over the edge of an abyss. You can't tell how far you're going to fall, you only know you'll never be able to climb out. I knew I had to escape, so I began secretly planning my exit. One morning I would steal some money and go. But where to? Back to London? I could hardly pick up where I had left off. Or so I thought.

'And it wasn't long – just as soon as the novelty of being clean had worn off – before I started using again. Secretly using. On and off. A little bit to begin with. I thought it was just me wanting to get high, get out of it, have a break from the hopeless mess underneath that refused to go away. Really, I know now, I was trying to precipitate the end. In NA they say that addiction is a disease, one that progresses irrespective of whether you're using drugs or not. I'm not sure I entirely believe that, but I do believe that people use drugs as a form of catalyst to change. By scoring a phial of pink powder from a dealer in the market, I was saying, "Something needs to change here. I don't know what or how, but something needs to happen."

'It wasn't long before Ralph had sussed me out. It turned out he had been secretly using as well. We spent the next nine months dabbling and battling. Getting wasted, giving up, getting wasted. It was awful, awful. There is such an air of irony and inevitability about having a habit. As soon as you resolve to kick off, just as soon as the pledge crystallizes in your mind, you know that you're going to succumb. You may start off strong, you're going to really do it this time, but as soon as the sickness sets in it's like a flame melting wax and your resistance just falls away, dissolves. And being sick in the tropics is the worst, the very worst. The suffocating heat drains you of every last ounce of energy. You can't move. You can't sleep. You can't eat. You might feel you want to fuck but you don't really and when you do you just feel disgusted with yourself.

'As I said, we had nine whole months of this, with

the promise of an indefinite period to follow: withdrawing, getting high, withdrawing, getting high. It was like
one endless, nightmarish *déjà vu*. And when we were
doing the drugs we were dealing – or, rather, Ralph was
dealing. To the travellers who were staying with us. We
didn't need the cash, but Ralph wasn't capable of bypass-
ing moneymaking opportunities. It was the buzz of the
thing.

'Then I missed my period. I knew pretty much
straight away I was pregnant, I could sense it – but smack
interferes with your cycle and it wasn't until I missed
again that the reality became something I couldn't avoid
any longer. It was confirmed in the toilet of a chemist in
the outskirts of Penang.'

Lizzie ground out the cigarette she was smoking and
lit another.

'I took a walk along a railway embankment, a shanty-
town either side. There were children playing in and out
of the tracks and monsoon drains. Tears were streaming
down my face. I was alone, miles from anywhere, the
only person on earth. I was railing at God, imploring
him, deriding him. Why had life dealt me such a fucking awful hand? What had I done to deserve this? Please
couldn't I wake from the nightmare to find everything
sorted? I was almost revelling in the misery. It seemed
like you couldn't have had a bigger problem than I had
at that moment in time.'

There was a long pause.

'So it was ironic what happened next. Because it was
right then that I got picked up by the narcotics police in
their green van. They had stopped at a junction ahead

and were waving at me. In my innocence I thought they were going to give me directions, that they had come to protect me. That this was some form of divine intervention, even. But, no, quite the opposite.

"You, you, English, get in . . . now . . . now . . ."

'They took me to a sub-station about an hour inland, put me in a cell and interrogated me. It was terrifying. They knew exactly what we had been up to in the camp, every last detail. They could keep me in now, they said, bust our house, and I would get somewhere between ten and fifteen years, depending on what they found there. Or I could co-operate, do as I was told. In which case I would be released. The officer who brokered the deal had a wide face and thick, pockmarked skin. He had on a pair of reflective sunglasses. I never got to see his eyes.

'The agreement was that I would inform them when Ralph bought the heroin. They knew he met a young Chinese boy, a runner, in a restaurant by the bus station. All they wanted was advance notice of when this meeting would take place. They wanted to arrest both Ralph and his supplier. It would help bust a syndicate. They gave me a phone number.'

Lizzie couldn't go on. It was obvious what she was going to tell me next. And that she had to tell me, because she had gone past the point of no return. But she couldn't actually speak, form the words. So I sat next to her and put my arm around her shoulders. Together we stared at the floor.

'I didn't do anything for a week or even ten days,' she went on eventually. 'What could I do? I was paralysed by fear. It was an impossible situation. Then one night I saw Ralph staring at me in a weird way. Everything was getting really freaky by now, and I was paranoid, so paranoid. Who knew what was going to happen next? Were the police just going to burst in? But I wasn't expecting what he came out with, not at all.

"You're pregnant, aren't you, Lizzie?" he whispered, looking me up and down and smiling.

"What do you mean?"

"Look at your belly. And look at your face: you're fuller. You're pregnant, aren't you?"

"Ralph, it's the heat."

'By the way he held my eye I knew he could tell I was lying. I remember he was holding a spirit level in one hand and pulling at his beard with the fingers of the other. With his workmen he was building some new huts. Because he was so busy that day he let it drop. That night I made up my mind to act.'

I was stroking the nape of your mother's neck.

'I don't really know what Pete knows. But the truth of the matter is, the fact of the matter is, Phoebe, I had Ralph busted the following day. He was going to meet his man. I did exactly as the police told me. They picked him up with two grams of pure heroin. In Malaysia, Phoebe, you get the death penalty for dealing.'

'Jesus, Lizzie!' I couldn't help whispering.

'I had Ralph busted. I did.'

I had taken your mother's hand and squeezed it until she looked at me. There was terror in her eyes, a terror I've only had occasion to dread. 'It's okay, Lizzie,' I tried to reassure her.

'It's *not* okay. It's *not* okay. But now you see why, don't you?' she breathed.

I knew immediately what she was referring to, but I knew, too, that I must force Lizzie to actually come out with it. 'See what?'

'See why I couldn't watch Lily Rose grow up with the knowledge of what I had done gazing up at me, reminding me . . . every day, every night. Knowing that one day she would ask me about her father. And what would I say? I haven't been able to live with the guilt, but I haven't been able to live with the secret either.'

'Where is Ralph now?' I asked.

'In prison outside Penang.'

'You know that for sure?'

'I had someone write to him, pretending to be a pen-pal of prisoners abroad. Everything I do is so dishonest, underhand. He's been in for six years now, Phoebe, and still his case hasn't come to court. The guilt has never let me alone. Not for one minute. I've tried to deal with it, but it has never let me alone. It won't.'

I made us tea and we sat talking late into the night. Forget about honour among thieves, your mother had dealt the most cowardly, spineless, underhand blow that was possible, really. Yet I made my mind up without hesitation: I must be generous. What else could I do? Compound the guilt. Why? And there was some substance to my reasoning. We went through it over and over again, me using my fingers like an abacus. It was Ralph who had broken the law. Not Lizzie. It had been his choice to deal heroin, no one else's. He would have been arrested at some point in the future. That went without saying. It would have been only a matter of time. And, okay, it had been cowardly what she had done, but where drugs were concerned anything went. A lot of people, more people than might admit it, would have done the same in her position. I might have acted the same way, given the impossibility of the situation. She had suffered enough already. It was time to let go of this.

Lizzie was staring at the ceiling now, her hands tied together as if in prayer. Was this how she had looked on the railway embankment in Malaysia, I wondered, self-piteous, broken?

'And where's Lily Rose? Where's Lily?' she couldn't stop whispering. 'I miss her so much. Where is she?'

That was a question, of course, that no one could answer.

I never spoke to Lizzie again. Not so much by choice. It was just the way things turned out. I thought to begin with perhaps we could have made an arrangement to meet, that we could have taken our friendship on – but where could it go with a secret like that haunting every word, ghosting every gesture?

I next saw her about three years later. I was driving through Denbigh Square behind King's Cross. Scarlett was with me. We had just been to her friend's tenth-birthday party. So you would have been nine.

And there was Lizzie, or a shadow of Lizzie, among a group of what could only be described as vagrants. She might have fallen in Bombay, but now she had properly fallen. I remember not being able to believe what I was witnessing, and driving around the square, three, four, maybe even five times. But it was Lizzie, all right, with those high cheekbones, more pronounced now, and that way of sitting forwards with her legs crossed, one finger over the bridge of her nose. She was wearing a pair of tracksuit bottoms and an anorak. She couldn't have weighed more than six stone.

Ralph was in hell, too. That went without saying. Every now and again you would see an article in the Sunday supplements about what were euphemistically known as the 'correction facilities' in Thailand and Malaysia. Just dreadful. Sixty men to a cell, not enough room for all of them to lie down at once. How they ate from troughs, a soup of fish entrails and rice. The dysentery, the insects, the heat. In the Malaysian top-security prisons the convicts were shackled with leg irons, and one detail stuck in my mind. The prisoners spent all their daylight hours polishing the steel, which had become rusty in the humidity overnight, so that when it opened the sores about their ankles the wounds didn't become infected.

It didn't come as a surprise when Jack phoned to tell me Lizzie had died. 'She's dead, Phoebe.'

'I'm so sorry, Jack.'

Jack had wanted to talk, you could tell. He sounded exhausted, broken. Lizzie had been living in sheltered accommodation outside Basingstoke, he explained. She had been through any number of treatment centres for rehabilitation (paid for in part by old Mrs Dunne), but each time a short period of abstinence had been followed by relapse. And each time the relapse had taken her further down. 'There was no helping her, Phoebe. She just didn't want it enough.'

Her death might not have been a surprise, but the funeral was a dreadful jolt. The first person I saw in the church was old Mrs Dunne seated in a wheelchair adjacent to the front pew, grey, stiff, her mouth turned down. It's unfair, I know, but as soon as I caught sight of her that was where I laid the blame, beneath the veneer of stoicism and so-called respectability.

Mr Dunne was much greyer about the temples. 'We lost the battle, I'm afraid. But thank you for coming down, Phoebe,' he said, with the faintest bow of the head.

Mrs Dunne was inconsolable. 'My baby, my beautiful, beautiful baby . . . gone.'

Jack gave the eulogy, concentrating on Lizzie's sporting achievements, before my friendship with her, and her work for the charity. It was a glossy sham and his clumsy words seemed only to expose the family's culpability further.

It was a shock to see Pete there. It wasn't until we were at the graveside that I noticed him, in spite of his being the only black face for miles around. He told me afterwards it was only by pure chance that he had happened across the notice in *The Times*. He was working as a PE instructor for a private school in North London and he had found the paper open in the staff common room. 'And I never read *The Times*,' he said.

I had travelled to Salisbury alone on the train. I got a lift back to London in Pete's car.

'Ralph died maybe six, eight years ago,' he replied to my question. 'Of blood poisoning. The conditions in those prisons – nothing comes close to it. No sanitation. No medication. Nothing. An infected insect bite can take you out.'

'How did you hear?'

'A British prisoner wrote to tell me, one of Ralph's friends. I think Ralph wanted everyone to know before he died. He was actually on Death Row.'

'Death Row?'

'Not that that means much over there as they virtually all get a reprieve. But a pretty poor place to spend the last years of your life.'

'Did you tell Lizzie Ralph was dead?' I asked him carefully, as I didn't know how much Pete knew.

'I never saw Lizzie,' he answered. 'I thought about telling you so that you could tell her. But then I thought, What's the use?'

'Did he know that Lizzie had had a baby?'

'He knew.'

'How did he find out?'

'I don't know, but I do know the Malaysian police taunted him with it.'

'How did it happen?' I then asked.

'How did what happen?'

'How did he get busted?'

Pete didn't look at me as he said, 'Let's just say he got busted, Phoebe.'

And that was Pete's way of not engaging with the truth, by not discussing it.

*

The statement is over.

'Is that it?' I ask.

'That's it, Georgia,' Dr Murdo answers.

I turn away, then back to face him. There is no expression of pity or surprise or seriousness on his face: he just looks at me straight on.

We say nothing for about ten minutes, until Dr Murdo can't take the pressure any longer. 'What are your thoughts, Georgia?'

'It looks like I'm responsible for everyone's deaths,' I reply.

Dr Murdo lifts one arm high into the air to remonstrate. 'Georgia . . .'

But I stop him with a wave of my own. 'Can I have a glass of water, please?'

'Tap?'

'Mineral,' I insist.

'I'll have to go down to Reception?'

'I'll be fine.' I nod. 'Honestly.'

Once Dr Murdo has closed the door behind him I turn back to the quadrangle. The action of moving and then moving back has altered the sound of breaking water. It is as if I am listening down a different corridor, that's the only way I can describe it; a bit like when you move away from a stack of speakers at a gig and find yourself in one of Sula's 'pockets of calm'. I've still got Fudge's hair between my thumb and forefinger – in fact, I've got a few now. I can feel them there on my fingerprints, the finest pieces of wire you've ever felt.

ACKNOWLEDGEMENTS

The author gratefully acknowledges the generous assistance and expertise of James Gurbutt, Andrew Kidd, Karl Miller, Gilly Sheard and Liv Stones.